DALLAS NOIR

EDITED BY DAVID HALE SMITH

Series concept by Tim McLoughlin and Johnny Temple
Dallas map by Aaron Petrovich

Published by Akashic Books
©2013 Akashic Books

ISBN-13: 978-1-61775-190-5
Library of Congress Control Number: 2013938543
All rights reserved

First printing

Akashic Books
PO Box 1456
New York, NY 10009
info@akashicbooks.com
www.akashicbooks.com

ALSO IN THE AKASHIC NOIR SERIES

FORTHCOMING

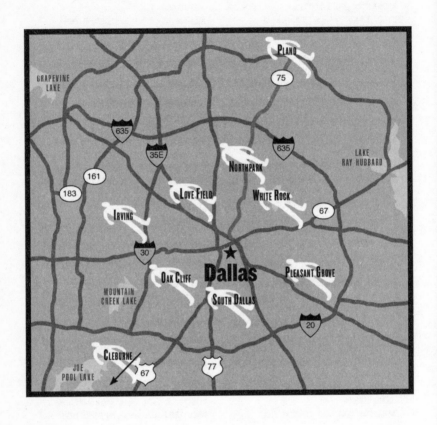

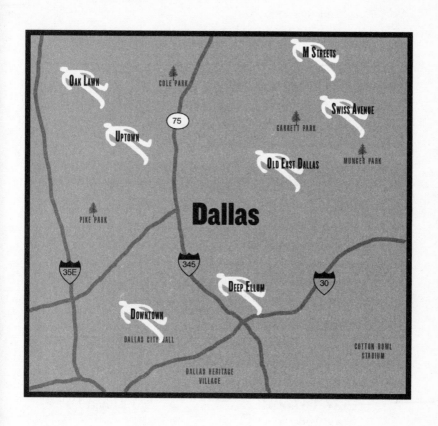

TABLE OF CONTENTS

PART III: MAVERICKS

INTRODUCTION
A Permanent Black Scar

My favorite line in my favorite song about Dallas goes like this: *Dallas is a rich man with a death wish in his eyes / A steel and concrete soul in a warm-hearted love disguise . . .*

The narrator of Jimmie Dale Gilmore's perfect tune "Dallas" is coming to town as a broke dreamer with the bright lights of the big city on his mind. He's just seen the Dallas cityscape through the window of his seat on a DC-9 at night. Is he just beginning his quest? Or is he on his way home, flying out of Love Field, reminiscing after seeing the woman who stepped on him when he was down?

Dallas itself is like a marvelous piece of fiction. It is a city created out of nothing. Nobody even seems to be certain why it's called Dallas. Founded because it sat on a navigable spot in the Trinity River, the city was originally envisioned as a port from which ships could travel to and from the larger gulf port at Galveston. However, only a few boats ever successfully made the journey, and none without encountering major trouble along the way. The river is too shallow. It barely exists anymore, except when one of our terrifying Texas thunderstorms turns it into a dangerous flood. Despite this apparently doomed beginning, Dallas seemed to will itself into existence and flourish against all odds. Two major railroad lines eventually crossed paths here, the town became a major cotton exchange, and it has been pulsing with life and growing ever since.

In a country with so many interesting cities, Dallas is often overlooked—except on November 22 every year. The heart-breaking anniversary keeps coming back around in a nightmare loop, for all of us. On that day in 1963, Dallas *became* American noir. A permanent black scar on its history that will never be erased, no matter how many happy business stories and hit television shows arise from here.

In a stark ongoing counterweight to the JFK tragedy are those two iterations of the TV show. Dallas is not a TV show. It's a real city with a booming downtown, a flourishing arts district, generous philanthropists, and ever-sprawling suburbs that boast some of the most beautiful neighborhoods, best schools, and lowest cost of living in the US. My parents moved to Dallas when I was in elementary school. We were welcomed into a diverse neighborhood with hills and trees in the 1970s that included Jews and Gentiles living next to each other, academics sharing ideas with entrepreneurs over backyard beers, and artists howling at the moon alongside frog-giggin' cowboys and avid deer hunters. All of my early memories were made here. I love this town. And for the past forty years, my capacity to be surprised by it has not diminished one bit. I hope the stories in this collection will surprise you too.

In the February 2013 issue of *Texas Monthly* magazine, Pulitzer Prize winner Larry McMurtry wrote: "Dallas is a second-rate city that wishes it were first-rate." Perhaps Dallas has a certain image that makes it easy to underestimate, or to dismiss with blanket assumptions and odd assertions such as McMurtry's. Like a beautiful woman with poison under her fingernails, this is a town of dangerous paradoxes. Art and commerce in constant battle. Immense wealth and crushing poverty. An obsession with private schools and competitive youth sports. Country club kids with good drugs and guns in the glove boxes of their cars. Professional athletes, interior decorators, gangbangers, and narco-traffickers jammed into a nightclub, dancing the night away during an ice storm. Texans with more money than taste, gilding the wide streets with latter-day châteaus. The "eighty-thousand-dollar millionaires" driving rented Aston Martins and Range Rovers up to the valet lines.

Business is combat in Dallas. And everybody—even the old-money rich—is leveraged in mountains and mountains of debt because they are always rolling the dice on another deal. In this atmosphere, nasty surprises lurk around every turn. There are winners and losers. And in good noir stories, they are often one and the same.

Forget the typical bad-news headline stories every city has about murders, rapes, and other nasty violent crimes (the kind used on the screen crawl and daily front page to sell newscasts and newspapers). Dallas has those too. But the other true crime of the century may have been the savings-and-loan crisis that bubbled up and then ran unchecked for nearly a decade in Texas, with the Wild West of Dallas as the epicenter in the 1980s. Before Enron and Bernie Madoff and even the subprime meltdown, there was Danny Faulkner, who was caught perpetrating a real estate fraud that bankrupted five savings and loans and cost the US government (meaning you and me) one billion dollars. Faulkner and a group of buddies turned Dallas into their own personal cash machine. Through a scheme of insanely friendly loans from their thrift-banker pals, they figured out how to buy large chunks of land for pennies along Interstate 30 in East Dallas County. Then they flipped their new properties like Bisquick pancakes, often many times over in the same day, jacking up the land value on paper by several hundred percent in a few blinks of an eye. They promised beautiful condos and bountiful returns.

Their astounding fraud happened in plain sight, with dozens if not hundreds of people involved in the deals. Everybody had their hand in someone else's pocket, like a dirty daisy chain. Everybody got paid. Until the last guy in the chain ended up holding property that was worthless. Then there were no buyers for the cheap condos. When the final property owners couldn't pay their debts, the lenders went under in a huge collapse.

At the height of Faulkner's success in the mid-1980s, he was worth millions. An illiterate house painter from Mississippi, he drove around Dallas in a fleet of Rolls-Royces and flew in his own helicopter. The FBI started an investigation. It wasn't pretty. More than a hundred people were eventually convicted in the scheme. Those collapsing Texas S&Ls were the early-falling bones in a domino effect that crippled the nationwide independent banking system and eventually resulted in a lovely US government bailout to the tune of an estimated $500 billion.

Dallas' very own Danny Faulkner was the poster boy for the entire debacle. For decades afterward, the interstate highway along which he and his pals did their finest "land development deals" was lined with acres upon acres of partially constructed, unsold condos with no roofs and vacant concrete foundation slabs. A man named Faulkner, from Mississippi, creatively developing a small parcel of land . . . but it's not fiction. It's Dallas history.

This kind of real-life brave citizenry and lendy-spendy atmosphere make terrific fodder for noir fiction. That's what I've tried to gather together in this collection. To paraphrase Frank Underwood, current leading man of great hamartia on the original Netflix show *House of Cards*, it's always such a pleasure to find someone who's willing to put a saddle on a gift horse rather than look it in the mouth. When Johnny Temple of Akashic Books approached me and asked me to edit *Dallas Noir*, he gave me an incredible gift. And I knew exactly where to put the saddle. An anthology of brand-new dark short fiction, set in the city known for perhaps the worst crime in American history, to be published on the fiftieth anniversary of that infamous event. Sign me up.

I didn't ask McMurtry to contribute a story, so I don't know whether he would've written something or not. I wanted to get as many voices as I could from writers who actually live in Dallas now, or come from here, or have deep connections to this town. I found some great pieces. Editing this anthology together was even more rewarding than I thought it would be. The stories feature some of the finest writing set in and about this city that I've ever read. There are tales here from a few writers you may recognize from the crime fiction trenches, but also ones from a debut writer, a poet, a teacher, and a National Book Critics Circle Award winner. You'll find a story about when defense against the West Nile virus turns into a lethal rooftop brawl. Another features the most exquisite femme fatale in the history of residential real estate. There are murderous swingers killing each other for drugs after an orgy, a lonely waitress in desperate trouble, the deadliest Civil War battle reenactment ever, and a tale of haunted guilt so dark it's like Edgar Allan Poe on Tex-Mex. This collection reveals a Dallas fiction scene that is dark and exciting, growing and writing its own new story.

With all due respect, Mr. McMurtry, you have it wrong: Dallas is a first-rate city, and it's the ultimate noir town.

David Hale Smith
Dallas, Texas
July 2013

PART I

Cowboys

PART 1

HOLE-MAN

BY MATT BONDURANT

White Rock

By the time Anders opened the newspaper, four of them were on his left foot, proboscis planted deep, their hairy black torsos pumping with effort. He mashed them with his hand, leaving a bloody smear, and wiped his palm on the brittle St. Augustine grass. Nine in the morning, Saturday, late July, already ninety degrees, and a dark fog of swirling mosquitoes hung above the back alley. Anders's two-year-old daughter Blake was pushing a miniature stroller around the tiny patch of grass. Beyond the grass the blue eye of the pool, and the eight-foot wooden privacy fence, the steady atonal thump of roofing hammers pounding throughout the neighborhood. It was the summer in Dallas when the West Nile virus was killing off a dozen senior citizens a week. City Hall was in a public relations panic, and in the evenings low-flying planes crisscrossed over the neighborhood, blanketing the city with dense fogs of pesticides.

Anders and Blake were both wearing a visible sheen of 65 percent deet, stuff Anders got online because you couldn't legally buy it in stores. It helped, but the sticky residue was difficult to scrub off, leaving a pungent odor reminiscent of public restrooms. Anders was irritated for several reasons. When he was putting the trash in the alley that morning, he looked through the chinks in their fence and saw that the house across the alley had a pool that was mostly empty. This represented a blatant disregard of one of the principal codes of suburbia. Standing water meant larvae, meant mosquitoes.

Anders's pool was like something out of resort brochure, expertly cleaned and with a water quality that almost made you cry to look at it. The pool service kept it sparkling and inviting, a crew of men coming weekly to vacuum, backwash, apply chemicals. The pool took almost the entire backyard, the edges of it coming within four feet of the house on the garage side. Anders put a potted palm tree on the deck and a plastic owl on the diving board to keep the ducks out.

He was a fleshy man, over six feet, with the broad back and pillow shoulders of swimmer. A former collegiate water polo player, Anders had insisted on the pool when they moved to Dallas, but he'd been in it maybe a dozen times that summer, mostly due to Blake's lack of interest and the horde of mosquitoes that descended about a minute after you exposed your naked flesh.

Blake had a sippy cup and her Batman mask buckled in the seat of her toy stroller. She was murmuring to the mask, and Anders could see a half-dozen mosquitoes on her face and neck, like a slash of dark freckles on her fair skin. *Fuck!* Anders swiped at her face, then scooped her up like a football, Blake hanging onto the stroller, and ran inside the house. He set her down and she continued pushing the stroller through the kitchen, murmuring to her mask. Anders was getting a wet paper towel to wipe her down when he heard the slow crunch and thrum of footsteps above him. Someone was walking across the roof.

This was East Dallas, the broad swath of suburban neighborhoods with teardrop cul-de-sacs, wide concrete avenues, and brick ranch-style homes built tight together. A network of alleys ran behind every house and everyone had privacy fences with lumbering automatic gates that opened to the garage. Front yards were landscaped and unspoiled, tended by feverish bands of Mexican men who descended upon the neighborhoods in droves at all hours, eight men at a time cutting, edging, trimming, cleaning gutters, pruning trees in a yard barely big enough to hold a racquetball court, knocking the whole thing out in about ten minutes. Sometimes in their enthusiasm they did yards they weren't contracted for, but it didn't seem to matter. So a gang of Mexicans running across your roof with backpack leaf blowers and pruning saws wasn't too unusual—but Anders knew that his normal day was Tuesday. This was Saturday.

He stepped out the front door to look but there was nobody on the roof, at least on the front side. His square plot of front yard grass was neatly trimmed and edged, his hedges cut with razor-like precision. *When was that done?* Some of his neighbors a few houses down and across the alley had crews scrambling around, men carrying ropes, saws, stacks of shingles, stepping from roof to fence to neighboring roof like circus performers. Somebody was *always* getting their roof done, and Anders never understood how this was possible. In North Texas hail the size of golf balls was a yearly occurrence, but it seemed that some in his neighbor-hood were getting their roofs replaced several times a year. He decided that he would have to get a better look at the pool across the alley before he reported it to some kind of authority.

So Anders got on his roof. Easy enough using the side fence gate; low slope, no gables, a brick chimney for the gas fireplace that they never used. He hadn't been on the roof before, and he was struck by the ease of access and the powerful monotony of the vista. The same roof layout was repeated in rows as far as he could see, some partially obscured by the swelling branches of oak and pecan trees, alleys running between the rows like rivers, the privacy fences cutting clean lines. He walked up to the peak over the garage, next to the alley, and stood for the best angle.

The house directly behind him was a rental; that he already knew. It was the exact same house as his, the 1960s ranch-style, with large windows covered by heavy shades, cracked and buckled cement patio, sunbaked landscaping. The vegetation was withered and clearly uncared for, and small drifts of rotting leaves lay in the corners of the house and fence. Must be the only one on the block, he thought, without a lawn care contract. Dominating the backyard was a deep in-ground pool, a couple feet of water in the deep end choked with leaves and debris, a turgid swamp of muck and algae growth, the air above vibrating with movement. Dragonflies swooped and cut through the outer edges of the cloud of mosquitoes, like cowboys culling the herd, and formations of brown swallows lined up and took turns plunging through the fog, mouths agape. The water must be thick with larvae, Anders thought, a new batch erupting every few minutes.

He noticed a roofing crew on a nearby house looking in his direction, motionless, hammers dangling in their hands, shingles balanced on their shoulders, long-handled spades for scraping tar paper cradled akimbo. Then, as if on cue, the pounding of roofing hammers began again, and Anders realized that all the roofers in the neighborhood had gone silent when he got up there, as if they were tethered together by some unseen cord. When he came inside Megan had ground beef in the skillet for tacos, Blake sitting at the table using her plastic scissors to cut shapes out of tortillas.

Anders and Megan came from West Texas, flatlander kids who met at a fraternity mixer at Texas Tech when Anders became enamored of the pretty girl who delicately vomited into her solo cup. He offered a new toothbrush and paste from his room in the frat house, and this was the anecdote they often depended on to set what they felt was the appropriate tone of their relationship; they were uncomplicated, casual extroverts who were not humiliated easily. Megan went to his water polo matches and whistled and catcalled from the bleachers every time he came out of the water, Anders flexing and posing in his Speedo. Anders was a three-meter man, or "hole-man," the position in water polo that demanded the most strength and a vicious nature. The hole-man posted-up with his back to the opponent's goal like a center in basketball, and all the offense ran through him, while a hole defender—the biggest, nastiest man on the other team—fought him for position and to deny the ball. It was something akin to freestyle wrestling a powerful psychotic in eight feet of water with a ball coming at you every ten seconds.

Anders was in sales, at Dell computers. He didn't know shit about computers, hated sales, and his job remained foreign and separate, like some bizarre cultural ritual he performed daily without any knowledge of why it was done. He wrote this off as something that was a matter of course, and that it was best not to get too involved in one's vocation. What he did for a living didn't define him; rather, he was a slightly flabbier version of the man he was in college, the vortex of the party, always in the throes of whatever action, with Megan as his running partner. He had other dreams and he was bound to realize them. He was the hole-man. Everything went through him.

But moving to Dallas a few years ago when Megan got her nursing job called this extroverted notion of themselves into serious question. They hadn't met anyone in the neighborhood other than the androgynous lunatic of indeterminate age who lived next door, and the university literature professor down the block with his strangely beautiful trophy wife, who both seemed to do little more than drink gin cocktails by their pool and grouse about how Austin had a much better "literary scene." Anders believed it was the simple arrangement and logistics of the neighborhood that was responsible: because all the garages faced the back alley and everyone had privacy fences, people entered and exited their houses by their concealed back entrances. No children playing in the front yards, no gatherings of adults meeting by chance on pleasant afternoons. Anders was convinced that many of the people in his neighborhood had no idea what the lawn crews were doing with their topiary or hedging because they'd never even *seen* their own front yards.

Later that afternoon the doorbell boomed as Anders was having a beer and watching *SportsCenter*. Blake was napping, and the girl had the sleeping habits of a paranoid bloodhound. The slightest sound, movement of air particles, or change in barometric pressure and she'd spring up and seize the bars on the crib, loosing a soaring shriek that would ring in your ears for the rest of the day. Megan was on the computer in the kitchen and when the doorbell went off they both looked at each other with real anguish, as if they were on separating ice floes. They had a note taped over the doorbell button that read: *Please Knock Softly, Sleeping Baby*. Anders and Megan gesticulated at each other in frantic pantomime: *Who the hell rings the goddamn doorbell like that?* Anders sprang up and raced to the door, but as he grasped the knob it went off again, answered down the hall by Blake, the timbre of victory in her voice.

Anders flung open the door to find a short Mexican man in clean jeans and cowboy hat standing on the porch. A small group of men stood in the front yard. At the curb an enormous Dodge pickup, the kind favored by work crew foremen, idled with a throaty rumble.

Good afternoon, sir. My name is Salvador.

He smiled and bowed slightly, proffering a card.

Anders looked at the note covering the doorbell, then back at Salvador. He had a belt buckle the size of a small dinner plate in the shape of Texas.

I am asking, Salvador said, if you have some trouble with your roof.

Anders blinked. The men in the yard looked elsewhere, sweating in the shade of the oak tree. They weren't dressed like a normal work crew. These guys had pressed shirts and fancy cowboy boots like something a Texas congressman might wear. Behind him Blake's shriek had warbled into an approximation of a rebel yell.

My roof?

Yes sir. You been up on your roof, yes? Is there something wrong? We are expert roofers. Insured and licenses, we do all the roofs around here.

He held out the card again. Anders took it. It simply said *Salvador* and had a phone number on it.

I don't think so, Anders said. I mean, no, there isn't anything wrong with the roof.

Salvador shrugged.

Then perhaps, he said, you should stay off it, eh?

He pointed up, still smiling.

Is dangerous up there, you understand?

Anders nodded.

In the evening Anders sat on the patio drinking whiskey, his skin polished with a layer of deet. Inside Megan did a yoga DVD, her arms folded behind her head like a Hindu goddess. The even, stentorian breathing of Blake was audible on the baby monitor in the kitchen. Overhead jets droned invisibly, lining up for the pattern into DFW. All through his young life Anders was a social animal of the first order, and so he was completely unequipped to handle the developments of the last couple years. It felt as if his life was telescoping away from him, disappearing from view as night fell on the world outside this tight bubble of responsibility.

It took about a year of living in Dallas to really hit him. It was the early spring and Anders had been in the pool alone on a Saturday afternoon, Blake and Megan napping. The water was a cool seventy degrees and the mosquitoes had yet to issue forth from whatever underground lair they hibernated in. Anders read somewhere that the ancient Egyptians believed that insect life was created spontaneously from the effect of the sun on the muddy banks of the Nile. This bit of extrapolation made complete sense to Anders. How did they survive the winter, when

Dallas might have a foot of snow, a couple weeks of freezing temperatures? How deep in the soil did the larvae and eggs have to be planted to stay alive? Anders was thinking about all these things as he treaded water in the deep end, unconsciously putting up his hands to work on his leg strength, an old drill from his water polo days, when he suddenly became aware of his loneliness. Surely, on a day like this, in a pool like this, and people like himself and Megan . . . he didn't know how to finish this thought. Anders paddled to the shallow end and stood, hands on his hips. The wooden privacy fence gave the impression of a bowl that opened up onto clear, empty sky. The casual, muted sounds of occasional birds, the distant deep *whoosh* of the freeway. The dull thump and whack of work crews, roofers. He tried to picture the interior lives of these houses, these small brick-and-mortar capsules of life. There would be people inside, going on about the business of dreaming and living. But doing *what*, he couldn't imagine. It was blank. He was just over thirty years old.

On Monday Anders called the Dallas Public Works Department to notify them about the house across the alley.

I can see them right now, a literal cloud of mosquitoes.

I understand, sir.

Saturday there were about five of them on my daughter's face. We just walked outside. And with the West Nile Virus epidemic . . .

We will send someone over to check it out.

I think there is something strange going on over there. At this house.

What do you mean, sir?

Well.

What's strange?

I just think someone needs to take a look.

* * *

Blake struggled in her long pants and long-sleeved shirt, but after a block she collapsed, her head lolling at those amazing angles that only a toddler can endure, her face shining beneath the sun shade. Anders wanted to get a look at the front of the house across the alley, so he decided he'd take Blake out for a walk in the stroller. If they could hack the heat maybe they'd go the mile to the "lake," as it was called in Dallas parlance, which in reality was a runoff cesspool and duckshit depository. A narrow grass park surrounded the lake and each heavy rain left a thick watermark of cans, bottles, packaging, and plastic grocery bags. The members of a boat club bravely raced one-man dinghies on the weekends around the circuit of the lake, their zeal for victory moderated by the potential horror of capsizing into the murk. The turtles that rose to the surface to accept bread crumbs were the size of manhole covers, their backs carpets of lush algae, their soft exposed necks festooned with pale leeches. In the evening the surface of the lake roiled with the froth of mutant life, larvae, distended, globular fish, tadpoles that never fully transitioned into frogs.

But it was too hot for more than just a few blocks. The wide cement road was hazy with heat flares, the lawns down the road distorted and shimmering like oil on water, lifeless. Megan swore that a pair of young twins lived across the street, but Anders couldn't believe it. How could two young boys, subteen boys, live in a house and never play in the front yard, never swagger down the street on aggressive bikes, never make a yelp or holler, never clip a ball onto the roof, never climb a fucking tree? Two cars idled farther along, one an aging Hyundai compact that pulled away only to glide to the curb a few houses later. The flat lines of the roofs, all with girt-garnet asphalt shingles. The hedges had the same flat-edged look, sharp corners, heavy lines. The landscaping of Frank Lloyd Wright. The next block was the same again, this time two cars and a pickup, idling, tinted windows, pausing and drifting away as he drew near, like scuttling cockroaches on the kitchen counter.

The front of the house was dormant, heavy drapes pulled and the front stoop littered with leaves and lawn debris. The yard was black dirt with the occasional bunch of crabgrass and about a dozen ancient copies of the *Dallas Morning News* moldering in plastic bags cloudy with condensation. Nothing moved. Blake moaned and shifted, her face slick with sweat, so Anders turned back.

When nothing happened he called back on Wednesday.

I just wanted to check if someone went by there. This house I reported.

I'm afraid I cannot tell you that, sir.

What *can* you tell me?

I can tell you that the complaint was filed and acted upon.

What does *acted upon* mean?

I don't know, sir, but we have it here as resolved.

How is it resolved? The pool still has water in it. The mosquitoes are still horrendous. I can see them streaming over the fence.

Sir—

They are biting my daughter, my wife! You are aware of the West Nile problem?

I'm sorry, sir, but the file says it is resolved.

Well, can I report it again?

I'm afraid that wouldn't do any good.

What? Why?

Have a good day, sir. Goodbye.

Thursday evening Anders put his foot in his pool. Warm, like a vat of fresh urine. He thought about jumping in but he felt a bit sick, like he was coming down with something. The light under the diving board illuminated the sculpted cement bottom with patented Pebble Tec surfacing, six parts deep blue, two parts aquamarine. Anders had it done when they moved in and the color was perfect. To him it looked like the blue of a whale's eye in the deep valleys of the Pacific. He swatted away a mosquito trying to land on his lips. Anders had already weathered painful bites on his eyelid, between his toes, his inner ear. He gripped his drink and, staring at the limpid face of his pool, began to recount all the bad decisions he had made in his life.

Sometimes at night Anders heard the faint muttering of lips, the working mouths of the strangers who surrounded him, whispering in their sleep. Or not whispering; more like weeping. The yawning jaws and stifled sobs of men and women weeping in their catacomb beds, lying like sewing needles under the coverlet, the shuddering sigh and gasp of ragged sorrow. He didn't know if he was dreaming or awake. The city wept. Nothing mattered. Nobody mattered.

He felt a sharp pain like someone was pushing a thumbtack into the back of his neck, and when he slapped at it his hand came away with a splotch of blood the size of a quarter. That was somebody else's blood, he thought, someone else out here in the neighborhood. The notion made him feel dizzy with a kind of unwanted intimacy. He wiped his sweaty face. The feverish quality of the dreams and his general distorted sense of waking life worried him. He hadn't felt well lately, not at all.

Later that night, after a few more whiskeys, Anders crouched on the peak of the roof weighing in his hand the "mosquito bomb" that he'd picked up at the hardware store. It was about the size of a golf ball, designed for large bodies of water, up to a hundred thousand gallons. The tricky part was lobbing it in there. It was only about twenty yards across the alley, but the mosquito bomb was light. He would really have to whip it. If he missed he had two more. Even at night, the heat was punishing on the roof, his shirt soaked down the back and his feet slipping in his flip-flops. He rose up and launched one. He could tell immediately the trajectory was no good, too high, and it fell just over the fence, short of the pool.

Anders fished the second bomb out of his pocket and gave it the full arm and overshot the pool, the mosquito bomb hitting the dusty sliding glass back door with a solid *pock*. The door looked like it hadn't been opened in years, so he fished out the third bomb and dropped it neatly into the green muck, dead center.

He was crabbing down the roof to the side fence when the sliding door was flung open and a young man stepped out, a flabby twentysomething white guy in a black T-shirt and wearing some kind of wool hat. He looked around the backyard and pool with a slack-jawed expression. Behind him Anders saw what looked like dozens of waving hands, delicately fingered. The room was full of plants, tall ones, the ceiling hung with twisting cables and hoses, racks of lighting, misting systems. Anders immediately knew what this was. Last year he and Megan sat through the first three seasons of *Weeds* on DVD, before it got really stupid.

Then a young woman stepped out, also dressed in black, her hair streaked with raven and vermilion, her face the pasty pallor of a Welsh miner. The young man slung his lantern jaw around at her and she raised an arm and pointed directly at Anders, now with one foot on the side fence, balancing.

Anders dropped to the ground with that peculiar, surprising drunken dexterity that rarely happens when you need it, rolling over in the grass and to his feet in one motion. Inside the house he checked on Megan and Blake, both of them sleeping soundly. He locked the doors and windows, turned the alarm system on. He peered through the blinds of his back window, his pool glowing dully from the ambient light of Dallas, the dark fence, no light or movement on the other side of the alley. Anders looked up the nonemergency number and made the call to the police.

The operator took down the information and said they would send someone by shortly to talk to him.

Why do you have to come talk to me?

Procedure, sir.

But I don't want to talk to you. I want you to go over there and bust a drug house. They are growing a ton of weed over there. *And* their pool is breeding mosquitoes.

We need to take statements about what you witnessed.

But I'm telling you now!

I'm sorry, sir. The officers will be around shortly.

Anders made himself a drink and was taking his first sip when the doorbell rang, booming through the house. *Again?* He could see a police officer standing on his porch. It had been about three minutes. The baby monitor registered the scuttle of blanket and stuffed animal as Blake scrambled to her feet to begin her ardent vocalizations.

The cop introduced himself as Officer Meyer and shook Anders's hand. He was a young man, maybe thirty, wearing wraparound sunglasses, his neck raw from razor burn. At the curb an unmarked car sat idling, another cop in the driver's seat, his face illuminated by the blue glare of a smart phone. Anders repeated what he had seen on the roof and Officer Meyer scribbled in a small notebook, nodding his head. Down the hall Blake's siren pitched into something akin to an Apache blood lamentation.

It's good that you called us, sir, Officer Meyer said. This is important information.

He tapped the notebook with his pencil. Officer Meyer had veins running across his biceps and his uniform was snug across the chest, like he had recently gained weight. The shoulders of his shirt had epaulets with gray bands, something Anders had never seen before.

What are you going to do? Anders asked.

I'm afraid I can't reveal that, sir. Operational details.

When he smiled he revealed a swath of misdirectional teeth like a collapsing fence line.

Okay, Anders said. I understand. Don't forget about the mosquito thing.

Of course, sir.

It's really ruining our summer, you know? For the whole neighborhood.

Officer Meyer grinned again and glanced back at his car for a moment, shoving his notebook into his back pocket. Anders realized why his uniform looked strange across the chest: although Meyer had the silver Dallas Police Department badge over his breast pocket, he had no name tag. Did cops still wear name tags? Anders couldn't remember. The night air shifted for a moment and Officer Meyer sort of sighed and relaxed his shoulders. Anders batted away a pair of mosquitoes that circled his face.

We will take care of it, sir. Just do me a favor?

What?

Stay off the roof.

We need to call an exterminator, Megan said the next morning.

Anders was trying to find his least wrinkled dress shirt in the closet, Blake wearing her Batman mask and clinging to his leg.

We've got rats or something, Megan said.

What?

I could hear them through the ceiling.

She drank her coffee in the doorway, bathrobe askew, a pair of Anders's old boxers visible underneath. Unchanged, he thought. He felt like he was withering away and his wife hadn't aged a day.

Footsteps, Megan said. Running around all night. Creepy.

Friday evening the people two houses down were having a barbecue, so Anders lacquered himself up with deet and sat sweating on the chaise lounge, drinking a watery Jack Daniel's and listening to the laughter and music. A squadron of mosquitoes hovered over his exposed skin searching for a weak spot. Blake trundled her stroller around the patio wearing a full-body caftan and a broad-brimmed hat with netting tucked into her collar that Megan had rigged up. Anders turned on the pool light, a great glowing eye in the deep end. Haven't been in the damn thing in almost a month, he thought. Maybe I will tonight. A wave of nausea passed through him and he watched the glassy film of the pool for a moment, thinking about powerful chemicals on his skin, in his blood, rearranging his DNA, juggling the color-coded molecules of his being. He felt like shit. The people at the party started playing "puka shells," Megan's name for Kenny Chesney, so Anders figured he'd better get inside and start bedtime for Blake.

They bathed her together, Anders playing counting games as Megan scrubbed the day's accumulation of grime, sweat, and chemicals off her skin until she was pink and shining. Then Anders read three books to her in the big chair while Megan tidied up the room. Soon he turned off the lights and left them there, cuddling together in Blake's bed, Megan asking a set of questions that Blake answered with a tiny, angelic voice. Anders stood in the darkened hallway, swaying, listening to his wife and daughter.

What was your favorite thing you did today? *Play with stroller an Batman.* What would you like to do tomorrow? *Play in backyard wid Batman an Daddy. The 'squitoes make Daddy mad.* What are you most thankful for? *The planes.* What planes? *They make rain. The rain for 'squitoes.* What do you want more than anything in the world? *Daddy to be happy. Is Daddy happy, Momma? Is he?*

Later, Anders perched on the peak of the roof over the garage like a ruined gargoyle. The party a few houses down had gone quiet at eleven o'clock and Anders had now been squatting on the roof for several hours, watching the house across the alley. There were lights on and he could see the dim outline of moving shapes through the heavy curtains. The kitchen window had louvered blinds turned up slightly, so from this angle he had a fair look at the sink and stove area. The young woman who'd spotted him before came into view, filling up a blue teapot. She put the teapot on a burner and lay a cup and tea bag beside it on the counter. Then she stood at the sink, washing her hands, the crimson streak in her hair shining. In the kitchen light she looked young, her face sweetly composed as she stared at her hands under the water. Can't be more than twenty-five, Anders thought. Somebody's daughter. How do you end up here?

In the distance the droning sound of engines, semi trucks gearing down on the freeway, deliveries, drug couriers, dark workers, vans of illicit goods, carjacked SUVs, midnight road machines tearing up asphalt and laying it down, fresh and new.

The young woman dried her hands and then someone to the side handed her a large Ziploc bag. She held it up to the light, appraising the contents. Anders took out his phone and switched to camera mode, holding it forward and trying to get the images to congeal. Too dark and too far away. He needed to get closer, and with a better camera. He could see the spray of steam coming from the teapot spout, and heard the thin sound of a whistle growing louder.

Amigo.

When he spun around there were two men standing on the roof behind him, a pair of dark silhouettes where the garage met the house. They stood with a practiced familiarity, at ease, one with a long-handled spade resting over his shoulder. Anders rose from his crouch, stuffing his phone into his pocket.

Yes? What?

Amigo, one of the men said in a low voice, we have tried to tell you. Of the danger here.

What danger?

The roof.

Anders glanced down the line of houses to his left and right, the rooftops empty. The sluggish night breeze pushed the trees into a slow rotation, branches creaking, and for a moment he thought he saw the limbs of his neighbors' trees full of forms, bodies in all manner of repose, the trees throughout the neighborhood thronged with men.

I can get on my own roof if I want, he said.

Give us the camera.

The man with the long-handled spade on his shoulder stepped forward, and in the shifting moonlight Anders could see his face, a middle-aged man, weathered, tired eyes. He held out his hand.

This will go badly for you.

This is *my* house. My roof.

Not your roof.

What?

Our roof. You see?

The second man stepped into the light as well, his arms loose, hands empty. He was younger, long hair pulled back into a ponytail, a utility belt around his thin waist. The other man took the spade off his shoulder and brandished it in front of him like a medieval pike. He began to move to the right and Anders backed away before he realized that he was now cut off from the side fence and the way down.

We have no choice now, the ponytailed man said. He had just the slightest touch of an accent, like he'd been educated in excellent American schools. My friend, he said, you have made a terrible mistake.

He started forward, his posture still relaxed, and Anders again stepped away, now backed into the far corner of the garage roof. The night air suddenly seemed to compress, a dull rattling roar developing to the west, and like some kind of biblical plague unleashed, all manner of animal and insect came sweeping over the roof; a platoon of chattering squirrels, streams of birds, a million flying bugs of every type whacking into them in a hard panic, and all three men crouched slightly and turned away from the onslaught. The next moment a dual-prop plane came roaring low over the trees, dumping a blanket of heavy mist scented like peppermint and bleach that settled on the men like a fog. Anders gouged at his eye sockets with his fists, coughing, his clothes instantly damp and his skin sticky, opening his eyes to see the man with the spade drawing it back like a axe over his shoulder. He took a wild chopping swing, slanting downward, and Anders dropped to his hands and knees, the spade cutting the air above his head before sinking into the shingles just beside him. Anders instinctively reached out and grabbed the shaft of the spade as the man tried to work it loose. There was a momentary frantic tug-of-war, but Anders outweighed this man by at least fifty pounds and a twisting pull brought the guy stumbling down the roof and flying over the edge with a short cry of alarm.

The one with the ponytail was quickly there beside him and Anders felt a sharp pain under his arm; as he twisted away in shock he saw that the man was holding a long, curved pruning knife in his outstretched hand like an offering, the blade wet and red. Heat spread across his side and a thin finger of pain began to creep through his chest. The chemical fog settled down around their waists and they both coughed, covering up their mouths with their hands.

When the man stepped forward and slashed at him, Anders caught the blade on his left forearm, the knife rattling across the bone of his elbow. Anders got his right hand on the knife arm and, rolling backward, used his momentum to toss the ponytailed man over him and off the roof, Anders doing a back somersault and going over the edge as well, his fingers trailing over the gutter as he fell into space. Silence.

In his first moment of free fall Anders found himself trying to look at the stab wound in his side that blazed with heat, then the next moment he considered the landing. Then he heard the ponytailed man hit the water of the pool and relief washed over him just before he tumbled in headfirst on top of his assailants.

There was a flurry of limbs and water and Anders allowed himself to stay under, opening his eyes and getting his bearings. The underwater pool light was blinding to his left, but directly in front of him the legs of one of the men kicked frantically, and Anders saw the curved pruning knife falling to the pool bottom, coming to rest with a clink beside the long-handled spade. The next moment the water was enveloped in a crimson cloud of blood, *his* blood.

Anders ground his teeth and grabbed a handful of the man's pants and climbed up his back, pulling him under. He got his legs around the man's torso and pivoted his hips, forcing the man down so that he was horizontal with Anders astride him, a position they called "horseback" in water polo. The first man, the one who'd swung at him with the spade, was doing a furious dog paddle just a couple feet from the deck edge, his breath coming hard. The guy under him twisted and clawed at his legs but Anders got his ankles locked and began to squeeze, forcing the air out of the man's chest, the dull pop of cracking rib bones reverberating in the water. The other man reached the deck edge and turned back with a look of terror, mucus running out of his nose.

Dios mío, por favor!

Anders reached out and got him around the throat, yanking him off the wall. He got a forearm under his armpit and across the back of his neck and he cranked the man's head underwater. This man barely fought at all, quivering in Anders's arms like a sobbing child as he held him under.

When he released them, the man between his legs slowly drifted to the pool bottom, barely discernible in the blood-red water, his form a silhouette against underwater light. The second man bobbed on the surface, his back humped and hair spreading out like a halo, and Anders pushed him away toward the diving board.

Anders was panting, suddenly exhausted, the sound of his exhalations seeming to echo in the small canyon of the backyard. The red water in the pool sloshed like a bathtub, and he looked around wildly at the dark windows of his house, the yard, the fence, the plastic owl perched on the diving board watching him. The pain under his side began to broadcast itself again and, glancing down, Anders could see the quick, steady pulse of blood that emerged from him like puffs of red smoke.

He heard a voice from above and saw another man standing on the peak of the roof, secured by ropes that led up into the trees, a phone held to his face, the glow of the screen illuminating his moving mouth. Anders treaded water and watched him speak, his voice faint and indecipherable. Anders held out an arm, slick with blood, and beckoned him with a crooked finger.

C'mon in, Anders said.

The guy smiled slightly and the next moment Anders heard men running in the alley. The back fence shook and a pair of hands gripped the top. Two pairs of hands. One hand held a pistol.

Oh God—Blake, Megan . . .

Anders turned and stroked to the shallow end, finding his feet and charging up the stairs. When he reached the back door the first gunshot came, splintering the brick framing of the door. He slung the sliding door open and dove into the house as the second shot spidered the glass, the third shattering it completely. Anders crawled across the kitchen floor, slipping on the glass shards, through the living room, heading toward the bedroom. A wave of weakness washed over him and for a moment he wasn't sure he could stand. In the backyard there was a babble of Spanish and the sound of men jumping off the fence onto the patio. Footsteps crunched across the roof in several directions. Megan appeared in the main hallway, white-faced, holding Blake tightly in her arms.

What is happening?

He figured he had maybe ten seconds before they were in the house. Anders rose up and ran to his wife and daughter and, taking Megan's hand, led her to the front door. Blake was shaking, her face stretched into a silent scream, tears streaming down her face. His daughter pointed at his shirt, torn and stained deep red, his arm with the deep slash across the elbow exposing a white nub of bone. Megan clutched at him wildly with her free hand.

Run, he said. Don't look back. Down the street toward the avenue, and scream for help, as loud as you can. *Go!*

Anders opened the door and, pushing them before him, they all ran out past the trimmed hedges and across the dark front lawn. Megan ran swiftly, barefoot and soundless, with Blake watching over her shoulder as Anders pounded after them, his legs heavy and awkward. Megan began screaming.

Help us! Please, somebody help us!

The street was empty, the line of houses that stretched before them dark and endless. He was staggering behind them as they ran down the middle of the street, and the stars that he knew were not there began sparkling, expanding, as if the night sky was descending. He heard himself screaming, his voice clotted and strange.

Please help us!

The lights began exploding around him like flashbulbs, and Anders stumbled and fell to his knees. Megan and Blake were now farther ahead, becoming dim shapes.

Get up!

He saw Megan and Blake slowing, stopping.

Keep running!

More lights began to gather, emerging from the murk, and Anders thought of the muddy banks of the Nile, a man in a white-belted tunic carrying a reed basket, watching the tidal flats, burbling with gaseous emissions of carbon life. And the thinly wound cocoons of grublike flesh that sprouted six arms and pushed out of a squalid burrow to crawl the river bottom, avoiding carp and crayfish, scuttling up the bank, driven out of the water by a preternatural urge, standing now, amazed at the fresh wet wings that unfurled like flags of champion nations on a battlefield. That first flight must have been glorious! And then to navigate a land of such immensity, of moving worlds beyond comprehension, and, when finally alight on some shifting alien landscape, dipping your proboscis deep through the skin of giants, feeding on their hot coursing nectar, swelling to three times your natural size. The courage of such a thing! The majesty!

He could see other shapes around his wife and child, forms emerging from the houses, other voices, and Anders saw the lights in the houses coming on, open doorways streaming with light. People were rushing out across their lawns, men and women and children, people putting their hands on him, the sounds of their concerned voices, asking, *What's the matter, what's the matter, what's the matter?*

THE REALTOR

BY Bᴇɴ Fᴏᴜɴᴛᴀɪɴ

Swiss Avenue

B y their early thirties they'd made an outrageous amount of money. It had started with a group of eight investors, most of them lawyers who'd joined the same downtown firm within a couple of years of one another. Even though they'd been full-fledged professionals then, their lives still centered on whatever sport was in season, but now they played in the bar association leagues. Touch football in fall, basketball in winter, softball in spring and summer; it didn't occur to them not to play. Only one of their group was married by the age of thirty. The rest of them continued as always, making and spending money, dating the women they met in bars. When Brice's mother fell ill, he tried to be as good a son as possible from long distance, shuttling from Dallas to Omaha every couple of weeks. His father had died when Brice was in law school, but his two sisters still lived near their mother. Strictly speaking, they could have managed without him, but Brice was determined to do his part, and it turned out to be the longest ten months of his life, juggling his law practice with the almost ceremonial pace of his mother's death.

That same year, his friend Steve left the firm to start a high-tech company with a former frat brother, live-streaming college sports over this new, suddenly ubiquitous thing called the Internet. When Steve appealed to his old friends for capital, Brice invested $40,000, half his inheritance, and figured he'd never see that money again. The truth was, he hardly cared. It was as if the money would always connect with the hospital smells of latex, catheter bags, the ammonia stench of disinfectant that could still turn his stomach. His mother had suffered, badly. He'd seen it up close. Those last few weeks he'd done little else but sit by her bed and hold her hand.

So he wrote the check and kissed that money goodbye. Thirty months later the company went public and made them all millionaires many times over. A year of extreme partying followed. They chartered private jets to Cannes, the Super Bowl, skiing in the Alps. Every birthday in their group was celebrated lavishly, spectacularly. They became famous in Dallas for their parties, their guy-fantasy trips abroad, and what had once been a nice, steady supply of good-looking women morphed into a scene. All you wanted, quantity and quality; that first year had been insane in its pleasures, though Brice came to realize that having money made you a harder person. It was necessary. You couldn't trust people the way you had before, because so many of them wanted something from you. But it had its kicks, this new dynamic, it gave an edge to the sport of getting women into bed, and what you did with them once you were there. The more you had, the more you were allowed to take, apparently, and if Brice got what he wanted with virtually no strings attached, it was their own fault, they offered. There were times when his behavior was downright shitty. He didn't necessarily admire every aspect of this person he'd become, but he was experimenting, pushing boundaries. It was part of his education in this new way of life.

He started shopping for a house in the spring. He'd already bought an Aston Martin, and upscaled his wardrobe; aside from women and the trips with his friends, he couldn't think of anything else to spend his money on, so he started driving around on weekends, dropping in at the open houses. Realtors, he quickly decided, were shallow, often desperate people, which made it easy and satisfying to mess with their minds. He'd kept his old beat-up Camry for everyday use, and that was the car he usually took on his house-hunting rounds, parking right in front of whatever tricked-out Italianate or Georgian mansion caught his eye, so the realtor inside would be sure to see his humble ride. And how they snubbed him! They'd hardly give him a minute of their precious time, but if the house was interesting he might return in his Aston for the next open house, often as not with one of his flashy girlfriends. Then, of course, the realtors fell all over him. It was a joke, their blatant shamelessness, and he wondered if it was this crude everywhere, or if Dallas was different, more mercenary. Since coming into his money, Brice's opinion of human nature had dropped considerably.

He wasn't in any rush. People said it was a buyer's market, and he liked walking through the houses, seeing how people lived. He felt informed; so many different ways to go about life, and he liked inserting himself into the various possibilities. Then things got busy at work—he was still practicing law—but he took most of August off to travel, and didn't start looking again until early fall.

He met Laney on a Sunday afternoon in September, at an open house she was holding for one of the grand old mansions on Swiss Avenue. Her name tag was pinned to the sweater of her trim skirt suit, *Laney Shaver*, and she gave him a smile as he slipped inside, dodging the jam-up of middle-aged couples in the foyer. She wasn't all that special—*cute* would be the operative word for this youthful, pretty woman in her late thirties, early forties. She was fair-skinned, with auburn hair cut short, and a slim, fit frame, not much in the way of a chest. She was dressed as if for church, and for some reason this appealed to him, the notion that she'd gone to services this morning, then headed straight into a busy afternoon of selling real estate.

"Beautiful house," he said when she caught up with him in the dining room. Her gear was here—MLS fact sheets, the sign-in form, the big satchel that all women realtors seemed to have.

"Isn't it? I really love the old houses. Especially the ones that've been completely updated!" She laughed. Her voice had the bright timbre of a socialite's, slightly breathless, and she didn't quite close her r's. "Are you looking for something over here?"

He shrugged. "Just looking, mainly. Highland Park, University, Preston Hollow . . ." He let his voice trail off. "But it's nice over here."

"It's very nice. And if you work downtown it's a straight shot on Swiss, five minutes max."

"I'm not sure I want to be that close to work," he answered, which got a laugh. "I guess these walls are real plaster?"

"Real plaster. You don't see construction like this anymore. Now, step back, just take a second and see how it does in the light. There's a kind of glow. Plaster has a warmth you don't get with any other material."

Brice nodded. He did see it, he told himself, even as he was aware of wanting to think he was seeing it.

"It calms people down, I've noticed, that glow. Even the most hyper kids'll come into a room like this and you can see them settle down, it's almost like a drug."

"Interesting. Too bad I don't have kids."

"But grown-ups like it too!" she cried, spinning it for a jokey sales pitch. There were voices in the foyer, new arrivals. She gestured at him as if to say, *Help yourself*, and headed toward the front.

He took his time touring the house. It was a rambling, wide-bodied place in the Craftsman style, built, according to the MLS fact sheet, in 1911. Five bedrooms, four full baths and two halfs, a third-floor office/media room, a solarium, finished basement, pool with Brazilian teak deck, detached two-car garage with upstairs guest quarters. Miele appliances in the kitchen, a fortune in granite countertops. The house was fully modernized, though some of the small classy touches had been retained: the dumb-waiter, the claw-foot bathtubs, the ornate cast-iron trapdoor for the basement coal chute. This was a house for a big, rambunctious, well-to-do family, and Brice conjured up a sepia-toned image of five or six lively kids clattering up and down the stairs, a staff of longtime servants who never complained, and the handsome mother moving about in long skirts, her hair pulled back in a prim Victorian bun. Cheerful father returned home in the evenings to a rowdy hue and cry from the kids, a demure yet promising kiss from the wife. He was a wise, strong, loving man who took the trolley downtown every Monday through Friday and made piles of money. The hot tub came much later, obviously.

Brice's Camry was the only car parked out front by the time he made his way back to the dining room. Laney was packing her sales materials into her satchel-style purse. It was after five; the open house was over.

"So what do you think?" she asked brightly.

"It's great." His car was clearly visible through the front windows. "But probably not the right house for a single man."

"Sure. Unless you were looking to expand someday."

He chuckled. "Sure, someday. But I'm not in any rush."

"No reason why you would be. But it is a lot of house for one person. Did you see the Willet window downstairs? Come on, I'll show you," she said, reacting to Brice's blank look. She led him down the narrow, winding staircase off the kitchen to the basement, most of which had been converted to a walk-in wine cellar. Set high in the wall, shot through with late-afternoon sun, was a small stained-glass rendering of grapes on the vine, done in a highly idealized pastoral style.

"That's beautiful. I guess I didn't notice it before."

"It has to get the light like this to really jump out. It's Willet glass, early twentieth century, very rare. They found it through a picker in upstate New York and had it installed with the remodel."

"Nice. Who are these people, by the way?"

"Doctors. Husband and wife."

"And they're selling—"

"They bought a bigger place down the street."

"What, they have twenty kids?"

Laney smiled. He'd already told her he wasn't interested, yet she was talking to him like she had all the time in the world. But Brice was starting to see the house in a different light. It could be the perfect house for a bachelor, if you were thinking of taking your game to the next level. With the chandeliers, the twelve-foot ceilings in the formal rooms, the grand staircase, and acres of hardwood floors, you could have some world-class parties here. What woman wouldn't be stoked to walk into a house like this? He imagined Gatsby-style blowouts of elegance and excess, women running around the place in their underwear.

He asked about the cellar, not idly; he was learning about wine. As they made their way upstairs he quizzed her about mold, roof, foundation, HVAC. Were the sellers motivated?

Laney thought for a moment. "Fairly motivated. Tell me this: how much money do you want to spend?"

He lowballed his range. She didn't bat an eye.

"I don't think they'll go for that. I'll check, but I don't think . . . I know of some other things I could show you. If you're interested."

"Sure."

"We'll need to get your agent involved, of course."

"I don't have an agent."

"You don't? Brice, you really need an agent. I think I should be your agent."

He laughed. The way she stood there, so trim and poised, so tastily self-contained, sparked off a longing in him. There was a tautness about her frame, a tensile balance that seemed to hint at spring-coiled energies expertly held in check. This could be fun, he told himself. She wasn't at all the kind of bombshell he'd grown accustomed to, but she was cute, fiercely cute, she had her own little mojo going. He had to fight the urge to ask her out right then.

"All right," he said. "So why don't you be my agent?"

That poise he was seeing, as it turned out, was twenty years of formal study in dance. She'd started in Dallas at the age of five, at Miss Hilda's Dance Academy in Snider Plaza, and continued through college and beyond, spending most of her twenties in New York, "dancing and starving," as she put it. There appeared to be no husband in the picture, past or present. She drove a small white Lexus sedan that wasn't particularly well maintained, and had a desk and phone at the offices of Whitley-Brown Associates, a storefront operation in Lakewood that resembled a boiler room, with a dozen or so lady brokers all sharing the same space. His first time there, he parked the Aston right in front of the plate-glass window. All those women were beaming at him when he walked in, their eyes flashing, cheeks flushed—the Aston had clearly caused a stir—but Laney was cool. She offered a breezy "Hel-loooo," and led him right back out the door to her car.

This was annoying. She ought to gush at least a little, Brice thought. At a certain point it was appropriate for a woman to acknowledge, in theory at least, all the things a wealthy man could do for her, but Laney just showed him to her Lexus and off they went, Brice thumbing through MLS fact sheets while she drove too fast and described the day's prospects.

That first day they saw six houses. A few days later they saw six more, and by the weekend he'd lost count. This was not a woman who wasted time, he gathered. Within his stated price range of $800,000 to $900,000 she'd found an exhausting array of prospects, but after a week of noncommittal looking he sensed she was growing impatient with him. On Saturday they were stopped at a signal on Preston Road, and the moment the light turned green she gunned a left across two lanes of oncoming traffic.

"Nice," he murmured.

"Sorry. Does my driving scare you?"

"Not really. You've got skills."

She laughed. "I do?"

"Sure. You're fast, but you aren't reckless. You anticipate."

"Oh, so that's what I'm doing."

"I bet you never get tickets."

She laughed again. "Almost never!"

"Just to show you how safe I feel, I'm going to unbuckle—"

"Stop." She was giggling.

"I'll just reattach it here, right here behind me so it doesn't ping—"

"Stop!"

"There." He straightened up in his seat.

"Brice, buckle your seat belt!"

"Why? I'm fine, I'm perfectly safe. Nothing's going to happen."

"You're perfectly nuts is what you are."

This was the way they developed with each other, a kind of razzing semiflirtation carried on at arm's length. She did not, he suspected, take him entirely seriously. His buying power made him a serious client, but personally she wouldn't engage on any meaningful level. They joked around. Or he joked; mostly she smiled and nodded, as if indulging him. Maybe a man of thirty-two just wasn't that interesting to her. Not experienced enough, not tested. Perhaps he couldn't help but come across as somewhat clueless.

None of this would have mattered if he weren't oddly taken with her. It didn't make any sense. She was cute, sure, she had a neat little body, and her pared-down style was a nice change from the overproduced Dallas look. Laney didn't wear much makeup. She could knock her hair into place with one pass of her hand. Objectively speaking, he could do better—did do better, all the time. That she was so cool and private about herself was part of it, he decided. The challenge of cracking that facade, of wanting the one thing that seemed beyond your reach. He was savvy to the basic psychology of it, but the burning thing that egged him on, that had to be chemistry, pheromones.

Over time she dropped a few details about herself. She'd gone to a small liberal arts college in Vermont, but never mentioned when she'd graduated. Her parents were dead. She had a sister, a niece, and a nephew in Houston, and a condo in East Dallas, the location of which she left appropriately vague. On Saturday mornings she taught ballet to preschoolers at a studio in Preston Center, for fun, she said, just to be around dance and because she adored those little girls.

One day when they were driving down Fairfield Street, in the heart of Highland Park, she pulled up near the corner of Miramar and pointed to an empty lot.

"That's where I grew up."

He waited a beat. "You camped out?"

"Hush! There used to be a house. We sold it after Mom died, to a builder. I hated to do it but he made the best offer, and of course he razed it first thing. Then the economy tanked and it's just been sitting like that for the last three years."

"That's lousy. The house you grew up in."

"He swore he wasn't going to tear it down, but I knew. They always do. Just before we closed I came over and took a bunch of pictures."

"Is it for sale?"

"Not officially. He's just sitting on it. I hear through the grapevine he's waiting till he can get a million dollars for it."

They were silent for a moment.

"You never told me you grew up rich."

She laughed. "I didn't!"

His head swivelled left and right. "Looks to me like we're in the middle of Highland Park."

"Well, it wasn't always like this. It was middle class." She caught his look. "Okay, nice middle class. Not like it is now—"

"Obnoxious?"

She nodded and laughed again. He wondered if she knew it would make him want her more, the idea that she'd grown up in Dallas's most exclusive neighborhood. He was really trying with her. He watched his language, opened doors, insisted on paying when they stopped for snacks, even though she could write off the expense. He was aware that the past two years had coarsened him, but that was a stage, he told himself, a necessary period of adjustment. He was a better man than that. With time he could work himself back to the way he used to be.

In early October he and his friends chartered a 727 and flew to Tokyo for the Japanese Grand Prix. "The ultimate road trip," they christened the adventure, which was extravagant enough to make the "Seen on the Scene" column of the *Dallas Morning News*, with the names of Brice and his buddies highlighted in bold.

Laney didn't see it. Or pretended not to have seen it. On their next outing she asked where he'd gone, and he gave her the basics: Private jet. Japan. The final race of the Grand Prix season. Parties. Lots of parties. She could fill in the rest for herself.

"Sounds exciting," she said mildly.

Brice tried not to be irritated. "And you, what've you been doing?"

"Working!" she cried.

"The whole time?"

"The whole time. I told you, realtors never take a day off. When everybody else is off, that's our busiest time. And when everybody's at work, we're working too."

"Come on, there must be some time . . . Christmas. What about Christmas?"

"Okay," she allowed. "I admit, I've never worked on Christmas Day."

"How long do you think you can keep this up?"

"Excuse me?"

"This kind of pace, how long can you do it? It just seems like you'd burn out sooner or later."

"Well, I don't know, Brice, I guess I can do it as long as it takes. Till I win the lottery, how about that?"

"Do you like it?"

"Sure," she replied in a droll voice, "I like it fine. I like it better in the months when I've sold a few houses." She was gently mocking him, he realized. The conversation had gotten away from him. He regrouped.

"Well," he said, "I missed you, over in Japan. I missed our house-hunting trips together."

"Aw, that's sweet."

"And I missed your driving."

She laughed. "Nobody's ever said that before!"

It was Saturday, a warm Indian summer afternoon. She was wearing a skirt, pumps, a lightweight jersey top with the sleeves rolled up to her elbows, her casual sexiness setting off a jangling in his gut. When she unlocked the door of the first house and let them in, the atmospherics gave him a titillatory rush. The strange house, the two of them alone, her cool efficiency with the keys—it all had the feeling of an affair, that sexed-up charge of sneaking around.

"You like it?"

He realized he was grinning at her. Sure, he said. Seems nice. In fact it was just another over-the-top builder's special, seven thousand square feet of architectural bombast. She showed him several more in the same style, and they finished the afternoon at a '60s modern in Highland Park West, a dark place with a cheap-looking mansard roof, skinny windows facing the street, and a master bathroom tiled entirely in black. The master bedroom got them both sniggering, its floor-to-ceiling mirrored walls and antiqued Roman columns modeled on a strip club owner's idea of class. Their walk-through ended at the backyard pool. The yard was enclosed by a high double-slatted fence, reinforced by a hedge of ten-foot high ligustrum.

"Very private," Laney deadpanned. She directed Brice's attention to the lagoonlike pool. "Look, they painted the guanite black, to hold the heat." She knelt by the side and swished her hand through the water. "Feel."

Brice knelt beside her. He flinched when his hand touched the water, its blood-warmth faintly repulsive, mismatched to the day. It was moving toward evening, and the air had already taken on a chill.

"So." Laney stood. "What do you think?"

"It's okay. I don't know. It just seems . . ."

"What?"

"Well, kind of shabby. Off. A step or two below what you've been showing me."

"There's a reason for that. For what you want, your price range, we've seen about everything that's on the market right now. We're starting to scrape the bottom of the barrel."

"Okay."

When he didn't say more, she spoke briskly, motioning him to the nearby chaise lounges. "Let's sit. We need to talk."

He couldn't help smiling. He had a notion of what was about to come. They sat.

"Have you seen anything you're seriously interested in? As in, something you'd like to make an offer on."

"Maybe. You've shown me a lot of nice—"

She raised her hand. "Stop it, stop being so polite. Is there anything that stands out in your mind, okay? If you had to make an offer right now, is there one you would pick?"

"I don't know. Maybe if I went back and looked through all the material . . ."

She was shaking her head. "No, unh-unh. I want you to tell me what it is you're looking for. What exactly do you want, Brice, that's what I'm asking."

"Just what I said when we started out. Something nice, in the Park Cities, Preston Hollow—"

"No, I'm talking about the big picture, okay? What do you want in your life? What do you want out of your life?"

"Oh." He chuckled, but she wasn't smiling. He flailed for a moment, then got himself together. "I want the same things everybody else wants, I guess. A family. A nice house. You know, just a decent, normal life."

"You want a family. And a house."

"I do."

"A house I can help you with, but you've got to work with me here, buddy. Give me some reaction, something to go on. We've looked at fifty-six houses so far—is there anything in that bunch you really like?"

"Well, I liked a lot of them. But not enough to make an offer, I guess."

She sighed, looked away.

"The house on Swiss, I liked that. Where we met. That house had, I don't know, character. I guess you could say I could see myself living there."

"That's a lot of house for a single guy. You said so yourself."

"Hey," he smiled and held out his hands as if pleading, beseeching, "I didn't say I was gonna stay single the rest of my life!" She laughed. They were flirting, it seemed. It was finally out in the open. Brice felt incredibly happy.

"Really."

"Really."

"You've never said anything about it before."

"Well, I am now. You wanna have dinner?" He pitched it half as a joke, a zingy one-liner. She laughed loudly, appreciatively. "And I think that house would be a great investment," he added.

"I think you're right." She leaned back and gave him an appraising look. "I told the owners about you, by the way. What your upper range is. They said thanks, but they aren't ready to come down that far. Yet."

He was confused. Surely by now she'd figured out that he'd lowballed his range. He could easily meet their price, she had to know that. And yet she played along, wouldn't call him on it.

"I'm serious. How about dinner?"

She cocked her head. She was smiling. Then she laughed. "You really are serious, aren't you?"

"I really am." All in, he thought. The couple of seconds she made him wait, it felt like his face would crack.

"Screw dinner," she said at last. "Let's go look at that house."

It was deep dusk, almost dark when they arrived. "Let's go upstairs," she said as soon as they were inside, and halfway up the stairs she took his hand. His legs went weak, mushy, like he was sixteen again and getting with girls for the first time, almost sick with the hormone rush of it. Stupid. No way he should be this nervous, this absurdly worked up. A faint wash of light filtered up through the stairwell to the master bedroom, where they managed to get most of their clothes off before he scooped her up in a bulldoze charge toward the bed, Laney screeching, laughing, locking her legs around his waist, and down they went with a mighty thump, his weight forcing a satisfied *ahhh* from her chest. She laughed. She was game. He loved the feel of her whippet body as they shucked the rest of their clothes, and once they were naked he pulled back and grazed the length of her, her skin yielding, springing back at his touch. The thrash and torque of her response were marvelous, but he wouldn't lose himself in it. By this point in his life he'd learned some things. He knew how to ward off messes, entanglements, awkward situations, though right now he was tempted to let himself go, let the infatuation get the better of him. And when the infatuation passed? By then she'd be thinking certain understandings had been reached. She'd have assumptions, expectations. It wouldn't be fair to her.

All the crazy shit that goes through your head during sex, he thought. You wanted it to be clean, no more or less than it was, yet so much else was always pressing in at the edges. They were well into it when she climbed on top. He laughed at the deliberate way she took charge, and she chuckled, nodding, acknowledging the moment, approving his good-natured acquiescence. She settled onto him with a dreamy half-smile, planting her hands on his chest and rolling her hips. She seemed so pleased with him, that was the thing. Once again he was conscious of the need to be careful. She was on top, but it felt like he was the one who was barely hanging on, and he watched her all the way to the end, when her eyes closed and her face clenched and her fingernails curled into his chest.

He wanted to see her when she was most herself, as if that knowledge might give him some sort of advantage. She collapsed on him when they were done, her embrace so jumbled and headlong that he saw possibilities even in this, her spontaneous tenderness. For what seemed like several minutes, they didn't move.

"I hope nobody's planning to do a showing right now."

Her laugh was deep, languorous. She turned her head so she could see him, flipped the hair out of her face. "Not much chance of that. The house-buying crowd's all watching *60 Minutes*." She rolled off of him.

"That was nice."

"Ummm." She was leaning over the side of the bed, rummaging through her satchel from the sound of it.

"Don't tell me you're looking for a cigarette."

"Nope. This." She propped a pillow against the headboard and sat back. Her solar-powered pocket calculator was in her hands. "You can get this house for one point two." She'd just told him her other client's bottom line. The red needle-thin numbers appeared on the screen: *1200000.* "How much can you put down?"

"How much do I need to put down?"

"Ten percent. Twenty if you don't want to carry mortgage insurance."

"All right, twenty."

Her fingers on the keypad made a light snicking sound. She turned the calculator his way. *240000.* "Can you handle that?"

"I can handle it."

"Good! Which leaves a balance of . . ." More tapping. The numbers blinked onto the screen. "The going rate for jumbo mortgages is around six and a quarter. Which would give you a monthly payment of seven thousand, give or take. How much do you make?"

"Two fifty, two sixty. Maybe better if my hours are good."

She hesitated, as if surprised. "Then we'll have to get the owners to finance part of this. A second note for, say, two hundred fifty, three hundred."

"They could do it?"

"The question is, *would* they do it?" She laid the calculator on her smooth little belly. "But even then it'd be a reach for you. I don't know if the banks will go for it."

"How about if I just pay cash?"

She turned to him. "How about if you just pay cash," she echoed in a flat voice. He laughed. She really didn't know by now? It was impossible to read her face in the near dark.

"Yeah, cash. You know, wire transfer, cashier's check, paper sack full of bills. However they want it."

"Really. However they want it." A kind of challenge. She was turning sassy, playful. Like flipping a switch, he was hard again.

"We can meet with my banker tomorrow," he said. "He'll start setting it up."

She tossed the calculator overboard and slid toward him. "Well congratulations, player. How do you like your new house?"

That it was an all-cash sale greatly simplified things, though there was still a lengthy checklist to work through. The title insurance company found an array of minor encumbrances that had to be cleared. A new survey was made, various inspections done; the property insurer had its own high-handed list of demands. Laney guided him through the process, dropping by his apartment in the evenings with the latest batch of documents to be reviewed and signed. Sometimes she stayed for dinner. Sometimes, with a little cajoling and wine, she'd stay the night.

They weren't really dating. They seemed to have skipped that stage, though Brice supposed all of their house-hunting trips might qualify as dates. He didn't invite her to any of the parties or dinners he had with his friends during these weeks. To introduce her to his group seemed complicated; it would raise too many questions he didn't feel like answering. How to explain his attraction to this older woman when most of his friends were seeing women not much more than half her age?

He tried to imagine how Laney would see his friends, and it was then that he realized he'd grown tired of them, of the perpetual adolescence they encouraged in one another. He just wanted to be with her, only her. Which was hard, because she was always working.

His new neighborhood turned out to be more marginal than he'd thought. The low-income apartments nearby spun off a constant seep of minorities and homeless types. One day Brice was coming up the front walk to meet an inspector and was startled by an elderly black man sleeping in his bushes. A few days later a different black man rang his doorbell. He offered to wash windows, clean gutters, whatever Brice needed, but the man was ragged, empty-handed, not even equipped with a coat against the chill. He fussed when Brice said there was nothing for him to do, then grew belligerent when Brice refused to give him a handout.

These encounters were depressing, vaguely suggestive that he was making a mistake. He moved in over the weekend before Thanksgiving. There wasn't much to move, and his possessions seemed to get swallowed up by the house like a boy flopping around in a man's suit. He spent most of Sunday getting the kitchen and closets organized. The day was overcast, solemn, cool: fall bordering on winter. He kept encountering stray drafts as he moved about the house, and realized it was going to be a beast to heat.

Laney arrived around five with a bottle of champagne. She helped herself to a Diet Coke from his fridge, then took a walk through the house while he put the champagne on ice, the tap of her heels across the hardwood floors marking her progress. He caught up with her in the master bedroom. She was standing in the middle of the mostly empty room, laughing.

"Brice, really. A futon and a weight bench? You're too much."

"I'm planning on getting furniture, duh."

"Glad to hear it. I could help you with that, if you want."

"Great." He felt a sudden surge of hopefulness.

"There's an interior designer I know, she does great work. I'll have her call you."

"Sure. Fine." He followed her out to the hall and down the grand staircase. "You're staying, right? The champagne's chilling. We can celebrate."

"Can't," she said over her shoulder. "Gotta work."

"Now?"

"Got a bunch of comps I need to run. Next week starts tomorrow, bright and early."

He tried not to feel desperate. "Then come back when you're done. I'll fix dinner."

They'd reached the front door. She turned to him and smiled as it swung open, then leaned close and handed him her empty Coke can. "Another time," she said sweetly, and gave him a quick, dry kiss.

He stood in the doorway and watched her go. As she drove off he became aware of the house at his back, its silence, the vast bulk of it breathing out, like a live thing waiting to see what he would do.

IN THE AIR

BY DANIEL J. HALE

Deep Ellum

Diego Smith woke up in an empty bed with a head full of hurt. Muted carnival sounds and flat daylight seeped through the tall windows. The aroma of fresh-brewed coffee wafted about the open second floor of the converted firehouse to mingle with whiffs of French perfume. Diego sniffed his skin. He smelled nothing but faint traces of Ivory soap. If he'd been with anyone last night, he'd showered after she left. He reached for his cell phone. The nightstand cradle stood empty. Diego pulled on the jeans he found atop one of the moving boxes lining the wall, and, cold concrete beneath his feet, he stumbled into the kitchen.

He found a shot glass, a half-bottle of Don Julio, and the carcass of a lime strewn across the granite countertop. Diego's hankotsu was missing from the magnetic knife holder on the wall. It wasn't in the sink or in the dish drainer. Besides, a hankotsu wasn't the proper tool for cutting citrus. The handmade Japanese boning knife had cost a fortune. Diego realized he'd once again brought home a little thief. He thought, *I'm too old to be living this way.* By the time his father was twenty-seven, he was already married with a baby on the way. Diego knew his mom had been right—it was time to settle down.

He poured a mug from the automatic coffee maker and looked out the window. Fair Park's giant blue-spoke Ferris wheel spun slowly against the overcast sky. People crowded the entrance to the fairgrounds across the street. Diego figured his brother was already inside working the throngs of humanity. Alex's campaign manager had asked Diego to steer clear today. The Smith boys had barely spoken in nine years, and they were polar opposites politically, but Diego didn't want to be an anchor around the neck of Alex's campaign. Besides, the movers were due to arrive in a couple of hours. They'd probably been trying to call.

Diego's cell was nowhere to be found in the kitchen. He wondered if the little thief had stolen it too, but the phone sometimes slipped out of his pocket when he watched TV. Diego topped off the mug and, with metered steps, made his way toward the cluster of leather furniture surrounding the flat-panel bolted to the far wall of the loftlike space. The scent of perfume he'd noticed when he woke up intensified as he approached the couch. He found a long-legged brunette lying there, her midsection covered with a black cashmere throw.

"Carole?"

Her emerald eyes crept open, and she spoke in a throaty voice. "Mornin', cutie."

Diego stepped back, sloshing hot coffee onto the hard glazed floor.

Carole Bennett sat up on the edge of the couch wearing panties and a bare-midriff T-shirt, no bra. She smiled and said, "You look more like María-Consuelo every time I see you. She'd be so proud."

"Mom hated you." Diego placed the mug on the poured-concrete coffee table and folded his arms across his bare chest. "What are you doing here?"

"I found you drunk as a skunk at the Monkey Bar last night. I took your keys and drove you home." She leaned back and draped her arms over the top of the low-back couch, leaving her taut belly exposed. "You're welcome."

Hoping to God he hadn't slept with her again, Diego glanced toward the stairs leading down to the garage and the street. He said, "All right, then."

Carole gave a laugh. "What? You want me to vacate the premises?"

Diego found his eyes drawn to the small, hennalike tattoo encircling her navel. He felt a stirring that angered him.

"I didn't just happen to run into you last night. I hunted you down." Carole's smile had faded. "Your father's pulling the plug on the Latino youth center."

"He can't do that." Diego sat on the edge of the coffee table. "I gave up half of my inheritance to fund it."

She leaned forward. "Reginald changed his mind."

"He can't just change his mind. The documents were executed months ago." Diego stood and started to walk away. He paused, then turned to face the green-eyed brunette on the couch once more. "How do you know this?"

"My BFF's a paralegal at Wadley, Adams & Snow. Her boss said your father decided sending Alex to Washington would do more for the Latino population than the youth center ever could."

Diego's whole body felt numb. It took a few moments for the words to come. "My brother and I may be half-Mexican, but Alex is the whitest guy I know. He barely speaks Spanish. All he'll do in Washington is help rich old WASPs like my dad hang on to their money and their concealed-weapon permits."

"Well, you need to talk to Reginald." She paused before saying, "Right away. The lawyers are taking the papers to him this afternoon."

Diego glanced at her and asked, "Did you see what I did with my phone?"

"You were looking for it on the way back here last night. You probably left it at the Monkey Bar."

"May I borrow yours?"

"It's in my car, and we came here in your convertible." She bit her lower lip. "Besides, we both know your father would never answer a call from my number. You better go talk to him."

Diego dressed in a chambray shirt and a pair of boots he pulled from one of the moving boxes against the wall near his bed. He hurried into the bathroom to brush his teeth and run a comb through his inky black hair.

Carole appeared in the doorway dressed in a chocolate suede jacket, tight jeans, and a pair of high-heeled shoes that made her taller than him. "Before you have your little heart-to-heart with Daddy Dearest, I need you to drop me at Highland Park Village."

Diego frowned and said, "I'll flag you down a—"

"No." She put her hands on her hips. "I am not taking a taxi."

The silver Aston Martin convertible's engine roared to life as the enormous firehouse garage door rolled open. Carole tossed her chartreuse-colored purse onto the passenger floorboard and slipped into the red leather interior. Diego breathed in her scent. She had added a layer of perfume. Hermès. 24, Faubourg. Floral. Subtle. Expensive. Carole had worn it nine years ago, back when she was engaged to Alex, before she took advantage of a drunken eighteen-year-old virgin and ruined five people's lives.

Diego drove out into the warm, cloudy October day. As they passed the entrance to the fairgrounds, he glanced over to see his brother standing in shirtsleeves, smiling and shaking hands with the crowd. Diego was compact and dark-haired, like their mom. Alex had turned out as tall and blond as their father. Campaign staffers in T-shirts swarmed through the crowd of fair-goers passing out flyers extolling the reasons Alex Smith would be the best voice for Texans and their right to bear arms.

Even if Alex had stabbed his younger brother in the back yet again, Diego didn't want him to see Carole in the car. He didn't want Alex to have the wrong idea. Diego made a quick turn and accelerated down Exposition.

Carole said, "Why'd you sell the firehouse?"

"I needed the money—my investors forced me out of the restaurant."

"But that was your concept." She looked at him and arched her dark eyebrows. "I heard the place was doing really well."

"It was, but the backers wanted to squeeze more money out of the operation, and I apparently cared too much about my employees." Diego brought the Aston Martin to a quick stop at a red light.

Carole swept back her chestnut hair with a stroke of her hand and gave him a sidelong glance. Her eyes were an intense green. Scary eyes.

Diego had always found it disconcerting to look directly into them. He focused on the traffic signal and said, "The investors let a lot of my staff go when they ousted me. The firehouse and . . ." Diego tapped the steering wheel, "this ridiculous car will finance my new restaurant and help my employees stay afloat until we can open."

"God, it's hot." Carole pulled off her suede jacket, the short T-shirt again exposing the firm flesh of her belly.

From the side, Diego could see that her once-flat stomach was now a bit distended. She looked great for her age, but she was thirty-five after all. He wondered how he'd look when he was her age.

After a space of silence, Carole asked, "Why didn't you just ask Reginald to back you on the new restaurant?"

"Are you kidding?" Diego glanced at her. "My dad thinks I'm the world's biggest bleeding heart." He shook his head. "Maybe he's right. But at least I can sleep at night."

"The alcohol probably helps."

Diego shrugged.

The light turned green, and they made their way past the vacant lots, derelict buildings, and dive bars of Deep Ellum.

Diego realized he had no idea what he'd say to his father. The aroma of ribs grilling on mesquite wafted into the convertible. He wondered what he'd done with his boning knife. Even with the ADHD and his drinking, he never misplaced things, not since Alex went to college and Reginald Smith sent his younger son to survival defense training.

Diego turned to Carole. "Did you notice what I did with my hankotsu?"

She shot him a strange look. "Your hand what?"

"Hankotsu—it's a type of knife. Japanese. For boning."

Carole smiled. "Really?"

Diego shook his head.

"Seriously, I have no clue." Carole shifted the greenish-yellow purse from the floorboard to her lap.

They passed the hospital where María-Consuelo Smith had died months earlier. Diego remembered the days and nights he spent there with her breathing in air that had been scrubbed of every smell that made life worth living. He missed his mom, and he wanted to cry, but he wouldn't. He had to stay strong for the children she vowed to help.

The Dallas skyline loomed large. Diego accelerated north on Central Expressway. A combusted diesel smell filled the space between the sunken freeway's beige concrete walls. It was always a few degrees warmer down here than at street level, thirty feet above. It reminded Diego of Death Valley.

As they neared Mockingbird, Diego peered up to see his brother's handsome face smiling down from a billboard on the access road overhead. Alex looked the part of the Ivy League–educated Texan, a successful man in his midthirties surrounded by a patrician wife and three photogenic kids. But Diego knew it was just a picture. There had never been much love in Alex's marriage. His politically connected wife had worked for a gun-control lobby after she graduated from Smith, but she swallowed her beliefs to support his career. Diego wondered if his brother had the 9mm Beretta strapped to his ankle under the navy-blue suit he wore in the campaign photo.

Diego glanced at Carole and said, "Is this all about hurting Alex?"

She was holding her long brown hair behind her head. "I figured I owed it to the Hispanic community to let you know." She shrugged. "Getting Alex is a nice fringe benefit, though."

Diego looked at her again. "Getting Alex?"

Carole shook her head. "Getting back at Alex."

Diego exited Central and headed west on Mockingbird. He missed the yeasty smell of the old bread plant long since torn down. They passed SMU's Georgian campus, and Diego breathed in fresh-cut grass. Well-kept homes with meticulously landscaped lawns floated past the convertible. They skirted the Dallas Country Club, drove under its golf cart overpass, and pulled into Highland Park Village.

The exclusive shops and boutiques filling the Moorish-Spanish buildings were abuzz with activity. Smells of good Tex-Mex filled the air as the convertible crept through the parking lot. Carole pointed out a black Audi SUV with temporary plates. "This is me."

Last time Diego had seen her on the street, she'd still been driving the red Mini Cooper that Alex had given her as an engagement gift. The mom-mobile seemed out of place, not to mention expensive. He wondered what Carole did for money. As far as Diego knew, she didn't work. Her only brother had been murdered in prison. Her parents died long ago in a bad part of Garland. Then again, as Diego had learned in the restaurant business, women like her always found a way.

"Thanks for telling me about the youth center."

She turned to him. "Don't forget your phone."

Diego found a space for the Aston Martin and left it parked, top down, while he went inside. The small bar on the restaurant's third floor wasn't open yet, but a busboy let him in. He checked under the tables and in the spaces between the seat and the back cushions on the banquette, but he couldn't find his phone.

He returned downstairs to find Carole waiting for him. She held up a smart phone and said, "It was ringing under the passenger seat of your car. I didn't answer."

Something about Carole's smell had changed. The floral scent was now mixed with something deeper, richer, and reminiscent of leather. Diego wondered if her skin or clothing had absorbed the smell of his Aston Martin's upholstery, but he couldn't obsess about that now. He took the phone and tried to walk past her.

She placed her fingertips on his chest and said, "I don't care if you were only eighteen, and I don't care if it ruined things with Alex—the night I deflowered you was one of the best nights of my life."

"You say, 'deflowered.'" Diego backed up a step so that her hand fell away. "I say, 'destroyed my family.'"

A text message alert chimed. Diego checked his phone, but the sound had come from the chartreuse purse hanging from Carole's shoulder. She pulled out her phone, looked at the screen, then hurried away without a goodbye.

Diego spoke to the manager for a moment before leaving the restaurant. Carole's new SUV was gone. He hoped he'd never see her again. He wondered what he'd say to his father, but he couldn't waste time thinking about it. Now was a time for action. Diego unlocked his phone and saw that he had forty-seven missed calls, twenty-three voice mail messages, and sixty-two texts. He dialed his father's home number. It went straight to voice mail.

The Aston Martin made quick work of the traffic on Preston Road before it squealed onto megahouse-lined Armstrong Parkway. Diego raced to a halt in the driveway of the enormous Tudor set far back from the road. He killed the engine and opened the console to retrieve his father's house key, but it was missing. As a joke gift for Christmas years earlier, Reginald Smith had given his son a National Rifle Association medallion key ring. Diego kept his father's house key on it. The medallion wasn't worth stealing, and it was too big to lose. *First my boning knife, now this.* Diego wondered if drinking had begun to affect his memory. It seemed to be another sign that it was time to find a nice girl and start a family.

He got out of the convertible and approached the front door. It had been months since he set foot inside the house, not since his mom had died. He didn't want to be there, but what lay at stake was more important than his comfort level. Diego extended his hand to ring the doorbell, but he noticed that the front door stood slightly ajar. He pushed it open and said, "Dad?"

A loud sound like a rapid busy signal came from somewhere inside. He followed the noise through the big house into the kitchen. The old-fashioned phone on the far wall was off the hook, the receiver dangling by its short spiral cord. Diego took a step toward it before he noticed the gray-haired man in the pin-stripe suit splayed out on his back on the kitchen island. A black-handled knife stuck out of his chest. It took a moment for Diego to realize it was his father.

Diego rushed to his side. "Daddy?" The coppery scent of blood mixed with the reek of feces and urine. The smell made him gag. His father's eyes were closed. Diego couldn't tell if he was breathing. Blood had turned his white dress shirt red. The knife had been plunged up to the hilt. It had surely penetrated his heart. If his father was still alive, pulling out the knife would kill him. Diego felt for a pulse, but there was none.

Time slowed then seemed to stop when he noticed the Japanese characters covering the knife's handle. Diego couldn't read

them, but he could have drawn them from memory. His father had been stabbed with his missing hankotsu.

As it dawned on him that he'd been framed for his father's murder, sirens pierced the thick walls of the big house. He hurried to one of the front windows to see two police vehicles screeching to a halt on Armstrong.

Instinct told him to flee. Diego ran through the kitchen, past his father. *I'm sorry, Dad.* One of his boots caught something and sent it flying under the breakfast nook table. Diego only caught a glimpse, but it was enough to know that it was the NRA keychain his father had given him. There wasn't time to grab it.

He dashed out the back door, past the pool, and through the gate. Diego found himself in the long, narrow park that ran between the backs of the houses on Armstrong and those on Bordeaux. It smelled like excrement. People walked their dogs there. Diego dashed down the length of the green space to where it ended at Douglas. A beat-up landscaping company pickup stood parked along the street. He was relieved to find the keys in the ignition. There was no one around. He jumped in, started it up, and drove away.

Not knowing where to go, Diego headed back through Highland Park toward Central Expressway. The smell of sweat and stale cigarettes almost overpowered him. He cranked down the driver's-side window and fresh air flooded the cab.

My father's dead. The realization slammed into Diego like an oncoming semi. Even if they'd spoken only occasionally in the months since the funeral, even if they'd agreed on almost nothing, Diego loved his dad. He felt tears welling up inside, but he held them back. He had to figure out what to do. He had to think.

Diego didn't know how Carole had done it. He didn't understand how she'd had time to slip in the back of the house on Armstrong and kill his father before he arrived. It didn't make any sense. The man hated her. He would never have let her inside. Besides, he was a lot stronger than her. She'd had an accomplice. But who?

Diego needed help. There was only one person he could turn to.

Keeping the pickup just below the speed limit, Diego drove east on Mockingbird. He crossed Central and pulled into a grocery store parking lot near the DART light rail station. Hoping that would throw the cops off his trail long enough to buy him some time, he got out of the cab and started walking away.

A gruff voice behind him said, "Excuse me, son?"

Diego wondered how the police could have found him so quickly. He considered running, but that would just get him killed. Diego looked back to see an older Caucasian gentleman holding a canvas shopping bag in each hand. "Sir?"

The man said, "I had to fire my yard crew. They just weren't no good." He paused a beat. "I hear you people are real hard workers. Could I have you come out and give me an estimate?"

It took Diego a moment to realize why the man was asking what he was asking. He hadn't seen the well-dressed son of a privileged upbringing with a two-hundred-dollar haircut and thousand-dollar boots. All he saw was a Mexican gardener dressed in denim stepping out of a lawn-service pickup. Diego didn't know if "you people" had referred to the landscaping company or to the Latino population in general, but he smiled. Affecting an accent, he said, "If you call the number on the truck and tell them Luis sent you, we'll send someone right out."

Diego rode the light rail underground. People cast him strange glances, and he realized he was crying. He dried his eyes and tried to ignore the cheap aftershave and body odor and cigarette smoke–saturated clothing filling the car. He changed trains downtown, breathing in huge gulps of fresh air before continuing on to Fair Park.

When Diego stepped off onto the platform, he glanced over at the beautiful old station house that had been his home for three years. A large moving van stood parked alongside. There were no police vehicles there, at least not yet. He thought about going inside and grabbing his passport and the cash he kept in the floor safe and running to Mexico, but he knew that would be a mistake. He needed to clear his name.

Carole was a common enemy. Alex would help. He had to.

Security was tight at the State Fair of Texas. Diego felt sure his brother couldn't have made it inside with the 9mm Beretta strapped to his ankle, because even the coins in Diego's pocket set off the metal detector. He bought a ticket and blended into the noisy, smelly, swirling crowd.

When Diego was a boy, he and Alex lived for those three weeks of Fletcher's Corny Dogs and rides and cotton candy and Frisbee dog shows and funnel cake and Big Tex. The brothers would have gone to the fair every day if their parents had let them. That was back in the days when the Smith boys were still buddies, when Alex was Diego's guardian angel, before Alex went to Harvard and Diego's afternoons were filled with survival defense training classes. It occurred to Diego for the first time that the memory of those happy times at the fair might have been the reason he'd bought and renovated the old fire station across the street.

Fair Park covered more than two hundred acres. Diego could have wandered the place for hours without finding his brother. He dodged the trajectories of the disabled in mobility scooters and young couples pushing baby strollers. He passed a uniformed policeman, but the officer paid him no apparent attention. Diego knew it might be only minutes before his face was beamed to the screens of all the law enforcement phones.

In the distance, against a sky that had darkened to the color of lead, Diego saw the Texas Star spinning slowly. The Ferris wheel was the tallest in North America, and it was the focal point of the fair. Alex would be there. Diego could feel it in his bones.

He strode down the midway as quickly as he could without looking like a man running from the law. Carnival barkers and stuffed animals and blue awnings and games of chance and rubber duckies and more stuffed animals blurred past. Smells of cotton candy and fried food filled the air. The occasional whiff of vomit pricked his nostrils.

Diego approached the Texas Star, its multicolored gondolas swaying overhead in the warm, humid breeze. He found Alex smiling and pressing the flesh and looking every bit a winner. A large all-access state fair pass hung from the lanyard around his tall blond brother's neck. Alex's forehead and the blue button-down shirt he wore were dotted with perspiration. Diego had only seen his brother break a sweat when he played sports. The pressure to win the election must have been intense.

Alex was glad-handing an elderly woman when he spotted Diego. His expression changed to something less than happy. The older of the brothers approached the younger and, words angry, said, "What are you doing here?" He seemed to regain his composure, and his tone lightened. "I thought you were going to steer clear of the fair today, baby brother."

"Something happened." Diego could feel tears welling up inside once again. He choked them back and said, "I need to talk to you. Alone."

A man Diego figured to be his brother's campaign manager approached and gave Diego a harsh look. Alex waved him away before turning to say, "I'm kind of busy here. Can it wait?"

"No, it can't—Dad's dead."

"What?"

"He's been murdered. Somebody framed me. I think it was Carole."

Alex didn't react. He led Diego up the wheelchair ramp to the Ferris wheel's loading platform and flashed the state fair credentials around his neck. Alex exchanged a few quiet words with one of the attendants. The man ushered the brothers into an empty gondola, shut the doors, and locked them inside. They sat facing each other. The bars and mesh surrounding them allowed a view while keeping desperate people from jumping to their deaths.

The big wheel began to spin. Moments later, Diego and his brother were hovering above the midway in the warm breeze. The Dallas skyline sprouted up in the near distance like an isolated forest in the middle of a prairie. Diego felt trapped, caged like an animal, but at least he had fresh air.

Alex said, "Start at the beginning. Tell me everything."

Diego recounted what had happened that day. He took a breath and concluded, "Carole didn't have time to do it. I think she was working with someone."

A gust of wind ruffled Alex's blond hair. "None of this makes any sense."

"I know—I'm screwed." Diego looked down at the floor of the gondola. He noticed a bulge above the cuff of his brother's left pant leg, and he wondered how Alex had gotten into the fairgrounds with the handgun strapped to his ankle. The all-access pass around his neck must have allowed him to bypass security. Diego then noticed a spot of something red just below the knee of his brother's pants. Alex had never liked ketchup on his corny dog—he'd always covered it with mustard.

The Texas Star spun again. It came to a stop with the brothers' gondola at the top, two hundred feet above the ground. The air was suddenly still. Diego caught a whiff of his brother's rich, leathery cologne—Hermès Bel Ami. Their mother had given each of her boys a bottle for Christmas long ago, before anyone knew how sensitive Diego's senses of taste and smell were.

Diego said, "I wish Mom was here. She'd know what to do."

"I miss her too." Alex grimaced. "But it's up to us to figure a way to get you out of this mess."

Diego nodded and took another breath. In the still air, intermingled with the leathery scent of his brother's cologne, he caught a whiff of something delicate, floral, and distinctive. It took him a moment to place the aroma. A wave of recognition shot through his body. He remembered how Carole's scent had changed at Highland Park Village while he'd been inside looking for his phone. Diego again noticed the red spot on the left leg of Alex's khakis. It felt like the bottom of the gondola had dropped out.

The events of that afternoon played like a slideshow in Diego's mind. Carole had met Alex while Diego was upstairs in the Monkey Bar. She had given Alex Diego's knife and the key to the house on Armstrong. They embraced. Her 24, Faubourg mixed with his Bel Ami. She "found" Diego's phone and brought it inside and delayed him for another few precious moments so Alex would have time to go to the house on Armstrong and . . .

Alex had murdered their father.

The tall blond man stroked his strong chin and gazed out to the horizon as if he were trying to figure a way to help his brother. But it was just an act. And Alex was carrying a handgun.

Diego thought, *Stay calm.* His brother couldn't read his mind. If he could just play it cool for another minute or two, he would get out of this okay. All he had to do was make it safely down to the ground. He'd slip away from Alex, run to Wadley, Adams & Snow, and tell them everything.

Diego was anxious for the Ferris wheel to turn, for it to take him back to earth, but it didn't move. He scooted to the edge of the gondola and peered down. People were pointing at the base of the Texas Star. Something was wrong. He thought about Alex's words with the attendant below. If his guess was correct, his older brother had asked the attendant to keep them up top and call the police.

Alex appeared distracted, still giving the pretense of figuring out how to help. Diego knew his time was running short. He pulled his smart phone from his pocket and replied to the first text message in his queue, one from the woman who'd managed his old restaurant. He typed: *Alex murdered Dad. Carole helpe*

His brother interrupted: "Whatcha doin' there, baby brother?"

Diego looked up at him and replied as calmly as he could: "Letting a friend know we're stuck up—"

Alex snatched the phone from his hands. He looked at the screen, then shoved the device between the bars and let it fall.

Diego didn't hear it strike the ground. He hoped it hadn't hit anyone.

Alex looked at his younger brother and asked, "How'd you figure it out?"

Diego thought about feigning ignorance, but it seemed ridiculous at this point. He shrugged and answered, "I smell her on you."

The tall blond man frowned, shook his head, and said, "Freak." He sighed. "It doesn't matter. If anyone asks, I've been here all afternoon." Alex leaned back and draped his arms over the seating area. "You'll never prove otherwise."

Diego knew what he had to do. He didn't like it, but it was his only choice. He brought his boot up hard into Alex's groin. When his brother doubled over, Diego yanked up the leg of his khaki pants and wrested the compact Beretta free from its ankle holster. He released the safety and pointed the handgun at his brother's heart.

Eyes wide, Alex looked at him and said, "You hate guns."

"Just because I hate them doesn't mean I don't know how to use them."

Nostrils flared, his brother glanced from side to side. Alex had become the caged animal.

"After you left for Harvard, Dad worried about me because I was so small and you weren't around to protect me anymore. He put me through personal defense training—*a lot* of personal defense training. I won't hesitate if I need to use this." Diego paused. "Why did you kill him?"

Alex shook his head. "I didn't."

"Then whose blood is that on your pant leg?"

His brother looked down at his khakis, then closed his eyes.

Diego took a deep breath of Bel Ami and 24, Faubourg and a faint whiff of fried food rising up from below. "You and Carole are having an affair. Dad found out. He cut off the funding for your campaign. You needed the rest of your inheritance. And mine too. Right?"

His brother gave him a blank stare.

"Why didn't you just lie like you always do?"

Alex looked away.

"You're my brother, Alejandro. Te quiero. How could you do this?"

Eyes wide, voice almost a growl, the blond man said, "You ruined my life."

"I ruined your life?" Diego felt rage welling up inside. "You cheated on Carole a week before you were supposed to marry her. She got me drunk and had sex with me to get back at you." He felt the tears streaming down his face. "I was an eighteen-year-old virgin with no tolerance for alcohol. She practically raped me!" Diego drew a deep breath and wiped his cheeks with the back of his free hand. "Nothing that happened to you was my fault. You brought it all on yourself."

Alex dropped his head into his hands. His shoulders began to heave.

Diego had never seen his brother cry, not even when their

mom died. He lowered the handgun and hoped the ride would be over soon.

As Diego lost himself in the knowledge that he'd never hug his father again, Alex sprang forth and tried to grab the Beretta. Diego held firm. He might have been small, but that gave him better physical leverage. As he twisted the weapon free from his brother's grasp, a loud bang pierced the still air.

Alex released the weapon and slumped back in his seat. Diego looked for blood, first on his brother, then on himself. The only red was the single drop on Alex's pant leg.

There was motion at the edge of Diego's peripheral vision. Beretta still trained on his brother, he glanced to the side to see the gondola's door swinging open. When the gun went off, the bullet had shredded the lock mechanism.

The Ferris wheel began to turn. Diego sat back, keeping the gun pointed at Alex. "We'll be on the ground soon, then we'll let the police take over."

Tears ran down Alex's cheeks. He said, "I'm sorry, baby brother."

Diego didn't know how to respond.

In one slow, deliberate motion, Alex raised his hands over his head and stood. Eyes red, jaw quivering, he smiled down at Diego. "I hope you can forgive me."

"Sit down, Alex."

The tall blond man took a sideways step toward the open gondola door.

Voice a hammer, Diego said, "Siéntate!"

"Or what?" Alex let out an audible sob. "You'll shoot me?"

Diego reached for his brother. "Give me your hand and sit down."

Alex inched closer to the open door. "Carole doesn't have any family. Promise you'll take care of the baby?"

"What baby?" As soon as he'd said the words, Diego realized

why Alex hadn't been able to lie his way out of the situation. He thought about Carole's distended stomach and the new mommy-mobile and her "getting Alex." It finally made sense.

Water pouring from his eyes, mucus dripping from his nose, Alex said, "Promise?"

Diego nodded.

Alejandro Días Smith turned and stepped out in the air.

THE CLEARING

BY EMMA RATHBONE

Plano

I always think about this thing that happened. It was when I was a kid, and I was sitting on the curb outside our house one afternoon. I would look back and the house would seem dark. I knew my mom was in there somewhere. I had a rock, and I was scraping it along the sidewalk. I liked the sound it made, along with the thin, chalky line. I just kept scraping it. I sat back.

It was hot. I remember that. Hot and bright. My mom had said earlier that day, "You could fry an egg on the pavement!" and I had considered trying. But instead I just went out and sat there. I don't know. The sun was pounding down and bright in my eyes. I don't remember what I was going to do that day. I don't remember if there was something I was waiting for or waiting out. I was just sitting there.

This was at our old place in Plano, Texas, on a cul-de-sac called Dalgreen Grove. It was before the area expanded with hot concrete plazas, spilling out over the plains, glinting with metal benches; before they built the freeway we weren't allowed to cross, and the multiplex on the east side of town.

Like I said, I knew my mom was in the house, vacuuming or doing the dishes or something. She was really fragile. I was a kid but I could tell. She was like the cranberry glass vases she collected and put in a display case. I always thought that one day she was going to fall over and crack with a giant *pop*.

So anyway. I was sitting there scraping my rock and this car pulls up. It was big and gray, like a Cadillac or something. I don't remember the exact make. It pulls up right in front of me and this woman leans out the window. Her hair was gray like the car, and curly. She was old. Maybe like around my mom's age. She says, "Little boy," even though she's already staring at me straight in the face. "What's your name?"

"Jonathan Meyers."

I don't know why I said both my first and last name. I remember thinking to myself after I said it, *Why did you do that?* Now I realize it wasn't that weird a thing to have done.

"You live in that house?" She pointed behind me. I looked back. My house was dark, dark even though it was such a bright day. And my mom was inside there, fragile. I nodded dumbly. I might as well mention right now that I was an overweight kid. I didn't like it. I couldn't help it. I grew out of it. What more is there to say? The woman leaned over and said something to the person in the driver's seat, who I couldn't see.

"Is there anyone home?" she asked, craning out the window again. When I was a kid, a fat little kid, I didn't have many friends and I thought adults knew everything. So I thought to myself, *Why is she asking me that if she already knows?* I said, "Yeah, my mom." I was looking up at the woman, squinting.

She said something else to the person in the driver's seat then leaned back out the window. "Does your mom like company?"

Even then, I knew it was a weird thing to say. When I think about it now, I can't imagine anyone saying something like that to a kid, sitting on the street. But even then, I knew. I glanced up at the woman and she pushed some gray hair behind her ear and now I noticed that she was old, older than I thought at first. The skin under her eyes looked like it was slowly dripping down her face. She had a square jaw and a bulky nose.

I said, "Um, I don't think so." I thought of my mom, inside the house, arranging her cranberry glass. The woman shifted back into her seat and they drove away. I guess I was pretty relieved.

I scanned the street. There was a wide crack down the middle of the cul-de-sac with grass bursting out in some places. There was a pile of newspapers lying next to Mr. Cunningham's mailbox because he never picked them up. The sun was still pounding down. It was pretty quiet. Across from us was a Korean family called the Lees. They had two small white dogs that would chase each other around and bark at Mr. Lee when he came home from work. The sprinklers were on in their front yard, throwing ropes of water across the grass.

I felt the rock in my hand, and figured I could go back to how I was before, just scraping it along the sidewalk. Then I noticed the gray car again, driving back down the street. It parked under the tree in front of the Perkins's house, the one with wide, shiny leaves. I just sat there watching them like an idiot. They got out of the car. The woman was big and she walked with a cane. And not only were her car and her hair gray, but she wore a gray suit like the First Lady of America. The person with her was a man, a younger man. He was tall and skinny.

They walked down the sidewalk, and then turned toward my house. They didn't even look at me as they went by. I don't remember if I was thinking anything in particular as this was happening. All I remember is that my heart was pounding. The man was pale and had a scattered mustache. The woman had a tattoo on her leg, under stretched nylon, but I couldn't see what it was. I turned and watched as they rang the doorbell and stood and waited.

I could picture it. My mom would be doing one of three things: watching television, wiping down a window, or moving the cranberry glass around. There were two pieces she liked the most. One was a small glass vase with tiny hoofs like a horse. The other was also a vase, a tall one. It was thin too, like it was only made for one specific flower. She could never figure out how she wanted them to be arranged. She would move them into different places and then stand back and look at them and walk away. Then she'd stop and put her hand on her cheek, turn around, and go mess with them again. That's probably what she was doing when the doorbell rang.

I watched as the door opened and my mom stood there, staring at the two people. She made a plank with her hand over her eyes to shield from the sun and then scanned the street until she located me sitting there. The man and the woman were saying something, and she said something back. I couldn't hear the actual words, I could only hear the notes and bumps of their voices. They started all talking at once and it reminded me of the way pine needles get tangled up at the edge of a creek. Don't ask me why.

The old woman's voice sounded urgent. My mom shook her head and started to push the door closed, but the man stuck his foot out so she couldn't. Then I watched my mom's mouth make a dark circle as they pushed her inside and closed the door.

I blinked and stared at the house. I turned back to the street. Everything was the same. It was quiet except for the sprinklers in the Lees' front yard. Then a plane flew by overhead and made a loud, scraping sound. I looked at the rock in my hand.

What I did next was get up—which took a lot of effort, because when you're big and fat everything takes a lot of effort, everything is like trying to pull a root out of the ground—and walk slowly toward my house. Except that it didn't feel like my house anymore. It was all kind of unfamiliar. For instance: I noticed for the first time that our walkway was made up of tiny brown shells stuck in circular formations in the concrete.

I opened the front door and my mom was in there, sitting on the couch in the living room with her hands folded, pushed down deep in her lap. The man was standing next to her. She saw me and said, "Johnny!"

"Tell him to come over here," said the man. One of his hands was in his pocket. "Tell him to come over here and sit next to you. Tell him we're not doing anything wrong."

"Come over here, Johnny," my mom said. "Come over here and sit next to Mommy."

She must have been feeling pretty strange. Because at that point she never referred to herself as *Mommy* anymore. I never even called her that anymore. But I went over there and sat next to her. I sat right on the part of the couch I didn't like, the part where I had spilled barbecue sauce once and it never really came out. My mom was wearing the blue and white checkered dress she always liked, it cinched around the waist with a small belt.

"Tell him," said the man. "Tell him what we're doing." He was thin but had cheeks that puffed out like a baby's.

My mom looked slowly up at the man, then she stared straight ahead and started talking. "This is Mr. Givens. Mr. Givens has brought his mother here, to look at our house."

"Tell him why," said the man.

"Mr. Givens's mother used to live here. When she was a little girl. She lived in our house. She grew up here. She just got out of prison . . ."

"Eighteen years," said the old woman. She walked into the living room and looked at me. "I was there for eighteen years. Texas State Penitentiary, Walls Unit. I just got out and I wanted to see my old house. The house where I grew up. This house. Is there anything wrong with that?" She looked at her son and then looked at me and then looked at my mom. She was leaning on her cane and there were sweat stains under her arms, seeping into the gray material of her suit. "Is there?"

"No, Mom," said the man.

Everyone was very still.

The old lady walked to our television and pointed at it with her cane. "This is new," she said. "We didn't have one of these."

She was breathing hard. "This is new too." She pointed at the mantel above the fireplace. "Fancy. They must have put it in after we moved. We didn't have anything like that. You, uh . . . you put things on it sometimes?" She looked at my mom. "Well, do you?"

My mom looked down at her lap.

"Answer her," said the man, and he moved a little bit closer.

My mom nodded her head and whispered, "Yes."

"What kinds of things?" asked the lady.

"Pictures. Family pictures."

"Well," the old lady slumped a little bit into her cane, "why wouldn't you? All this paint," she said, looking around. "All this paint. It looks good on the walls." I heard a car skid somewhere. The woman's son shifted his weight from one leg to the other. "You get the color from a catalog? A magazine?" My mom continued to look into her lap. The old lady turned away. "It feels different in here. You got all this furniture in here. It feels different."

She pointed to the couch where me and my mom were sitting. "That's where Clarry used to sleep. You remember Clarry?" She looked at her son.

"No, Mom."

"Well, you weren't born yet!" She laughed and then coughed. "He's always been a little dim."

Her son shifted his weight again.

I wasn't touching my mom as we sat there on the couch, but I could still feel her.

"That's where I used to read to Clarry," the old woman continued. "Lots of books, paperback books, we had stacks of them. I read them to him all the time. They were filled with filthy stuff, some of them. Those were the ones he liked. The filthy ones. The ones with women on the cover. Stacks and stacks of filthy books."

She started to say something else and then fell forward. She fell onto her hands and knees. My mom's eyes got as big as dinner plates.

The woman's son yelled, "Mom!" and ran toward her. "Get some water!"

The old woman was crawling toward the couch and she looked like a big gray rhino. Her son helped her onto one of the chairs. She was breathing really hard. "I must of lost . . ." she said. "I must of lost . . ."

"Get some water!" yelled the son, then looked at me. "Go!"

I got off the couch and then walked around it and out of the living room and into the kitchen. It felt like a whole different country in there. It was bright with the sun coming in through the windows and glaring on the sink. I got a glass from one of the cupboards and filled it up with water. My mom sometimes made me go to church with her, and there was this part where the priest seemed like he was preparing something with all kinds of quiet motions. And that's how I tried to be as I turned on the faucet. The water came out loud, like Niagara Falls. I filled the glass all the way to the top and got a napkin out of a drawer. Then I carried it out of the kitchen and back into the living room.

From the back, it looked like they were all friends. Like my mom had invited some people over for coffee. I walked around the couch and gave the old lady the water.

"What took you so long?" said the man.

The old lady's suit was crumpled and the petticoat under her skirt was sticking out. For me, at that time, I wasn't used to seeing that kind of thing and it was like a tongue sticking out at me. My mom was still sitting there staring ahead like she had never done anything else in her life. The man was standing next to his mother.

"They always had women on the covers," said the old lady. She was saying it to my mom. "And the women always looked scared."

I sat down next to my mom where I had been before. I couldn't stop looking at the old lady's slip.

"Clarry made me read every single one to him. There was one where a woman comes home to find her husband with another woman and then they all carry on together. And another one where almost that same exact thing happens. There was one where a husband makes a detective follow his wife around and the detective and the wife get mixed up together. I read Clarry one about a cowboy who tries to break a wild horse but he didn't like it because it didn't have any girls. Clarry couldn't read because he never went to school."

The woman put the glass against her lips and took a sip. Then she put it against her cheek. She looked like she didn't know what to do with the napkin. She crumpled it up and set it on the arm of the chair.

"Over there." She pointed to the corner next to the television. "Over there is where they were stacked. Stacks and stacks of paperback books. Clarry's favorite was about the Civil War. Well, it wasn't about the war exactly, it was about a man who was supposed to fight in the Civil War but he didn't want to go because he had a wild Indian woman for a lover. He wanted to stay with her. She was supposed to be real pretty. She had long black hair that went down to her waist. She would wind it up in different ways. They met one day when he was hunting. He saw her through the trees. She was scared of him at first, I remember that. She was scared of him but then they found a place in the woods where they could carry on together. She wasn't like the other girls he met and he liked her ways. He liked the way they were together in the woods."

The old lady took a sip of her water.

"I remember all of this because I read that book to Clarry. Guess how many times." She looked at me and my mom and her son. Her son had his hand on his back and was stooping forward. She looked at me again. "Well, guess!"

"One hundred times!" I said.

The old lady stared at me like she couldn't figure out where to put me. Like she wanted to place me somewhere else with her eyes.

"One hundred?" she said. "No. Five times. I read that book to him five times. I remember the man's name, in the book. His name was Colonel Legford. He left the army because he was in love with his wild Indian woman. She wasn't tamed. She had smooth skin. And her hair would come undone when they were together."

I looked at the old lady's skin. The more I looked at it, the more cracks and crevices I could see. I felt like if I poured water on it, I could straighten it out with my hands.

"I remember the clearing," she said. She was touching her chin. "I remember the clearing where they would carry on together. It was in the woods. Fifty steps away from an old tree stump next to a creek. And then the trees would part and it was like a room. The walls were made of leaves and the sun would come down and make it warm. The colonel and the wild Indian woman would wait for each other there. Then, when they were together the first thing he would do would be to take out her hair. It was always woven up."

The old lady was touching her own hair now.

"Her hair would come down like a dark waterfall. That's what it said in the book! A dark waterfall. Then they would start. The Indian woman took off her red leather things and the colonel took off his heavy boots and pants and they were jaybird naked together just like that, there in the woods."

I looked at my mom. Her eyes were searching around the room and her face was red. The man was looking back and forth between us.

"They would go to each other. The Indian woman made all sorts of wild forest sounds. They rolled around, panting on top of each other. Sometimes they would be sitting up. The colonel would always put his hand on the back of her neck. He had big hands. He sometimes felt like he was sculpting her, that's what the book said, sculpting her as they went along. And she would lean back and fling herself around."

The old lady's son coughed and she looked at him quickly.

"Then when they were finished, they would lie there and pick the leaves off of each other's skin. They were so wet they got leaves stuck all over them and so they would pick them off with the sun still coming down and making it warm."

Everyone was quiet for a second. The old lady was staring off into the distance. Her son was looking down at his shoes. My mom was red in the face and making short little breaths. I was hoping that the old lady would keep telling more of the story. But I knew she wasn't going to.

The doorbell rang.

"Leave it!" said the son, taking a step forward.

My mom slung her head to the side.

"Leave it," he said again.

I knew who it was. It was my mom's friend Henrietta from down the street who would come and visit at this time almost every day. She was pushy and always calling me "Johnny Morning" even though that's not my name. We all waited in silence for a few seconds and then heard her walk away. The old lady's son went up to the front door and moved the little curtain away from the window next to it and looked outside. Then he came back and give his mom a little nod.

The old lady slumped in her chair. She seemed really tired. "You ever have anything like that?" she said to my mom. She seemed to be shrinking under her gray suit, which now looked like it had way too much material for her.

My mom slowly turned her head to her. "What?" she whispered.

I pictured the old lady getting smaller and smaller and then disappearing under her suit, which would then be deserted and spilled out over the couch with all of its layers and panels.

"Like what I was saying before, with the colonel and the Indian woman. In the woods. You ever have anything like that?"

My mom continued to stare at the lady in silence, her eyes open wide.

"You think the colonel did something wrong by being with that Indian woman?"

The son kept glancing at his watch and then back toward the door. I wondered if the sprinklers were still going on in the Lees' front yard.

The old lady sat forward again. "Do you?"

My mom bit her lip and shook her head like she was trying to get water out of it.

What happened next is that the son said, "Ma, I think it's time to go now." A cloud must have passed over the sun because it suddenly became really dim in the room. The old lady tried to get up a few times but she couldn't. Then he helped her and propped her up on her cane and they started walking toward the front door. They didn't look at us or say anything as they went by. Before they left the old woman looked back at the living room one more time. Her eyes got all squinty, like the way you would look at an ocean. Then they walked out and we never saw them again.

My mom hugged me and started crying and rocking back and forth. We were like that for a while.

I think about that day all the time. My mom is really old now. About fifteen years ago she moved away from Dalgreen Court and into a nursing home in Denton, the next county over. It has square shrubs in front of it and you have to swipe a card to get in. I heard there was a bad fire, and our old house was torn down along with a few others. I heard they built it up again.

They poured concrete driveways and put potted yucca plants and gates on top of that.

Me, I had a wife and I have three kids. Some of the way I look spilled into them. But they're all out there now.

EN LA CALLE DOCE (FLACO'S BLUES)

BY OSCAR C. PEÑA

Oak Cliff

I t was nine fifteen Friday night when Estanislado Escobedo stepped off the Greyhound bus at the South Polk Street station, walked through the sliding doors of the terminal, and hailed a cowboy cab. The bus should have arrived at eight fifty, but had run into traffic leaving Houston. No time to catch a city bus. The taxi driver looked to be from the Middle East or India or Pakistan; like one of the hundreds of students he had seen at Texas A&I University in Kingsville, back in the late 1960s. Stan asked the man if he knew where the Dallas neighborhood of Oak Cliff was.

"Southwest—other side of the Trinity River."

"Good, take me there and drop me off in front of the Taco Bell at 505 West Illinois Avenue."

I

Dubose Williams is a freelance writer working on an exposé of fundamentalist churches for *Texas Monthly*. He's writing about some of the smaller evangelical churches within the Texas Bible Triangle: an area anchored by Houston, San Antonio, and Dallas. Williams is interviewing Plutarco "El Martillo" Paniagua, pastor of The Bread and the Water, a church in San Antonio. Hermano Plutarco is in Oak Cliff to attend a tent revival and has brought some members of his congregation up to Dallas to protest the planned opening of a topless club, the Prickly Pear.

"I read that you're from San Anto . . . Excuse me, Pastor Plutarco, I thought you were from San Antonio. How come it reads 'San Anto' here in your bio? Is that a typo?"

"Please. . . call me Hammer. Yes, I live in San Antonio. My bio was written by my good friend and cousin Jesus Chapa. Chuy was a pachuco before he was saved. That's the way he talks and he writes like he talks."

"Okay, fair enough. So what brings you up to Dallas? And why is your nickname El Martillo?"

"The answer to your first question is long and complicated. The quick answer is that we came for a tent revival and since we're going to be here we may as well join with other churches in protesting that topless club. But before I forget, can you write in your magazine that I want to thank all the church ladies who made taquitos and tamales for our Church Ladies Auxiliary fundraiser? Our travel ministry made enough money to buy a spare tire, the gas, and thirteen quarts of Pennzoil for the church van for our trip to Dallas."

"Okay, I guess . . . yeah . . . sure, I'll put something in the article."

"The answer to your second question is simple. I was born and raised in South Texas, down in Kingsville. My grandfather and father were carpenters and my old pops nicknamed me El Martillo because I was always banging on something. He thought I'd grow up to be a carpenter too, but as it turned out I liked to bang on the drums more than on two-by-fours, so I played music for years. Started in '67. I played with Chavez and the Chevelles, the Velmonts, Beto Leal y su Orquesta. Man, we'd play sock hops, KC Halls, VFWs, nightclubs, weddings, quinceañeras, bar mitzvahs. Well—maybe not those cause there weren't too many bar mitzvahs in Kingsville. I guess you never heard of the Velmonts, huh?

"But that's not really why you're talking to me, is it, Mr. Williams? Is it because you think I'm a fire-and-brimstone kinda guy? Do you think El Martillo means that I'm claiming to be the Hammer of God? Well, I'm not a Jonathan Edwards 'sinners in the hands of an angry God' type of preacher. Or do you just think that I'm selling God and religion to poor folks who don't know any better? Which is it, Mr. Dubose Williams?

"You wanna write a story for *Texas Monthly*? There's another reason why I'm here in Dallas; in this particular area of Oak Cliff. I'm meeting someone from my old band for breakfast tomorrow morning. I've asked him to come up from South Texas; we have another old friend staying in Oak Cliff who might be in trouble. You can join us if you want."

II

The old vato glides through the door of the Taco Bell, heels tapping spit-shined tangerine-orange Stacys, his khaki pants and snap-buttoned country western shirt creased and medium starched. The man's name is tooled across a belt cinched around his twenty-eight-inch waist. A bluesman, a poet, un blusero, Flaco orders supper—

"Señorita, un taco y una soda, por favor."

Then he starts to talk to someone who ain't there, kinda like he's singing—

I miss my wife and Lone Star Beer
And making love on Saturday nights.
Wish I could smoke just one more cigarette,
But I'm getting old
And I got sugar in my blood.

She died.
Who died?
My woman, pendejo,

A long time ago.
The only one I can cheat on now is my doctor,
so I sneak a bowl of menudo
On Sunday mornings as I make my way to church.
Ain't nobody gonna know but me and God
And He's got me talking to myself.

The girl behind the counter hands the bluesman a white paper sack. Salsa in his pocket, Coca-Cola in his hand, his supper wrapped in paper, Flaco slips into the night.

Stan had been sitting at a table along the back wall of the Taco Bell when he saw the old man walk in. He was just like all those guys Stan remembered from when he was going to Memorial Junior High back in Kingsville. They were all the same: skinny, wearing khaki pants, Stacy Adams shoes, and back then they wore those 3/8" belts. A thin strip of leather that satisfied the gotta-wear-a-belt rule the football coaches always enforced. His dad had called them *pachucos* and said the word as if it left a bad taste in his mouth. *Una bola de cabrones.*

I guess these guys never changed, Stan thought. *I know Flaco didn't; he still looks the same forty years later. Too bad his mind is going south. But he's here just like Plutarco said he'd be. It's been years since we were on the road together, playing beer joints during the week and weddings and quinceañeras on the weekends. Flaco was a good musician, playing accordion, sax, singing; hell, we were all good musicians, just never could get a recording contract. I just wish I knew what Hammer was talking about. Visions! Visions?*

His old pal had changed big time since he'd been "saved"; it drove Stan nuts.

Why can't things be like they used to be? All of us playing music, drinking beer, and dancing with pretty women.

Stan followed Flaco into the night, wondering where the old

musico was taking him. Oak Cliff wasn't a bad town; no different than other Mexican neighborhoods in cities like San Antonio or Houston. People walking around on a Friday night; families headed somewhere for a burger or one of those buffets where you could feed your old lady and kids for about forty bucks if everyone drank ice water with extra lemons. You could still tell who was a Mexican national and who had been raised in the US. The Mexicans were dressed up: men wearing cowboy hats and fancy, pointed boots they'd bought at La Pulga, the local flea market; the women dressed like they were going to Sunday Mass, they were even wearing heels. One thing probably hadn't changed— it was the end of the month and each one of those men would have twenties folded in his wallet, maybe a few fifties. Life was good here in Texas.

III

Stan met Plutarco for breakfast around seven Saturday morning at El Rincon Tapatio, a restaurant on West Jefferson Boulevard. He embraced his old childhood friend, then Plutarco introduced Dubose.

"Estanislado Escobedo, meet Dubose Williams. Mr. Williams is a writer for *Texas Monthly* magazine and he's doing a story on some of us preachers."

The two men shook hands. Dubose said, "I'm actually a freelance writer hoping to be able to sell a story to *Texas Monthly*. How do you say your name again?"

"It's easier if you just call me Stan." He turned to Plutarco. "He's staying at a rent-by-the-week motel, La Somnambula— which is about right for him because he sure seems to be sleepwalking. This, come to think of it, also describes me. I was up all night watching the entrance to that hotel like I was on a stakeout or something. Hammer! What the hell is going on, man? You had me drop everything, take a freaking Greyhound, and show up here to keep my eye on Flaco? Man, that's crazy. You said that you'd had a vision, like maybe you saw or dreamed something. I hope that vision don't include me cause I just wanna go home. I gotta get back to work on Monday and my old lady is pissed because I wouldn't tell her anything about why I was going to Dallas except just to meet you and she knows that I ain't no saint. But how was I gonna tell her that I was coming up so I could watch Flaco Huerta buy his supper at a Taco Bell?"

"Tanis, I did have a dream . . . more like a nightmare. I think Flaco's gonna kill somebody."

"Nobody's called me Tanis since my dad died. It's like everything is going back to when we were kids and playing music. What the hell do you mean? Kill somebody? Who's he gonna kill? He ain't never hurt nobody. All he ever wanted to do was play music, drink beer, and smoke cigarettes."

"A few months ago Flaco came by the church; he wanted to see me, wanted to confess. I told him, *Hey, esse, I ain't no priest, that's the Catholics.* He said he had found out that El Guero Poncho was living in Dallas, in a place called Oak Cliff. Said he was going to kill him. *Had* to kill him."

Stan was drawing a blank. "Who's Poncho?"

"You remember—the stories that Flaco's dad would tell us about his father being murdered? This guy Poncho used his blade because the old man was making fun of him in front of a woman. Man, everybody knows you don't ridicule Mejicanos, or treat them with disrespect; especially back then. It gets you killed. Anyway, Poncho had a stutter and Flaco's abuelo mocked him. Before anyone knew it, Poncho's left hand flicked out like un pinche rattlesnake and Abuelito was lying in a pool of blood. Dead. Muerto. El Guero Poncho left that little town, Doctor Cos, down in Mexico and took off, headed north across the border. People said, *Que se fue a Pensilvania.* But man, that happened like almost a hundred years ago, ninety at least. Flaco thinks

Poncho fled to Dallas. Somehow or other he thinks he's tracked him down—I know some people from a church here in Dallas, one of the members of the congregation is a cop. I talked to him and asked him to look into it, but I already knew that whoever Flaco thought he had was the wrong guy. Flaco's almost seventy years old, so whoever killed his grandfather died a long time ago. That cop didn't have much information except for the nickname so he never discovered anything. If he kills someone, it'll be an innocent man. We gotta stop him."

"But you don't know this victim's name, or if there is a victim; you don't know what he looks like or how old he is. I think Flaco is demented. Why did you call me?"

"Dementia. You think he has dementia and I agree. I called you because we've got a friend who needs our help and I can't do this alone. I have to be at that revival because I'm preaching. Maybe I'm wrong. Maybe Flaco isn't going to kill anyone. But what's it going to hurt if you follow him for a couple of nights?"

"Why this weekend?"

"That's the crazy part. I had that dream two weeks ago on a Monday night. It's going to happen tonight. I know because in my dream I was preaching this tent revival on Saturday night. Me and some people from our church were also going to be protesting a topless club later on today. It's called the Prickly Pear. Everything's just like in my dream. Tanis, I think I've received a sign, a premonition. I saw a man's body, but he had no face."

"You mean a sign like Moses and that bush?"

"Well, not that big, but still. I just know it. You need to go back to that Taco Bell and wait for him. He'll be there. Again. Remember that cop I told you I knew from a church here in Dallas? He followed Flaco for a few days; he eats supper at that same place every night between nine and ten. Orders the same thing. Did he sing that song?"

"Yeah."

Plutarco paid for breakfast, left a nice tip on the table. The three of us walked out of the restaurant.

I walked with the preacher as the men went their separate ways. We had gone maybe ten yards when Stan called out—

"¡Oye, Hermano Plutarco! You know what they got just a block down the street? The Texas Theater. I think that's where they caught that dude Oswald; the man who shot Kennedy, back in the '60s. I don't like that. Maybe that's another sign? Something bad."

IV

I decided to join Stan on his stakeout instead of attending the Pentecostal tent revival and listening to Hammer preach whatever it was he preached, so I was waiting outside the Taco Bell when Stan showed up around nine p.m. We went inside. Sure enough, there he was with his back to us, wearing a black vest and black felt cowboy hat; ordering his supper and singing his song. Again.

Stan wanted to see if his old friend would recognize him so he walked up, tapped Flaco on the shoulder and said "Oye, Flaco, como estas, amigo? Usted me recuerda? Soy Estanislado Escobedo. Te acuerdas, de la musica?"

Nothing. The man did not recognize Stan; almost looked through him.

Flaco turned, picked up his drink and paper bag, and slipped out the door. Stan and I started following. We must have walked five miles, Flaco eating his supper and drinking the Coke.

Stan was talking about the '60s as we walked, remembering how they would play music all night long, all kinds of music: rancheras, polkas, cumbias, R&B, and soul.

"Maaaan. Otis Redding was the best. Not that 'Dock of the Bay' shit for *American Bandstand*, but cool tunes like 'These Arms of Mine' and 'I've Been Loving You Too Long.' We had a tight sound—tenor sax, bari sax, two trumpets, a Hammond B3 with a Leslie speaker, guitar, bass, and drums. We were cool and man did the girls love it. Sunny and the Sunliners didn't have nothing on us when we played 'Talk to Me.' Jose y Carlos, two brothers, were on trumpet, me on bari and Gilberto on tenor sax, Bob on guitar, Jesse on bass, El Martillo en los tambores, La Vidi on the organ, and Flaco singing."

V

He was sitting at the table, a man in his seventies, wearing a white starched guayabera, looking more Hawaiian than Mexican with a white goatee and dark, squinting eyes; looking like he could have been a large old university professor—not large as in the University of Texas or Texas A&M, but retired-wrestler large—yet old and distinguished, like someone's grandfather; maybe five feet ten inches, weighing in at three hundred pounds. The woman, light skinned, had green eyes and her hair, dyed red, was big, stacked up like the day she was getting married back forty years ago, in 1971.

La Calle Doce restaurant featured Mexican seafood. Don Poncho and his wife Porfidia were regular customers. The food was good, had fancy names that raised the prices, but it was still Mexican style, or *estilo Mejicano*.

Dinner was being served. The ceviche, a dish of fish and shrimp cooked in lime and prepared with tomato, onion, and cilantro, and the sopa de mariscos had been a delicious start. The next course being served was braised short ribs and pan-seared grouper. Don Poncho was drinking ice-cold Budweiser and his wife sipped Pellegrino.

VI

Stan watched as his old friend stopped, then entered a restaurant on 12th Street. He hesitated—

"Maybe he's getting another drink or maybe he has to take a leak?"

Stan didn't enter the restaurant. He called Hammer instead, on his cell phone. I didn't stick around to hear what he told the preacher. I walked in.

It happened without warning. The waiter looked up. I watched as a crimson line slashed across the big man's face, starting at his right temple, angling downward, a dark red trail streaking toward the left side of his open mouth. Two points as big as dimes hit just above the heart; the line stitching down then up until it finally ended at his left shoulder. The woman sitting across from the big man was staring in shock as she studied her white shawl and realized that she had been spared. Her husband was oozing red from his right ear, across his face and chest, the table already soaked. Six .38-caliber bullets. There would not be an open casket.

He heard the shots while standing outside, waiting across the street from the restaurant. He'd seen the flashes and shadows peeking out from between the slats of the venetian blinds. Stan was already crying as he watched him leave La Calle Doce. A few people ran out screaming. Flaco didn't run, he just walked. I was right behind him. Stan crossed the street, joined me, and we started walking, Flaco about fifty yards in front of us. We headed east on 12th Street to the end of the block, turned left onto South Bishop Avenue, walked the block and crossed Center Street, walked another short block and turned right on West Jefferson Boulevard. Flaco had stopped. He was standing in front of the Texas Theater at 231 West Jefferson Boulevard when a unit of the Dallas Police Southwest Patrol Division pulled up and two cops got out, .45s drawn, ordering him to hit the pavement.

Flaco was singing, ". . . *and making love on Satur*—" as he turned to face the policemen, revolver in his right hand, six spent shell casings in the cylinder.

PART II

RANGERS

THE PRIVATE ROOM

BY MERRITT TIERCE

Uptown

Tonight they've put me on thirty men in the Private Room. The men are all white, fat, and over fifty. Sometimes parties like this will show up en masse on a hotel bus or in a drove of limos, if they're in town for a convention and everything is organized. But these guys trickle in, and by the time the last few arrive some of them have already been drinking for two hours. DeMarcus, my partner on the party, got everything started—introduced us, went over the set menu, helped them pick out their wine.

I wonder if it's a good thing that DeMarcus will be the face and I'll be backwaiting. You get to know the look of new money and the look of old; you can call on sight, with near-perfect accuracy, whether a person is a martini, a red wine, a Stella, a *Just water no ice extra lemon and a straw did I say no ice?*; you know that certain European accents doom your take. You have an entire catalog of these things in your head but still there will come that table, they're wearing jeans and when you ask them what they want to drink they say two Diet Cokes and iced tea and you think you know what you're in for—an appetizer as an entrée, split three ways, ten percent on a tab that's missing a couple digits. They're making out at the table, he looks twice her age, you can't figure out why the other one is with them. *Low class*, you think, *guess it's not my night*. Then you walk up with the second basket of bread they asked for and they say to bring out a bottle of Dom Rosé. After that they drink the 2000 Harlan Estate and order the big lobster tail. You start moving like you've got somewhere to be and when the bartender tries to play around with you instead of handing over the decanter, you snap at him because if they come through you stand to make five hundred dollars off a three-top.

Same thing with these types in the Private Room, the unpredictability. Sometimes they want a girl with their steak—a rival establishment across town employs only women—and sometimes they don't think a girl can do the job, or they seem embarrassed for you.

I won't be talking much from here on out, and with the look of them I'm glad of that even if it might have worked out better for us with me up front. I fill their wine glasses and pick up the cocktail napkins they've brought with them from the bar. Are you ready for another, sir? I say. One of them has already downed three Jack'n'waters and the hors d'oeuvres haven't even arrived. His nose is red and his eyes are pushed deep into a big waxy face. I ring up another for him and when I head into the well to pick it up DeMarcus is there, loading some other cocktails onto a tray. I point at the Jack and ask him if he'll take it with him so I can prep some mise en place. Who's it goin' to? he asks. You know, I say, Lushie. Ah, he says, big fella? They're all big, I say. Well, they're all Lushies too, he says.

Back in the room Lushie is standing, whiskey in hand, inviting everyone else to sit. He starts talking about their colleague who passed recently, due to an aortal aneurism. You can tell the others think this is a downer. They just got going on their buzz and they have to tell it to hold on a minute because it's making them want to laugh when they should be serious, so they start playing with their forks and staring at the tablecloth and especially they start drinking harder. You look across the table and the arms and glasses are going up and down quietly but nonstop like derricks. Lushie is using long medical terms with the somber educated air of a preacher bringing the word. *The word is—what? I think. Heartsick? Moderation? Death? Quit it all right now?*

Finally he drains his glass and sits all in one motion and the chatter folds back in around us and I can tell some of them feel like they barely made it out. Now they're talking *merger, due diligence, cash flow, liquidity, execute,* and the deadly *amortization.* I have my language too, so though I think about asking Lushie if he wants me to mainline it for him I put it the nice way and say with a prompting lilt in my voice, Would you like me to keep those coming for you, sir? and I start making them double talls to slow him down, something Cal taught me. *He wants to drink, let him drink, and make him pay for it too—he feels that second or third double hit his ass and he don't slow down, more power to him. But you don't got to be running around for him like his goddamn lil' bitch.*

We take the order, DeMarcus on one side of the table and me on the other. We have an unspoken rivalry about who can get from position one to position fifteen the fastest. The pros get the order-taking down to a call-and-response that reads each guest's mind and draws out his selections for three courses with all pertinent temperatures and modifications in forty-five seconds or less, without letting him feel the slightest bit rushed. You expand your intake words, like *Certainly* and *Absolutely* and *That won't be a problem, sir*, you let them hang rich and pillowy in a smile and the guest thinks only of how accommodating and efficient you are, he doesn't hear the ticking of the giant railroad clock in your head that is Chef, waiting on the line for this order because a big party will affect the cook times for everything in the house. I'm a position behind DeMarcus since one of my guys takes forever to acknowledge me, even though I'm standing there next to him saying, Sir? Sir? Have you had a chance to decide? At some point you have to give up and wait for the friends he's talking to to advocate for you, give him a sign with their eyes that he's being rude. I hear DeMarcus talking to his seat 8 about what side dishes he wants on the table with the entrées. This guy calls him "Mark"—DeMarcus is sensitive about his name, at least in the restaurant, and I don't blame him. He'll truncate it like that if he feels he needs to, though I think his name sounds regal and hip in the parking lot late at night when his brother swings by to get him and they ask me to climb in for a puff. On my side, on Lushie's right, there was one black guy. Guess he's their EEOC compliance. He's the only one of the lot who doesn't order a steak—he asks for the salmon, well done, and wants to make sure some greens will be on the table. Then I bend over by Lushie's ear to get his order, and he does that thing fat people do where they sit facing forward but they tilt their head back and up toward you like a flower looking for the sun. He says he'll have the rib eye. Maybe he's thinking the same thing I am about that because when I ask him what he'll have for dessert he pauses piously and says, I don't believe I'll have dessert tonight. I'll pass. You'll pass, okay, I say seriously while making notes like a doctor.

I leave the room to ring up my half of the table and while I'm at the POS my friend Asami comes up behind me. I've got some fucking Martians tonight, she says. I know, I say, they're everywhere, and I debrief her about the Private Room. She's telling me these stupid Botoxies at her table are doing the Sandra Oh thing to her again. It always goes down the same way. The ladies see her and she's taking their cocktail order and one of them says to another, Oh, you know who she reminds me of? and then turns to Asami and says, You know who you look just like? and Asami usually gives them this big gorgeous grin and says, *I bet I know exactly what you're thinking*, or, *No! I have no idea, who's that?* but she's telling me that tonight instead she kind of lost it and said to them, I don't look anything *like* Sandra Oh, she's Korean! But I don't look anything like her anyway!

Back in the room I'm clearing the hors d'oeuvres and getting everybody cleaned up and ready for the salad course when the Boss stands and starts telling jokes. The Boss is the one DeMarcus spoke to at the beginning about the wine—he'll be paying the tab and apparently the reason for this fete is some deal he signed with Lushie. I lent them my pen earlier when they set the contract down in front of him and he started patting his pockets. So two doctors are banging this nurse, he says. She gets pregnant but she doesn't tell them till she's seven months gone, so they send her to Florida to have the baby. They're gonna figure out how to raise it and do right, and of course she'll come back to work at a much higher salary than before because they both have wives and kids. So she delivers and one doc calls the other and says he has bad news. What's that? says the other doc. Well, she had twins, says the first doc, and mine died!

Grinning, he lets the laughter die down and then he goes, Okay, how 'bout this one. So one doctor says to the other, Are you fucking the nurse? The other doctor says, No, why? And the first doctor says, Good! You fire her!

Now he rides the laughter, shouting, How do you know your wife is dead? Sex is the same but the dishes start to pile up!

I catch DeMarcus's eye across the table and I can see the laugh he's stifling pulling at the corners of his mouth. He gives me a look like, *What are you gonna do? It's funny*, and I shake my head like he's a traitor. I wonder: if he and EEOC weren't here, would the Boss be telling nigger jokes too? The Boss continues with the jokes and the room is getting stuffy. I tell DeMarcus I'm going out to get Danny, the GM, to check the thermostat. It's hot as fucking hell in here, I say. The HAR-HAR-HARing is so loud I don't even have to whisper.

When I come back I'm moving around the table, setting out steak knives and crumbing, and when I get to the Boss he puts his hand on my elbow and says affably, We're not offending you with any of this, are we? Ha! I say to the Boss, you think I haven't heard this before? I give him a matronly smile with this but he's already patting my elbow and turning away.

The air conditioner must have gone out again. It's a chronic problem in this room, and I notice that jackets are off and collars unbuttoned. EEOC is the only one who doesn't seem to notice the heat, or else he's deliberately resistant to shedding any layers around these guys. The building is really old, it was built in the '40s, and though the owner is a millionaire he's notoriously cheap. It might cost $15,000 to replace the AC but he won't do it. He made his money in the '70s by investing in the development of the first heart stent. He keeps demand up, feeding all these people meat slathered in butter.

I corner Danny in the bar. Danny, you got to do something about the AC, I plead, I really don't need to see these guys take off any more clothing. Danny says All right all right sista I'm on it and I know that means *I don't give a fuck if they get heatstroke and die in there.* At least I've made the gesture of looking out for them, at least if one of them bitches to him on the way out about how hot it was, it won't be news to Danny and I'm covered. He'll be ready to say *I know brother I know, we had our man working on it all night, I can't fucking believe it went out while you got all your guys here, you of all people, I know it was a big night for you, how was everything else?* But when I get back in the room I think maybe the heat has sobered them up some because in the din I hear the Boss say, But I can't tell this one in mixed company. They've killed our last four cases of the 2002 vintage and we've had to move on to the '03, so when he says this I'm facing into the corner of the room, opening another bottle. I roll my eyes, looking down at the landscape on the Joseph Phelps label, but I don't leave and I hear him mutter something about he'll tell it later so I go ahead and pour around the table and take a coffee order. I say Would you care for cognac or espresso with dessert? I never say cappuccino or latte even though we can do it.

I learned that from Nic Martinez, in this room. I was assigned to be his bitch and he resented having to split the take with me because it was a preset and he could have done it on his own. I didn't fuck up anything on the first three courses but at the end he heard me say coffee cappuccino and he pinched the back of my elbow hard. In the corner of the room he said, Do you want him to like you? nodding at our busser. I didn't know what to say so I said What do you mean? It's not a trick question, he said. You put him in the back foaming milk for twenty minutes he's gonna hate you, and I am too. And don't say coffee, it's free on a preset. I thought he was off me forever because of that, but later the same week I walked past the Private and he asked me if I partied. I didn't know what he meant then either but I said yes and that was the beginning of something. He was resetting the table with his partner just like he'd done with me. I went home with him that night and he made me some microwaved apple cinnamon oatmeal and told me he loved my big juicy ass. In his bed when he said, Are you gonna get it? I lied and said yes and when he asked me if I got it I lied again. This is the room where Joe Ambrogetti bent me over in the dark, over there where the wine bucket is now. This is the room where Estéban kissed me one night—walked up to me with all kinds of purpose and kissed me. I kissed him back for no reason.

They're all finishing their desserts so we're clearing the last of the plates, but they're still drinking hard. Lushie is on his seventh or eighth whiskey and he's guzzling the wine too. The goal seems to be not so much pleasure as obliteration. Somebody puts their arm around my waist, a liberty taken with me fairly often because I'm small and just the right height. You sign up for a certain kind of life and shell out the dough for it, you expect the waitresses to permit you. I turn toward the guy to see what he wants. He's so drunk he's glowing but he's been here before, he keeps his words standing up as he asks, Sunshine, can we smoke our cigars in here?

No sir, I say, I'm sorry, there's no smoking in the building, it's a city ordinance. I tug away from his arm and notice that one of the others seems to be asking DeMarcus the same question at the other end of the table, he's gesturing with his cigar and when DeMarcus shakes his head he looks just as disappointed as the one who called me Sunshine. That guy sticks his cigar in his mouth anyway and starts chewing on it.

Everything is winding down and DeMarcus says he's going to go put the check together, which can take awhile on these parties. I say I'll stay in the room to watch over them till he gets back but I feel like I need to get out for a minute and everybody's topped off except Lushie. I can't keep up with him and I'm not worrying about it any longer, so I step into the hall and lean against the wall in the dark space between two stacks of chairs.

Benito, one of the bussers, comes around the corner into the hall and pulls a stack of the chairs away from the wall. When he sees me he jumps a little and says, Maestra! Me has asustado!

Sorry, Papi, I say. Benito is probably close to sixty but quite spry and often he'll help me out on my tables even when he hasn't been assigned to my station. I'll be holding a stack of cleared plates away from my body, leaning down over a table to answer someone's question, and suddenly I'll feel the weight of the plates being lifted from me. By the time I can turn to look he'll already be halfway to the dishroom. One of his sons, also named Benito though we call him Sanchez, is the barback; another, Orlando called Magic, works the salad line; and his youngest, whose given name I don't know because everyone calls him Niño, is also a busser. The sons all have their father's work ethic and Danny will joke with Benito that he needs to bring his other sons over too. Papi, you got any more where these came from? he'll say. Benito does, actually, and he'll say, Sí, jefe, sí.

Good peoples? he asks, with a nod toward the wall behind me, referring to my party on the other side of it. This question is strictly economic—it never means, Do you like them? It means only, Are they spending money?

Sí, Papi, I say, muchísimo vino.

Es bueno, es bueno, he clucks as he disappears around the corner with the chairs.

When I open the door this time I step into a thick quiet, the sleepy quiet of the overstuffed and oversoused. If they were younger they'd be boisterous and obnoxious, they'd be cranking up at this point, but those days are behind them and some seem calmed by the cigars they're holding in their teeth. The Boss is standing up at the end of the table opposite me, and at my entrance he pauses in the middle of another joke. He looks at me and says, Hi. Everyone else turns to look at me. I'm surprised at this late acknowledgment and I say hi back and stand still. In this job you learn to give them what they want and not take anything personally, but I've got Asami's frisky defiant burr up in my skin and I say, You're gonna stop now? This is the one I *want* to hear!

No one laughs at my joke. I'm like Lushie earlier, talking about aortal aneurisms. I turn around to get the hell out and I nearly knock down DeMarcus with the door. Whoa, he says, what got into you?

I am sitting on an upturned glass rack, vigorously working the spots off spoons still hot from the washer, when DeMarcus comes to tell me they're leaving. Cal thinks it's bad form to let your guests leave without telling them good night and if he caught me sitting here doing my sidework instead of seeing them off he'd call me out. *Just gonna let your people walk out like that, huh? How much money did that spoon pay you tonight? Make sure you give that spoon your card, Hey Spoon ask for me next time you bring in Knife and Fork I'll take great care of you. DeMarcus remind me not to have dinner at Marie's house, she one of those Don't let the door hit you on the way out hosts. Classy.*

I leave the silverware half finished and walk with DeMarcus back to the Private Room. We stand in the doorway while the men file out, shaking their hands like two pastors after a church service. Thank you, gentlemen. Thank you so much, sir. Thanks for coming in tonight. Appreciate your business. Congratulations, hope you enjoyed everything. How'd we do tonight? Everybody happy?

After we get out DeMarcus and I hang in the employee parking lot, waiting for Asami, who promised to share some of her stash with us. We have half a bottle of the party's cab and a full bottle of the chardonnay they left in the ice bucket untouched, and we drink both of them, pouring tall into Styrofoam cups. I make sure to leave a glass in the chard bottle in case Asami wants some. Other servers and bussers shoot out the back door like pinballs, letting the door crash against the side of the building and stripping off pieces of their uniform as they head toward their cars, calling, Good night, and other more exultant things like, Home fucking free! to us as they leave.

Niño is driving back into the parking lot from a beer run—whichever of the cooks or bussers gets out first takes his turn to buy a case of Modelo Especial or Bud Light before the stores stop selling at midnight. He lets down the tailgate of his pickup and offers DeMarcus and me a beer. There's something about the way Niño's navy workshirt is always starched stiff, and something about the way his hair is always trim and gelled, and something about the way he makes eye contact with you when he's taking plates from you as if to say, *Give me all that. I'll take care of it for you, no problem.* Sometimes he actually says things just like this. If you're female he might say *I got it, baby*, but you never feel condescended to, only happy he's in league with you.

He's so young, only nineteen, but his wife had twins in San Luis Potosí. He got the call after work one night a couple months ago, standing about where he is now. He was overjoyed, he began to cry, and everyone started hugging him and saying, Congratulations, Papa! and, Felicidades! and we all went over to the bar next door and bought him and everyone else in the place a shot of Patrón. He talks about how he's saving all his money to bring them over so they can be raised in America, he tells me he gave each of them one English and one Spanish name: Thomas Jose and Michael Alonzo. He calls them Pepe and Zozo.

I tip him more than I tip the other bussers, because he works so hard and I like his attitude. It pays to hustle, it pays to bend over, we both know this. You keep your standards high and your work strong but these are necessary for success; you keep your dignity separate, somewhere else, attached to different things.

When Asami finally comes out the back door I say Hey Sandra, how you living?

Dirty, fucking dirty, she says.

I pop a Modelo and hold it out to her. Here, honey, just wash it all away, I say.

Thanks, but I think some of it's gonna stick, she says.

Nah, says DeMarcus. Only if you let it.

That right, De? I ask. He shrugs, then says to Niño, What do you think, Francisco?

When DeMarcus says his name, which I repeat in my head several times for safekeeping, Niño suddenly seems older to me, but he doesn't have any more wisdom on the matter than the rest of us. All he says is, No sé, Marco. Es mi job, sabes?

DeMarcus has fantastic teeth and tight waves. He's tall and lanky and he smells good. He keeps taking care of me in the parking lot, passing me the green hit when Asami refreshes the bowl, lighting my cigarettes, opening beers for me. The two of us are having a good time—it's easier on the nights you make money. On the low-scoring nights you feel depressed as hell even if you tell yourself that's the way it is, inconsistent. You can't look at the money on the night, you have to wait for the week or even the month to look at it, and you can't start going home when they overschedule. You have to work it like a nine-to-five even though it's anything but. Asami is hustling hardcore right now, she's the speech teacher at an inner-city public high school in Fort Worth, but three nights a week she drives over here too. She can't stay out late like she used to. In the old times we'd wake up together at somebody's apartment and she'd give me a ride back to my car at the restaurant, the day looking gray as an old sock through our hangovers. I offer her the last of the chard but she says she has to go now or she'll be hurting too bad tomorrow.

You can tell she really loves her kids at the school and that's the job she takes seriously. Not that you can blow this one off—the turnover rate at the restaurant is ridiculous because new people don't realize quick enough they're in the army now and they better step up, Chef isn't kidding when he expects you to know all fifteen ingredients in the hoisin sauce that goes with the fried lobster. I've hung in long enough now that they've asked me to sub in for a manager on occasion, wear a sexy little dress suit and heels and help out when we're short staffed. So far I've said no. I know they see you in the suit and you do a good job and before you know it that's where they want you all the time, and then everybody else's fuck-ups are on you instead of just your own. Plus I'd never see my kid if I started managing and I hardly see her anyway.

All right, I'm out, love you guys, see you Thursday, Asami says, putting her bowl back where it lives in the glove box of her car. Peace, Mama, says DeMarcus, and I tell her to be careful driving all that way home. Niño and the cooks and bussers have cleared out so when she's gone it's just me and De, we get into my car and he cranks up my Erykah. *Push up the fader / Bust the meter / Shake the tweeter / Bump it*, he sings along, grooving in his seat. I saw her in Whole Foods the other day, he says. Damn, woman is a *woman*. Talk to her? I ask. Naw, he says, I'm gonna say "Excuse me, Miss Badu, got me a fine position of employment as a servant, can I take you out some time?" Whole Foods guy probably has a better shot than me.

Whole Foods guy didn't make three bucks tonight like you did, I say. Hey, partna, it was smooth, smooth tonight, he says, offering his fist for a bump. I work with you whenever you want, any time, he adds. Likewise, baby, I say, and then, I wish Asami had left us some. There's a long high pause while we listen to Erykah rock it and I feel him thinking something through. Got some at the house, he says finally. Is that an invitation? I ask. It is if you want it to be, he says.

His brother drops him off at the restaurant and picks him up when's it over and when B—I've never heard DeMarcus call him anything else—pulls into the parking lot I'm drunk and stoned and I have no idea where they live or how I will get back to my car but I get into the cab of the truck between them on the bench seat. It's an old green Ford, from before they started making everything on cars so round. It smells like smoke. B has the hip-hop station pounding and looks at me like he knew this would happen, his face still, absent. He nods, doesn't speak. I can tell he's on something that's taken him up so far he can see me from above. Crack? I tried crack only once and it didn't work and now I'm hoping I have some limits. He drives out of the parking lot and I feel DeMarcus relax next to me, he's realizing I'm committed, realizing I'm down. He puts his hand on my thigh and then we're making out, the cab of this truck is old-school huge and I swing myself into his lap, facing him, feeling him hard as glass through my thin dress pants. B turns up the music as he pulls onto the freeway. I am grinding on DeMarcus and it's not enough, I feel like my body will do this without me if it has to. I feel nothing but his hands on my hips and his lips all over my collarbone and the 808 kicking out of the stereo, a primal rhythm I can't resist any more than the blood pulsing in my cunt. She want it, observes B, looking over at us. He has gold teeth. Not solid gold, the kind with the gold edges.

DeMarcus unbuckles his belt and starts undoing his pants, it's like he has four hands because he's getting his pants down and turning me to face B at the same time, pushing me gently onto my knees in the middle of the seat, he's behind me reaching around to pull off my pants too. He can't find the button and I've got one hand on B's thigh and one hand on the headrest behind him, I'm concentrating on reminding my drunk self to not grab the steering wheel to hold steady. My pants are too big, I've lost weight from doing blow after work. DeMarcus can't wait so he just pulls them down, they catch briefly on my hips but he tugs and then he's pushing inside me and I'm pushing back.

B I'm in it, he shouts over the music and I watch B's face, he doesn't look at me right next to him, keeps his eyes on the road and says Tight? I feel DeMarcus slow down so he won't come and he says Shit fuck sweet pussy. Then he asks me do I want to get B in on it and I don't say anything I just take the hand that is on B's thigh and I rub his cock through his track pants. He still doesn't look at me. Suck on me, he says. I bend down and DeMarcus backs up, still inside me, until his back is against the door so I have room to be like a stretching cat between them. I suck on B long and right and he starts breathing deep and making sounds and he takes one hand off the steering wheel and puts it in my hair, puts it on my head, I can tell he wants to push on my head. I go faster hoping he won't and then DeMarcus starts moving again. I count when I give head or I repeat something over and over in my mind, one-syllable strokes. *Sex. Is. The. Same. But.*

The. Dishes. I say to his cock. This is mean head I'm giving now. It's firm and I'm not letting it be wet, but this B won't even look at me. There was a man once to whose penis I said *I. Love. You. So. Much. I. Would. Do. Any-. thing. For. You. Can. You. Tell.* and every time I got to that *Tell* I would moan Mmm and he would say Oh my God what are you doing to me but this is not that man. This is me in a truck on Highway 183, this is me drunk and high, this is me doing and being done.

B says I wanna switch and I feel the truck slowing down. He stops on the shoulder of the freeway and rams the gearshift up the column to park. I barely have time to get my mouth off him before he's out of the cab and then there's a damp *thwack* as DeMarcus pulls out of me abruptly, he opens the passenger door and crosses in front of the truck, trotting, he doesn't button his pants, just lets his long work shirt hang over everything. His brother is in the cab next to me pulling my hips down on top of his cock before DeMarcus has even gotten into the driver's seat.

DeMarcus glides the truck along the shoulder until he can get back on the freeway, and without being told I take his cock into my mouth, tasting myself. *I. Am. An. An-. i-. mal. Good. Then. You. Fire. Her.* I think about my daughter, how her eyelids turn lavender at night. I think about how my friend Hal, who also works at the restaurant and also has a daughter, told me I should never do anything I wouldn't want her to do. How one afternoon he said to me, You know, Rie, we're doing what we want. If we wanted to be with them we would. We have to face that and decide what's next. If I wanted to be with Blair I would move to Houston and work at Starbucks if I had to. It's just money. *She. Had. Twins. Mine. Died.*

B is hardly moving back there behind me although he's as stiff as his brother. I feel DeMarcus turn to look at him and I wonder what he sees to make him say B? B, you with us? Then I feel B drop down to the seat from where he'd been up on his knees against me, he moves so fast his cock goes sideways as it comes out of me and it hurts. I stop sucking on DeMarcus to turn and look at B, who's leaning against the passenger-side window. I think he may have passed out.

After five days of driving we stop in front of their house, which is small. The porch light is on and I see vinyl siding, a tricycle on the sidewalk. DeMarcus and I get out of the truck and walk toward the house, leaving B in the cab. Where are we and whose is that? I ask, pointing at the tricycle. Shh, he says, opening the door. In the front room an old man is sitting in an easy chair holding a can of Budweiser and watching television. Hey Pop, says DeMarcus. Where B? says the old man. Sleep in the truck, answers DeMarcus, I be back with him shortly, how you? The old man grunts in response, he never looks away from the television or acknowledges me.

Want to shower? DeMarcus asks me. I say How much? and he looks at me like he doesn't get it. When he said Want to shower? I thought *He wants to put me somewhere where I can't see what's about to happen with B* and I thought *I want to shower so much* and I thought *Some of it's gonna stick* and I thought *How can I ever get back from here?* and what came out was How much?

Do I smell like fries? I ask, trying to act like I am keeping it together, trying to pretend I didn't just say something incomprehensible. Yes, the restaurant is Zagat-rated and our party spent over four grand on one dinner that involved compotes, reductions, infusions, compound butters, a coulis, a pan jus, but somehow the smell of french fries is what I always carry home on me. He puts his nose in my neck and inhales tenderly. We're still standing right there in the living room in front of his dad. Crème brûlée, he says. Come on, I'll show you to the ladies'.

This is the thing about the service industry—you can get trained to be slick and hospitable in any situation and it serves you well the rest of your life. Once you figure out that everything is performance and you bend to that, learn to modulate, you can dissociate from the mothership of yourself like an astronaut floating in space. That's how you can show a fucked-in-your-truck girl down the hall to the ladies' and tell her her neck smells like crème brûlée in front of a zombie dad while some freebased flesh you're related to waits for you to carry it inside. That's how the crunked girl can get in the shower like she's told and stand over the drain and pee and not think about what might happen next.

I lose track of time in the shower. I wash my vagina and then stand there letting the water run over me. I'm hearing the water like it's a waterfall, loud and like I'm inside it, when I'm high I hear sixteen layers of sound. I hear someone come into the bathroom, hear a belt buckle hit the floor. DeMarcus pulls back the shower curtain and steps in behind me. Clean yet? he asks. How's your brother? I ask. He be all right, just gets carried away with the shit sometimes. Whose tricycle is that outside? I ask again. Excuse me, he says, stepping around me to get near the water, turning his back to me. My son's, he says finally. How did I not know you have a son? I ask. He turns around to face me but his hands are over his face, he's rubbing his eyes. He shrugs. Work is work, he says. Don't everybody got to know everything.

We get out of the shower and cross the hall into a bedroom. It's dark, the shades are drawn. B is lying on the bed with his back to the wall. A porno is playing on a television at the foot of the bed. DeMarcus is wearing a towel around his waist and disappears into the darkest corner of the room until he strikes a match and I see that he's lighting a cigar. He candles the end and then turns it and puffs three times until it's lit. He sits down on the edge of the bed and pats the place beside him. I sit down, I am naked and cold. I stare at the porno but I hate porn. De is watching it and his eyes are bloodshot. He says Let's lay down so we do, he is on the outer edge of the bed with his ankles crossed and I am between him and B, who is silent and still. I have my head on De's chest and I doze off lying on him while he smokes his cigar and watches a jarhead fuck a stripper on stage. She has her hair in two ponytails and he holds onto them like handles.

I wake up when I feel myself drooling on his chest. I wipe his chest and then my mouth. Sorry, I say. Happens, he says. No problem. You ready to go back? I'll drive you. Sure, I say, thanks. I notice that B is gone but I don't ask where he went. I feel something feathery on my skin. I stand up and can see by the bruised dawn light coming around the window shade that the bed is covered in cigar ash. Covered. Evenly, as if it is some new weather. His dad is not in the chair when we leave.

In the truck on the way back we don't say much. My head hurts. I see a sign that tells me we are in Irving. Working tonight? I ask DeMarcus. I'm off, he says. You? I say I am and he says You never take off do you? and I say I don't. We're quiet until we get near the restaurant and he says If you want that morning-after pill I'll pay you back for it.

I hadn't thought of that. Do I need it? I ask, more to myself than him. Couldn't hurt, he says. Yeah, all right, I'll let you know, I say. I don't tell him I already have a dose at home because the last time they gave me an extra. It was fifty bucks and I don't mind letting him pay it backward for me so I'll tell him how much it cost next time I see him.

As he drives away I get in my car and I think *We never even smoked the weed he said he had at the house* and then I stare at the back of the restaurant and wish there were more hours between now and seeing it again later today. It's seven in the morning and I have to be here at five this evening. I drive home, home to my clean apartment, to my clean bed. I take another shower and I take the first Plan B pill and I take some ibuprofen and I call my daughter's father because it's rare that I'm awake this early, when he's getting her ready for school. I ask if I can talk to her and then I hear her high-pitched voice say Hi Mama and I hear her crunching toast. I ask her what kind of jelly she's having today. I tell her I miss her. She asks if she can come up to the restaurant like last time, for a Shirley Temple. I say We'll see. I imagine Hal in the green apron, smiling and asking *What can I get started for you?* He is thirty-four and has braces.

I go to sleep at eight and wake up at three. Her school day. I make coffee and wonder if I have any diseases now. We've been warned there might be a test on the hand-sell wines this week so I review them. *'03 Stag's Leap Winery, Napa, $90 down from $120. Ruby red, plum, earth, green tea, velvety tannins, complex.* Wine is all words. People who know wine don't need your help and people who don't will believe anything you say if it sounds good. Our sommelier would think that was a shitty attitude to have.

I eat a piece of vegetarian sausage while I stand in the kitchen drinking my perfect coffee and reading over the hand-sells. I look lean and I wear a digital sport watch on my left wrist so sometimes my guests will ask me if I run. I don't say No I'm just snorting a lot of coke right now. I say that I do run and they say I bet you don't eat much meat do you? and I say No actually I'm vegetarian and they laugh at this because I have just shown them a tray of ten pounds of raw beef carved into the different cuts of steak we offer. I hype it, the tiny mystique of my being vegetarian and working there. I say Meat is my profession, which often leads someone at the table to say Well you're certainly a professional. I don't say *I know, because I've made a hundred people before you say that same thing in this same situation, I've made you remember your charming professional vegetarian server when it's time for you to put a number on the tip line* and I don't say *I'm not vegetarian because of the animals, I'm vegetarian because I hate the way meat feels in my mouth.*

At four I get in the shower, scrubbing everything hard. I

pluck my eyebrows, brush my teeth, do my makeup, fix my hair, file and buff my nails. They see your hands more than anything. I put on my pants and undershirt and grab all my tools. I put the second Plan B pill in my pocket and hope I will remember to take it when everything is madness at eight o'clock. I stop at the cleaner's to swap soiled for pressed, I have a good man on the corner of Greenville and Belmont who does my shirts the way I want them and doesn't charge much. He starches everything to spec, so my long bistro apron can stand on its own and the creases in my sleeves will be so pointy that even at ten thirty tonight when I walk up to my last table for the first time they will see those creases and they'll trust me just a little. My name is Marie, and I'll take care of you tonight.

NIGHT WORK
BY CLAY REYNOLDS
Old East Dallas

Samuel Grand Avenue, 6:30 p.m.

They came just at sundown, direct from the park, from the tennis courts, out the south entrance nobody ever used, wearing white. Mercedes convertible. Blue as sapphire. Not one of the nicest ones, but a nice one. Tan leather seats. Custom wheels. Not usual in this neighborhood, not even uncommon, more rare than that. It made everything around it look shabby, made the pavement look filthy. She got out. Not him. Everybody noticed that, particularly the homeys on the corner hanging out by the low-rider, a boom box on the car's roof, smoking doobies, a little crack, cigarettes. They noticed her right off. She was tall, maybe five nine. Legs to the sky. Short skirt, cashmere sweater cut in a V that didn't quite go down low enough over a mound of freckled cleavage. Her hair was blonde, ponytailed, pink terry cloth headband. And her eyes were blue. Cobalt blue. Blue enough to fall into forever. She didn't walk; she bounded. That was the right word. On the balls of her feet. The blasting salsa across the lot suggested a rhythm, a sway. She picked it up. Her hips moved underneath the pleats of her skirt when she bounded up onto the sidewalk, graceful, like an antelope, past the stuffed trash cans, nasty wads of paper sacks, broken shards of beer bottles, crushed-out butts and candy wrappers, into the store. Every move was velvet, smooth as a breeze. Delicate forearms, lightly laced with golden gossamer. Her calves curved like twin tan bows down to the pink tops of her socks.

Her thighs were slender, tight, ridged with muscle, rich as flan. Those legs caught the mind of every dark eye in the place. Even the bitches hanging by the video rack, drinking Slurpees, smacking gum, eating day-old donuts, reeking of Dial and cheap perfume, caught those legs, envied them too much to scowl, to do more than stare, to feel the ache of envy, afraid to catch one another's eye for fear of sharing the loathing. She went into the women's, in the back, past the stacked boxes, the beer poster with a half-naked cowgirl, past the racks of snacks and sweets, over the dingy linoleum, by the cracked wall, and through the dented door, out of sight. Everybody exhaled like something awful had passed and left them scared, safe, but revealed something true, something they didn't want to know. Outside, the homeboys checked him out. Young, groomed, confident, dark hair, good shoulders. An athlete, maybe. A tailback, maybe. Shortstop, maybe. Fast, probably. But not big, not mean, not really strong, and not fast enough. Money. Sure. White mohair sweater's arms knotted over the collar of a whiter polo, bracelet on his wrist, gold flashing in the dying light, more gold on a matte of dark, wiry chest hair. Money. Sure. Country club players slumming on the public courts, wrong part of town. Still in the car. Not noticing being noticed, he fucked with the radio or the CD. Looking for a tune, maybe, or a ball game, maybe. NPR, maybe. Fucked with something on the dash. AC, maybe. Trying to put the top up, maybe. Maybe he should have thought about that before he pulled up to this store in this hood. Convertibles are easy. The sun dropped behind the buildings. Tall evergreens on the edge of the park speared dark shadows across the street, the concrete lot, blackness crawling over the ground like blood on a bathroom floor. Streetlights came on too bright, store neon too loud in the urban gloaming. Cars passed without slowing. One cop. Didn't even look. A cell burbled. He answered, talked. Never looked around. The homeboys nodded, like they were all on a string and somebody dipped their heads. Like puppets. Muscles flexed, tattoos rippled, earrings sparkled in the electric glare. One got behind his wheel, fired the engine, gunned it once, let it slide to a low rumble, bounced it again. V-8 power under primer paint and dark glass. Quality rubber. Cranked up the CD. Mexican rap. Heavy bass. It permeated, even inside, through the heavy glass, the cinder blocks. If he heard it, felt it, he didn't show, didn't look. The others snapped down the boom box, stored it, got in, shapes in the car, the yellow glow of lighters pricked the smoked glass. He was talking on the cell, not watching, not listening. His hand moved in the air, struck the wheel, annoyed, not angry. Not the type to get pissed off, to lose it. Money. Sure. She came out of the women's, stopped, looked around. The bitches stared for a beat, then found new interest in old magazines. She'd had her piss, now she wanted to make it right. Buy something. Two dollars in her hand. She grabbed a pack of mints, put the bills on the counter, slid them forward with one long, pink, polished nail. The clerk, as young as she but five shades darker, fifty times more acute, stared at her. A question, maybe. A warning, maybe. Only blue eyes in ten blocks. Only true blonde in twenty. Beyond her world, beneath her notice, he said nothing, dropped his dusky face, made change. She offered a smile. He looked up as if he heard it. Teeth so white they hurt. Eyes so blue he wanted to lick them. She said something no one heard. Thank you, maybe. Then was gone. Through the door, iron-barred, steel-framed, opaque glass milky from dirt, handprints, scratches, crusty yellowed tape, and then outside. Bounding again. Off the curb, into the Mercedes. He dropped the cell, said something sharp and quick when she slammed the door, grabbed her shoulder belt. She laughed, stretched. Arms up, smile flashing, tits rolling. The homeys watched and waited while they pulled out. If he went right, toward the freeway, he was cool. If he went left, toward the barrio, he was fucked. Convertibles were easy. He went left.

His brake lights weren't even off before the homeys squealed out. The clerk watched, then picked up the phone, stood there, as if frozen, knowing it wouldn't matter, thinking about her goddamn eyes. He looked at the bitches, saw them watching too. "Is what it is," one of them said. They stared out into the gathering darkness and nodded when another agreed, "Night work."

Deep Ellum, 10:00 p.m.
There were four of them at the counter. Not one had ever been ugly. Not one ever would be. Six-inch heels, no stockings, perfect legs, skirts so tight you could see the rounds of their asses when they moved, not enough fabric in all four to cover a pillow. No blouses, just swatches of shiny, cheap cloth, stretched over stand-up tits. No bras required. Yards of skin. Coffee, vanilla, chocolate, tattooed in telling places. Ankles, thighs, bitch stamps between sacral dimples, just above the ass crack. And hair, acres of hair, flowing and clean and fresh, scented with flowers, fruit, almonds. Nearly as much hair as makeup, artfully done. They were eighteen, maybe nineteen. An assortment, a mixture, a blend. Perfect. They wanted snacks, smokes, the cheap ones, not premium. They flirted mercilessly with the buzz-cut behind the counter. He was swimming in it, and in sweat. It bubbled across his upper lip, his forehead, in heavy beads. He couldn't peel his eyes from those bobbing tits, flat, beaded bellies, pelvic grooves diving down into the tiny faux-leather kilts. Suggestive, not concealing. Movement constant, whirling and spiraling in front of him like phantasms. Tempting, luscious, out of reach, unreal. They were studded out: eyebrows, lips, tongues, navels, likely nipples and clits too. Paste diamonds, rubies, emeralds, plastic gold, stainless silver. Cool. Trendy. Out there. Manicures so sharp they'd cut glass, fingers twisting silky tresses, twirling in the air as they talked, cooed, and spun in front of him. A gust of sweetness he could almost taste, perfume radiating like shimmering tendrils.

Willing. Eager. Laughter like breaking crystal, high heels bounc-
ing on cold, dirty linoleum, lacquered nails tapping scratched
Formica. Three hard hats on a break from overtime, stale with
sweat, weary to the bone, lingered at the coffee machine, watching, gaping. They were dark, greasy, bristled, boasting more dirt
than pride. Heavy boots, stained jeans, second-hand shirts, filthy
bandannas. One opened his third packet of sugar. Another stood
with a forgotten cup steaming in his hand. The third just stared,
a hot dog crushed in his stubby fingers, oozing mustard, mouth
slightly open, salivating. Like cats watching a rookery, their eyes
captured the undulating movements and held them. When the
buzz-cut finally found his voice, they pulled IDs from tiny purses,
giggling, spiraling on their spikes, stretching their legs, straining
their stomachs, flexing their hips. "How do they move in skirts
that tight?" the hard hat with the hot dog asked. There was no
answer. They moved. The buzz-cut studied the IDs, fanned them
out in his fingers like cards in a rummy game. Eyes nearly crossed
in concentration as he tried to memorize a name, an address,
any detail while he pretended to verify, match a photo with a
face, but he couldn't focus, not with them so close, their scents
wafting, their eyes playing, their voices chirping and tittering,
glossed lips smirking when he returned IDs, and they danced
with each other, raked cards through the machine, punched buttons, waited without standing still even for a second while he
bagged their goods. At last, he pushed the plastic sacks forward,
his hand lingering, hoping for a touch, but they were too quick,
too experienced to let that happen, to let anything happen that
wasn't deliberate. They swept out as a wave into the night, then
jammed, legs folding, heels flying, laughter echoing, into a small
rusty Honda. Somebody's idea of a car. Dented fender, one headlight against the jet. When the engine buzzed alive, smoke bil-
lowed from exhaled tobacco, music burst from the open windows,
smothered their mirth, fueled their excitement. The hard hats

moved slow to the counter, paid up, stared while they pulled away, then went out and stood on the sidewalk for a space, sipping coffee, eating hot dogs, watching the Honda as it pulled away into the garish lights of the boulevard and turned toward the flashing neon and dark alleys, toward the clubs and bars. The buzz-cut also came out, sweat drying beneath his shirt, lit a smoke. He shook his head and, catching the eye of the hard hats, blew blue out of his nose and said, "Night work."

Harry Hines, Midnight

The pickup was old, older than the owners, rusty, had a caved-in right side, cracked windshield, mismatched tires, missing tailgate, ruined spare in the bed. The driver was large, bearded, hunched over the wheel, his eyes shadowed by a filthy, sweaty, shapeless cap. His arm on the window, thick, antiquely tattooed beneath coiling black hair. In the middle, a car seat with a sleeping baby. Another kid, maybe two, maybe three, crammed in next to it, only a tow crown visible in the indirect slant of the store window's yellow light. She sat enfilade, pressed against the passenger side. When she got out, slammed the door, he yelled something, low and mean. She shot him a scowl, came to the door. Short, light, she leaned heavy, levered with her hips and knees to push open the heavy glass. Inside, she stopped, recovered breath, found resolve, maybe strength, then strode toward the coolers. Deliberate. On a mission. She wore a uniform, yellow knee-length skirt, once-white sneakers run down at the heel. Waitress, maybe. All-night café, maybe. Swing-shift, for sure. Underarms stained, collar soiled, one missing button in front, tight in the bust and waist, but modest. It didn't hide a flat stomach, taut ass, firm legs. Built right. Not sexy. Sturdy. Solid. Cute. Best word for it. Precious might work, but that seemed wrong. Wholesome, maybe. Compact. Nearly perfect, for sure. And strong, though she'd put in a full shift, dealt fried grease and tepid coffee to overweight slobs, losers, and drifters who glanced from the TV only long enough to watch her walk away, then tried to see her naked. But just naked. Nothing more. An assessment, not lust. Nothing dirty. Nothing nasty. She conjured different dreams, past visions. A girlfriend, maybe, girl next door, down the block, up the hall, across the classroom, on the sidelines in a short skirt and bobby socks, church choir, maybe, picture in a yearbook, maybe, somebody's sister, somebody's cousin, somebody's best friend, maybe. Out of reach. They saw her in memory, the girl they met the last day of summer vacation, spotted getting off a bus, sitting at a stoplight, humming with the radio, waiting for the light to change, standing in the other line, looking the other way, looking like a girl somebody, anybody, might want to talk to. Nothing dirty. Nothing nasty. Just a dream. A girl to get to know, to send flowers to, to walk with in the rain, to marry. Maybe. A girl. Not a woman. A girl in the best sense of that word. Strawberry-blonde, feathery cut shag to her shoulders, green eyes that glinted, button nose, and a smile that would light the dark side of the moon. Her makeup was stale, but she didn't need it. Fresh. That's a word. She'd not lost that. Not yet. Two kids, hooked to a brute, lousy job, cheap rental, no money, no future, not much past, but she still had it. Knew how to flirt, but she knew the limit, the line between courtesy and come-on. Smart. She moved like she was gliding, skiing, lithe, easy on her feet, but now, here, tonight, also weary, weighted, resigned. She lugged a twelve-pack of Keystone and a liter of Sprite to the counter, heaved it aboard, glanced sideways at the pickup still idling off the curb, thought for a moment, then snagged some Skittles from the display and put them on top. She dug in the skirt pocket for a fold of bills, counted them out, added some change. Fingers, short but nicely shaped, delicate, ready to handle fragile things, smooth down a napkin on a metal counter, expertly pour a refill, clear a stack of plates, snatch up a sorry-ass quarter tip, wipe a kid's snotty nose. Nails blunt, painted with licorice, chipped at the tips, light-brown hair on her forearms, small beauty mark on one wrist, deep scratch on the other, just above the band of a cheap plastic watch. She asked for a tin of dip, then a pack of smokes, and, when she got it, zipped it open like a pro, put one on her lip before she remembered, then snatched it away and grimaced, grim, abashed, but not really apologizing, not looking up. The clerk, shorter, darker, forever internal and forbidding, counted the money, said she was light twelve cents, and she looked down, counted again, moving the bills and change around as if they would multiply with her touch. She glanced outside again, looked up, a plea in her sea-green eyes. Brows up, an antique scar between them. She knew the answer before the clerk, impersonal, insensitive, uncaring, shook his head. Her face went hard for a second or two, lines creviced around her eyes, her mouth, revealed her age, showed every month, every year since she pronounced herself grown. More bad than good. They webbed the veneer. Nothing soft remained beneath the alluvial surface. Iron under fascia. No rust. Not yet. But it was coming. Leather under satin, worn smooth with use, still strong, still serviceable, still salvageable. For a while. She smiled now, not just a grin, and displayed a chipped front tooth, slightly yellowed from smoke, from coffee, from life. Made her seem older, witness to too much for her age, for her time. As if she knew that, she sagged a little, defeated, not beaten, looked again out the window toward the pickup. Quick. Dreadful. Set her jaw. She put down the smokes, the loose one carefully on top, next to the twelve-pack, the soda, the candy, the snuff. "Be back," she said, shoulders squaring, her voice sweet, a chirp, but deliberate, like a mockingbird's. Then she stepped to the door—one movement, tugging it open and sliding out like a gust to the driver's side. The hulk in the cab's shadow sat still for a moment, listening, staring straight ahead, one arm draped over the wheel, fingers drumming. She shifted her weight, lifted one foot to give it a rest, dropped it toe down, knee bent, calf rocking, while she waited, like a carhop from an ancient time taking an order, flirting with a punk. One hand behind her back made a fist. She tossed her head like a colt. He said something, she barked back, her give as good as her take. He leaned, found a crushed wallet, then his hand extended, a bill in fat, dirty fingers, and she took it, spun neatly on one leg, and returned. Jaunting, almost saucy. At the counter, her face resumed its mask. Resignation, resentment, retribution. A jade glare at a stone clerk, who came to life, all at once. Broke his face with a plastic smile when she gathered her change, the beer and bag. She didn't look, didn't speak. She fished the lighter from her pocket, lit the smoke, inhaled deep, and blew a warm blue cloud over the clerk's false grin. "Fuck you," she said. Her tone now a knell, tolling deeper, resonant, acidic, edged by unformed tears. She hauled to the door, yanked it open, welled strength, stored and summoned, bounced it against her back, held the bundle of beer and bag against her chest, squinted against the smoke trailing from the butt in her lip. Spoke around it, "I mean it. Fuck you." She released the door, then twirled, burden balanced, trudged to the pickup door, got inside, slammed it. He pulled out with a squeal. The clerk watched them go, rubbed his eyes, pinched his nose, put his hands flat on the counter. "Night work," he said.

Oak Lawn, 1:45 a.m.

Behind him, Outside Security felt the pulse, the laughter, the low ebb of privilege, money, power filtering through the thick wooden barrier. A mass of masculinity. Handsome, in a way. Intimidating, in a way. Large, dense, well-defined. Polite, firm, impassive, circumspect, obsequious, blind, deaf, dutiful, obedient. Automatic. Ex-soldier, maybe. Ex-cop, maybe. Ex-pro player, maybe. Ex-boxer, maybe. Ex-con, maybe. Ex–all of it, maybe. Nameless. Beefy.

Forty-something. Strong. That was the word. Unmovable object. A block. Still athletic. No other ability, no potential. What he had was enough. Bald head, close shave, broken nose, mashed ears, solid chin, muscled neck. A body defined, chiseled, sculpted by iron and steel, sweat, steak, salad. No carbs. No booze. No tobacco. No drugs. Fit. Another good word. Off-the-rack suit, thick-soled shoes, white shirt, tasteful tie, Windsor knot. Coiled, even at rest. Ready. Gray eyes wide. Alert. Sentry. Guard. Picket. Invisible, but present. No one in. Not unless he said so. List memorized. Kept in his head. Authority, under his arm, in his pocket. Locked and loaded. Fully permitted. Nothing chanced. He scanned the restaurant. Dark, empty, quiet. That kitchen closed at ten. Tables cleared, white cloths replaced, folded linen and silver setups arranged. Regular staff gone. Waiting for tonight. Overpriced food served with style. Panache. Class. Good tips. The outer bar closed at midnight. Now deserted, scrubbed and polished oak and brass stretched down the wall, backlit. High glass shelves with top tequilas, vodkas, gins, whiskeys that ran a Franklin a shot. Brandies, cordials, liqueurs with names he couldn't say. Wines, vintage. Beer, imported, microbrewed. Varied clear pastels and earth tones of alcohol, awaiting orders. All quiet out front. Behind him, the door, oak-paneled, steel-lined. Three inches thick, but the deep bass vibe passed like light through tissue. Back room. Separate kitchen. Separate bar. Different staff. VIP. Twenty-dollar cigars. Dancers, players, gamblers, politicians, a police chief. Bankers, judges, doctors. Gangsters. Visiting CEOs. Mistresses. Whores. Men on their way up, women on their way down. Crowded, loud, smoky, secret, illegal. Wealthy people. Private party. Nothing to him. A paycheck. Never ask. Never say. Keep the List. Never ask. The door opened too quick. He pivoted as if on a spindle, arms out, hands ready. The din, the reek of tobacco, stench of alcohol, expensive perfume, sweet cologne blended into the waft. The flotsam of excess buffeted his

face. Jaw set, fingers flexed. Mental check of weapon, a quick impassive mask. She came out. Hair dark as thunder, wild and
straggled, froused over alabaster shoulders. Exposed, naked.
Black dress, too short, too tight, too young. Satin wanting to be
silk ripped open down one side. Bloodred fingernails held the
ragged edges partly together; one breast, bold but helpless, escaped, a pink nipple testing the ambience. Eyes blind with panic,
she slammed against him, bounced back. A wall. Pure sinew. A
rock. Unyielding, impervious. Unforgiving. She tottered on heels
too high, the dress rode up her rounded ass. Thighs like clouds.
Over her tangled nest of hair, he looked past the door, assessed
lights flashing wild, heavy music, hard, driving, blasting. Roar of
shouted conversation. A nude dancer pranced, crotch shaved,
revealed, unashamed. Well-dressed men and women watched,
laughed. Drank. Ate. Jewelry flashed. In the alcove beyond,
golden light over oak-trimmed tables, green velvet, vested dealers, chips stacked, cards sliding, dice flying. Waitresses in bust-
iers, black-mesh stockings, high heels, long hair, large breasts,
tall legs threaded through controlled chaos, balanced silver trays
in constant noise. He caught the eye of Inside Security. A nod. A
caution. Not serious. Not yet. He shut the door, stepped back.
She listed, swayed, looked up. Panic. Wild eyes welled. Violet
pupils, high, perfect brows. Mascara ran black muddy rivers
down soft pale cheeks, one blistered with bright prints. Whole
fingers. Pain. Perfect teeth, whiter than a wedding, gritted. A
long neck, chafed, red marks traced against the cream. Lips
messy with smeared gloss, cut, bleeding. A fresh scarlet trail on a
clipped chin. Her arms reached, long fingers loosing torn fabric,
forgetting, letting it fall. Grasped his muscles, dug sharp red nails
into cheap black fabric. Pleading. Desperate. Naked to the waist.
More new bruises. "Please!" Breath laced with booze, dope, sex.
Her eyes cut to the door, looked through it, beyond it. "Please!"
A lisp, lip bleeding. "Hurry!" Her head fell forward, pounded a

crown into his chest. A shield. Then up, into his face. "Please!" once more. He held her away, out from himself, off her feet, hands under her bare arms, her breasts, large, soft, swayed flaccid against her body. He felt the pulse of terror, smelled fear all over her. Soiled, exposed, helpless. Dangerous. New noise now. Shouts over the vibe. Anger. He looked once more into the tortured face. Considered. He felt the velvet of her skin beneath his fingers, the fragility of her bones. He decided, returned her to the floor like a delicate crystal curio, then slanted his gray eyes to the bar. She looked at him once. Quick. Verifying. Then scrambled, the shards of fake silk bunched, held closed, and passed through the publican's gate, dropped to the rubber-padded floor behind the long, heavy counter. He could hear her breathing when the door opened again. A man emerged. Not so fit. Not so tall. Not so strong. A player, maybe, run to fat and ruined by prosperity. Midthirties, maybe, but wrathful. Face dark with fury, marked by three long scratches, ear to chin, deep, crimson dollops on a white custom collar. Fists clenched. Platinum wedding band. Diamond horseshoe. Movado watch. Italian shoes. He jutted, nearly tripping, into the dim of the vacant restaurant, looked around. "Where?" No eye contact. Indirect confrontation. An insult. An order. A challenge. An accusation. Arrogance. Privilege. Condescension. Then, a collecting pause, an assessment. Calm. Control. Careful. Softer, now. "Where, goddamnit?" Outside Security's eyes slanted toward the side door. Exit only. An escape. No access, not even for cops, except those on the List. "Shit! Fucking shit." He rushed across, then out, holding it open with one hand, looked. Right, left, right again. He peered into the night, breath vaporizing slightly in the humid air. Another scout, a survey, a reconnoiter, final check. Thorough. Met by disappointment, frustration, then a shout into the shadows, voice cracking soprano. "Bitch! Fucking bitch!" A sag, a shrug, a return. Handkerchief out, pressed against his face, soaking it red.

Still no contact. "Got a smoke?" in enhanced baritone. A cigarette appeared in thick, hammer-hard fingers. A lighter followed,
and the first gray breath flooded out, struck unblinking eyes.
"Need an ambulance?" Now he looked. Up. Judging tone. Judging size. "She say anything?" A short moment, then a shake of
the head. Dark eyes studied gray, then narrowed. "You see anything?" A longer moment, a deeper beat, a bubble down deep
started to form, to rise, to burst on a solid surface. A desire to
assert. Indignation. Pride. Self-esteem. But then, priorities. A
shake of the head. One more look. Verification. Then a nod, and
the man stepped forward. Outside Security held the door as he
went through, holding his face, laughing now. Falsely vindicated.
He faded into the chaos, naked youth dancing on tables, wrinkled age lounging on leather, watching without looking, talking
in shouts, laughing in yells. Lasers flashed on expensive gems,
solid gold, Spanish silver. Music boomed, swirled through the
smoke. He shut the door, muting hell. A moment. Then two.
She emerged like a fawn from a grove. Crept forward, hand
grasping the rag across her body, face swollen, blood dried, hair a
twisted mat, eyes masked by ruined pencil and paint. Thirty, he
thought. Not younger. She sagged, knees buckled. He stepped to
her. Four paces. Caught her, steadied her, held her with one
hand. "My bag." A gasp, a sob. "My bag. Keys. Money." Her eyes
looked at the door in horror. He shook his head, definite, probed
his pocket, found a bill, pressed it into her palm. "Wait on the
corner. Behind the bus stop. Green cab. Ten minutes." She
looked at him again, hard and deep, to be sure. Her smashed
mouth mouthed silent thanks, then choked, "I'll pay—" He
shook her arm, pressed his face down into hers. "Don't come
back." She looked, nodded. Stumbled away, out the side door.
He followed, made sure, returned. His post. Pulled a cell from his
breast pocket. Punched a number, listened, then said, "Yeah.
Again. Night work."

Northwest Highway, 3:00 a.m.

He pulled up in a nondescript ten-year-old Chevy Impala—gray, no frills, no distinctions, no front plates—killed the lights, got out, stood for a moment in the amber glow of the arc lights, inspected the parking lot as if it was real estate he might buy. His gaze lingered on the dark edges, shadows bunched like lurking gangs of ghouls. One more sweep. Careful. He came in. Empty shop, golden light, a lone clerk. Tall, lanky, Ethiopian. Slim mustache and a small beard on the edge of a pointed chin, dozing on his feet, behind black laminate. A textbook open on the rear counter. The bell's jingle animated him. Reminded him. Instructions, policies. The man, older, bowed shoulders, thin face, sharp, hollow, lined, marked by clear eyes, light brown, never still. Not tall, not short. Nondescript. Average. That was the word. A dark blue suit with worn lapels, shiny creases, threadbare, clean. White oxford button-down, black tie, worn loose. Rumpled. Driving awhile. All day, maybe. More, maybe. Heavy shoes—wing tips with composite soles. Shined, high gloss. Nothing else looked kempt, neat, new. He was balding. Thin strands, well oiled, raced away from a forehead furrowed, and bushy eyebrows. Short, sharp sideburns, pointed ears flat against a peaked crown. A narrow mouth, sharp amber teeth. Thin lips. Grim. Like a knife scar, like a scratch on a new car. He waited, adjusted from the darkness outside, took in the clerk, nodded a greeting. Silent, unsmiling, ignored. The clerk waited, shifted. Unaccountably uncomfortable. Adjusted items in his reach. A pad, a pen, a small display of packaged fruit, dry cookies. Looked busy, not nervous, but he was nervous. The man inspected the shop. Constricted aisles, small, bright orange plastic booths, shelves of coffee appliances, clever crockery, upscale implements. A ravaged bakery display. Stale pastries, gummy sandwiches left from the day trade. He rolled his shoulders, his neck. Stretched without extending, flexed his fingers, one of which twisted in an awkward tangent, and again met the clerk's eyes. "Regular coffee?" Starting as if pinched, the clerk nodded to the coffee island in back. Thermos pots and bold carafes. Hot and ready. Checked every half hour. Instructions, regulations, policy. "Self-serve after midnight." The man stared, ugly mouth grim, eyes unblinking, then nodded, walked there directly, not fast, but steady. Like a cat, one foot in front of the other, confident, cautious. Eyes roaming. At the island, he studied the vessels, selected a paper cup and poured, added cream, sugar, stirred, then turned, faced the door, blew on the surface, eyes worked the shop over the rim. Sipped, tested the heat. The clerk watched, looked indirectly, furtively glanced, shifted, wanted to move, for some odd reason, to whistle. His head felt light, neck prickled, brow burned. Fear sprouted in his abdomen. His hands roamed, straightened candy, energy bars, gum, napkins, impulse items near the register. Something to do. He coughed a little, although he didn't have to, swallowed dryly, glanced again at the man, put his hand on the cell phone next to the register, pretended to adjust it, check it. Surreptitiously, he hoped, he punched in three numbers. Didn't call. Ready. The man noticed but didn't show it. He leaned against the island, crossed one foot over the other, drank deeper, looked around, eyes always moving. Watchful. Lights and appliances buzzed white noise, a barely audible hum, like the sound of pulse in the ear. The clerk turned oblique, watched the convex mirror overhead, fidgeted, wanted to walk away, maybe to run. He touched the textbook, then pushed a button on a wall-mounted console. A hiss, then music, low and jazzy. He offered a half-smile. Not returned. He resumed his blank stare, tried to see without watching, tried to hear without listening, willed himself not to shake. The man finished, refilled, added more cream, capped it, brought it forward. Same careful stride, slow and measured. Hands large but thin, thickly veined, hairy knuckles. Right at his side, loose, ready. Left held the cup lightly. He stepped close, set it down. "What's the book?" The clerk, alarmed, confused, recovered, relieved. "Uh, economics . . . finance. Studying . . . college." He baked with an invisible blush. The man nodded, dismissive. He touched the cup with the twisted finger, put his left hand in a pocket. The clerk named an amount. The man's eyes narrowed. The clerk tried to swallow, couldn't. The man looked at the cup, rediscovered it. "That's a lot." The clerk nodded, tried again to swallow, cleared his throat. A rasp. "Cup and a refill." Then, "Refills are half price." The man's eyes rose, quick and menacing. "You're serious?" The clerk nodded, pointed to a small hand-lettered sign, one of six posted around the shop, verifying instructions, regulations, policy. The man read the words slowly, his lips moving, as if they were in a language he didn't know. "Economics." The thin mouth's corners turned up. "Finance." He shook his head, but his eyes remained fixed on the clerk's. "Fucking bean-counters." In reply, a blank nod. Underarms awash, brow dripping, sweat rolling down his back, his sides. Primordial fear. Inexplicable. Instinctive. The man extracted coins from a pocket, studied them, replaced them, opened his coat. The wooden butt of a heavy revolver appeared beneath his left arm, tucked deep. The clerk's head snapped back, heart plummeted to his belly, crushed balls tingled, tried to withdraw into his body, legs dissolved. He wanted to slump. He sought balance, stepped away, hips blocked by the counter behind him. Throat closed, mouth arid as the desert that spawned him. A desperate need to piss. The man removed a battered brown wallet, pulled five crisp singles, cascaded them on the shiny laminate, adjusted them with the twisted finger. The clerk couldn't see them, only the pistol. The man looked right and left, up at the mirror, replaced the wallet, buttoned the coat, checked his watch, although there was a clock on the wall, just over the clerk's head. A reach into the side pocket produced a small, wrinkled piece of paper. He smoothed it out.

The clerk looked down. "You know where that's at?" A beat. A look. "Exactly?" A long stare, half a minute, maybe, and then the clerk made sense of the penciled symbols. At last, he wet his mouth, swallowed hard. "Two blocks down. To the right. Third building." His voice sounded small and far away. One hard nod. Affirmation. He replaced the paper, picked up the cup. "Keep the change." The clerk forced a smile, a nod. "Night work," the man said. "It blows." The clerk grinned wider. "Yes. Sir." Then the happy jangle of the bell, and the clerk breathed. The first of his life. He watched the man stop, survey the lot, get into the Chevy, start it up, pull out. Nevada plate. Brake lights flashed. A right turn. Even a signal. The clerk stared down at the money, the phone, scooped up the bills, punched them into the register, wiped the counter, mopped his face. Same towel. He looked at the empty shop, swallowed, breathed deeply again, heard the jazz, swayed slightly in the golden light, felt the cooling of hot sweat. "Night work," he muttered.

Inwood, 6:30 a.m.

If the cop, lazing against the photo counter, nursing sore feet, a bad back, feeling the weight of twenty-some-odd pounds of equipment and arms, worn all night, could have seen the horizon past the buildings and trees across from the front of the drugstore, he would have watched a growing silver glow warning the night of imminent mortality. Instead, he watched the fat man and the girl. The fat man trudged through the automatic doors. A high-pressure system. Invasive, huge, dominant, calm, confident as daybreak. He placed himself solid amid the wash of anonymous music misting from invisible speakers that seemed to mute in his presence. His head, an oblong ball mounted on a thick pedestal of neck based on a dense beam of muscle. Massive torso, draped by an ugly, stained, faded, flowered shirt worn half-buttoned. A hairless chest swallowed by a bulging gut. Shirt-tail out to cover a tortured waistband of cargo shorts worn low. Pockets bulged. He stood broadly. Boxy feet planted, like trotters flatly spread, crusty, yellow, jagged nails projecting over toes of flattened rubber shower-shoes. Dense hands, square fingers chewed ragged, raw, fresh-scarred knuckles akimbo at his sides, arms ink-sleeved with incomprehensible blue, green, and red designs—faces, whorls, symbols, and illegible words, chaotic collage. Hair, dyed ghastly yellow, stretched into a greasy miniature ponytail. Thin line of sideburns and curved, thick Fu Manchu affected a gangster style. Twenty years younger, a hundred pounds lighter, a dimension cooler. Tiny pale-blue eyes framed a vulture's beak, held court for a jowled face heavy with thick lips, perpetually pouting. He rested on spurred heels, recumbent inside his mass, poised in personal power, and took inventory of early shoppers browsing bright aisles, full shelves arrayed with the familiar at cut rates. And behind him, the girl waited, as if in queue for something she didn't want. Crouched in the shadow of his bulk, seeking invisibility in plain sight. Mindless patience, still as wounded prey, breathing lightly, hiding in full view. Small, black, timid, displaced. Wispy strands spraying out from poorly braided cornrows. She wore a man's white tee over cutoffs, floppy casings for rope-skinny thighs, balls of knees, shapeless calves falling like spikes onto bony ankles elling into too long, too narrow feet with peeling polished toes in worn leather sandals. Unshielded nipples dented white cotton, tiny juts betraying her age—too young, too old, already dying. Her eyes, black as ebony, unfocused, flickered dimly, looked dully at nothing. One orb slanted into an ugly bruise, the other dark pupil was matted by a bright, broken vessel, tinting the edge scarlet. Her right hand cradled her left in long, thin fingers chipped by red paint, the forearm crooked into her body under the tented points, held gingerly, like a baby. Her mouth, slightly parted, too wide, too crooked, lips swollen, nose misshapen in some exquisite way. Ugly. No other word for it. Except pitiful, maybe. She frowned when he shifted, reclaimed his shade, her acne-pocked cheeks wrinkling in a wince. He waited another moment. Checked the clerk in her company-blue vest, ignorantly busy, ringing up a sale, and then the cop, still leaning on the photo counter, watching him. Casual, calm, curious. With a nod, he snatched a plastic hand-basket and marched, heavy paced, lumbering to a rear aisle, the flattened rubber flipping and flopping against the callouses of his soles. She followed two steps behind, as if on a lead, her stalky legs stutter-stepped, nearly limped, as if hobbled. The cop unlimbered, rolled his head and cracked his neck, hefted his utilities, adjusted the black pistol at his waist, strolled forward, stopped briefly in the pretense of adjusting some novelties on display, but kept in view the man and girl, who, now returning, stopped at the cooler, opened a door, then came forward, him slapping, her shambling, nearly stumbling. At the counter, the girl, a pint of chocolate milk, package of cheap sugared pastries in her good hand, waited as he dumped the basket. A jumble. Gauze, peroxide, latex gloves, medicinal tape, iodine, painkillers, antiseptic, bandages, a sling. His head bobbed, she surrendered her loot, reluctant, timid, scowling when her bad arm moved. The clerk, bored, tired, glanced at the clock on the wall, scanned, bagged. "Morning," the cop said, stood off a yard or so, moved his hands to his belt, hooked his thumbs, rocked back on neoprene heels in the classic posture of surety policemen long ago adopted, perfected. A twirling nightstick was wanted. The fat man nodded, stared at the clerk, mouth closed. "Trouble?" The question hung between them like smoke suddenly exhaled in a small airless space, swirling without direction. The fat man's neck reddened. "Accident." Fat hands cupped, bunched the final items for the clerk, who finished, named a price. He dug a wad from a side pocket of the shorts, ignored the cop's startle, and counted out bills. Soiled, wrinkled. Head down, eyes focused, lips slightly moving with uttered numbers. The ponytail bobbed against the sickly orange orchids on his shirt collar. He turned, money in hand, faced the cop. Eyes pale. Direct. Cold as skim ice. "No big deal." The cop's chocolate eyes flared for a heartbeat. Gaze steady. "Report it?" The fat man's mouth parted. "Just a fender-bender." He took a wheezing breath. "No fault, no problem. Nobody hurt that bad." A confirming nod to the girl, his eyes still matched with the cop's. "Right?" She looked up, found the cop's face, drew away his stare. An instant cry, maybe. A flash, a signal. Maybe. One quick nod, her face found the floor. Her good hand reached for the sack with the milk, the pastry. "Nobody hurt that bad," he repeated. "Nothing can't be handled." For a moment, two, maybe, they stood en tableau, without breathing. Tension taut, atmosphere electric. Overhead, the music shifted to a waltz. The clerk, change made, now suddenly aware, now frozen, eyes on the cop. The girl pulled her arm tighter to her body. Bag dangling. One foot covered the other, one knob of knee folded over the other. Protective. The cop gave first. "She with you?" The fat man appraised her like a stranger. "Right." He swung his gaze to the cop. "Got ID?" The fat man gathered his bags. Casual. He stepped forward, closed the distance. The cop held ground. "No need. Stepdaughter." The cop glared. "Right?" the fat man asked the air. She raised her face. A plea, useless without words. Her head moved, barely. The cop studied, unwound, nodded, turned to the kiosk behind him, pretended to adjust a row of perfumes, soaps, bath salts. "Have a nice day." The fat man nodded, the ponytail bobbed. He tacked out the door, a ship unmoored, bags for ballast. The girl trailed like a dinghy on a line. Helpless but to follow. The cop watched them go, saw the yellowing sky, looked at the clerk. Her face a hundred questions. He hiked up his utilities, leaned on the counter, looked her in the eye. "Night work," he said.

FULL MOON

BY LAUREN DAVIS

Pleasant Grove

A cool rain was falling when Danny Contreras awoke to the nightmare and shouted, "Cuidado!" The face of his mother floating, a specter behind his throbbing eyeballs. Way too much crystal meth and tequila last night. Christ knows what else, but he craved hair of the dog. A shot and a rail. The sting in his septum. The burn of the añejo coating his guts. The thought eased the pain and he sat up and gazed around the room as if taking inventory—admiring the open floor plan, the midcentury modern furniture. Raising his arm, he squinted and tried to focus, but his wrist was bare. Oh yeah—the Rolex. He'd let the dope dealer hold it.

He reached for the phone on the night table. Five till nine. He called work and had the secretary he shared with the other midlevel investment brokers cancel his appointments. "Yeah, I know it's the third time this week."

No way was he fighting Central Expressway from Uptown to North Dallas this hungover in the rain. Fuck it—it was Friday. He had the weekend to get the devil out of his system. He could try normal again on Monday.

Normal. He thought about his mother, crying in the nightmare. "Cuidado, mi'jo!" she'd warned, but what was he supposed to be careful of? When she'd died two months ago, that's when he'd started to fuck up, feeling like his life was coming off the rails. He was in Thailand—running down profit margins on a sapphire mine. It was fucking paradise over there. He'd decided to stay on a few days. Get some R&R on the company. He'd stashed his phone in the hotel safe with his other valuables, and explored Bangkok, off the charts. He'd spent four days in an opium den. Shadows came and went in the red glow of the semidarkened room. Someone would lift the cold metal tip of the pipe to his mouth, and he'd suck until his lips were blistered. Oblivion. By the time he came out of his stupor, his mother had already been buried. "We couldn't hold up the funeral," his father had said when Danny called, after he'd listened to the frantic messages. "You knew how sick she was. Where were you, son?"

Danny brought the gold crucifix that hung from his neck on a heavy chain to his lips. Eighteen karat. He could pawn it for an eight ball, he thought, kissing the crucified Christ. Maybe two.

The rain had stopped by the time he'd made coffee, so he went outside onto his postage stamp of a balcony. He drank the whole pot, black, and tried to make sense of the nightmare.

It had been about the Christmas when he'd been twelve. His mother and his aunts were cooking. Mamá took a smoke break and carried in a tray of hot chocolate for the kids. There was a loud knock. It was Uncle Santiago. When Mamá let him in, he looked real pale. Shaky too. He said he'd been driving through a stretch of mesquite scrub outside Austin when he heard a voice whispering his name. It was warm that year. Mideighties—like it can be in Texas at Christmas, so his windows were down. He said he thought it was the wind, so he sang back, "Si, yo soy San-ti-a-go." That's when the sun went behind a cloud and a giant owl with an eight-foot wingspan flew out of the mesquite thickets ahead.

"I started to say the Hail Mary backward, and when I did La Lechuza flew off."

"You better go see a curandero," Aunt Mary said, stepping into the living room from the kitchen. "Somebody's put a curse on you, and you need to break it."

"A curse? Pinche cabróna," he countered. Everybody laughed, and he went out on the deck where the men and the beer were. Mamá lit another cigarette and began to tell the old Mexican legends to the kids. About the ghost of La Llorona, the weeping woman who steals naughty children out after dark, and about the witch-bird called La Lechuza. The omen of death. But Danny was twelve, and he didn't believe in spooks anymore. When Uncle Santiago was found dead the week after New Year's, Danny's father said he'd drunk himself to death, but the women at funeral had whispered a different tale.

Fucking crystal and tequila. Keep it together. He made a peanut butter sandwich, checked his unopened mail, and found a threatening letter from his landlord, so he decided to play the "money game." He paid one credit card with another, getting his credit limit raised enough to put the rent payment and the late fees on another card, leaving a final card maxed out and unpaid. He was good at manipulating money. That's what he did. MBA on scholarship in five years, the golden boy who'd showed a profit for the firm his first year, in spite of the crash of '06. His rise had been quick, but his career had hit a ceiling. For the last three years, he'd been treading water. Just another $75,000-a-year millionaire, jockeying on the concrete treadmill, up and down I-75, five days a week to keep the image alive—the high-rise apartment in the West Village, the BMW, the hundred-dollar haircuts. He wasn't quite thirty, but he was tired of keeping the balls moving in the air, all sleight of hand, prestidigitation— legerdemain. The thought of it was exhausting, so he loaded a bowl of hydro, hit it, and decided to crash.

It was getting dark when he woke. No headache, so he sat up and checked the phone. Only one missed call. From his father. He'd called every day since Danny had got back to the States. He'd avoided him—hadn't even been to visit his mother's grave.

He rang Kevin, the dope dealer, and the call went straight

to voice mail. Danny thought about hanging up, but he was too desperate for games. "Yeah, so, it's about six thirty. Give me a buzz when you get this. I was hoping I could come by and hang out. You still got my Rolex—right?"

If Kevin wouldn't answer, Danny would hit the streets. Friday night in Big D. He might get lucky. It had been awhile, but not because he hadn't had chances. He pulled it together with his best GQ-meets–Wall Street look and thought his years as a gym rat were still paying off, as he did his last line of crystal meth and rolled a joint for the road. On the way out, he checked his reflection in the full-length mirror and wondered if his clothes weren't starting to hang. But the crystal kicked in. *Naw*, he thought. *You still got it, Danny-boy.*

When he got to Hotel Zaza, he had to wait in line to valet the Beamer. The Dragonfly bar reminded him of something from an old black-and-white movie. The place was a sea of tall wineglasses and short skirts. At the bar, he opened a tab with his company AmEx and had a couple of shots of Patrón. He scanned the room, casually. As if he wasn't really on the hunt. A honey of a brunette in a tight red dress took a seat when the stool next to him opened up. He liked her direct approach and wondered if she might be a pro. When he asked her, she laughed but didn't say no. Fucking Dallas.

They talked, mostly about him, so he bought her a couple of fifteen-dollar martinis. She was eager to listen, grateful for the booze, and seemed up for most anything as she rubbed the inside of his thigh. He didn't object, but it was too early. He was more interested in hearing what Kevin had to offer. Danny couldn't even remember her name, and when the phone vibrated in his pocket at ten thirty, the brunette might as well have been dead.

From Zaza, he headed downtown, fishing out the joint he'd tucked under the driver's seat. He enjoyed driving through downtown at night. Through the shimmering tinsel of the lit skyscrapers that loomed along the nearly deserted streets. Especially when he was fucked up. Lately, he'd found Dallas more approachable that way. From the Commerce Street viaduct he exited onto Beckley. The car's radio whined, searching for a signal. Fucking Oak Cliff. It was a different world on this side of the Trinity River.

Growing up, Oak Cliff had been his turf. And as he passed the illuminated monolith of Methodist Hospital, he tried not to imagine his mother's last moments there, gasping for breath, craving one last cigarette. At Beckley, he turned onto Jefferson, coasting past the pawn shops, Mexican restaurants, and the brightly lit windows of the quinceañera stores with their quaint names and outrageous dresses.

"Cuidado!" a voice shouted.

Danny stomped the brake pedal, stopping just short of hitting a mariachi dressed in crimson velvet, weaving and jaywalking away from El Ranchito Restaurante.

"Pinche borracho!" Danny yelled, lowering his window, flipping his middle finger for emphasis, but the old mariachi just laughed and stumbled on his way. Rattled, Danny pitched the roach out of the window and tried tuning the car's radio again, without success. At Rosemont Street he detoured, creeping past his old home with his headlights turned off. When he came home to visit, before his mother died, he always thought the house seemed smaller than he'd remembered it growing up. But tonight, the two-story prairie-style looked big and empty, and Danny knew his father was inside. Alone.

At West Davis he put the headlights on again. He was getting close to Kevin's place. Adrenaline surged at the anticipation of the novelties he would offer. Meth for sure. Maybe some Thai stick. Hash or opium? He wanted something special to make the journey worthwhile. He enjoyed hanging out with Kevin—even though the guy was old enough to be his grandfather, he could match Danny drink for drink, drug for drug, and never got sloppy. Danny admired Kevin's business model too. He didn't cater to the in-and-out doorbell trade. There was a minimum. He offered an experience—he had clients.

Kevin answered the door in a white caftan. "Come in, Danny," he said with a hand flourish. Danny imagined this was what a real '60s drug pad looked like. He'd never seen one, and he'd never seen another place like Kevin's. All the legs of the upholstered furniture in the living room had been sawed off, and the amputated sofa, love seat, overstuffed chairs, and otto-man sat on layers of Persian rugs that covered the floor. There were rugs and black-light posters hanging on the walls, incense burning, beaded curtains in every doorway, and a mounted sixty-inch plasma TV over the fake fireplace. Kevin broke out some hash and motioned for Danny to sit. They played backgammon, snorted lines of crystal, and when Danny got too trashed to offer Kevin a challenge on the backgammon board, he switched on the plasma and they played *Grand Theft Auto* till a little past two. Kevin pulled out his photo album, just like always. Danny flipped through the laminated pages of old Polaroids of Kevin's days at Berkeley, the antiwar protests, pictures of parties where every guy had his arm around a skinny girl and a joint in his other hand. He said he'd been a chemistry major—that he'd dropped acid with Timothy Leary.

Danny knew he couldn't rush this part of the transaction, or Kevin would feel slighted. Finally, after another ten minutes or so, they got down to it. Kevin would give Danny five grand in credit for the Rolex, with the option to redeem it for six. He took two eight balls of meth and a quarter pound of some weed called Afghani gold. The shit had purple hairs. Kevin prepared a five-hundred-dollar grab bag of Thai stick, hash, and a ball of opium the size of a walnut. Danny was into him for just over three grand in product.

Danny snorted another line of crystal and stashed the rest in the trunk, except a Thai stick he decided he'd hit as he sailed along Hampton Road on his drive home. The radio's hum was soothing now, like wind or waves. When he topped the hill between Fort Worth Avenue and Singleton, he felt electric as he peered out at Dallas sprawled before him, a carpet of glitter. He looked at the full moon hanging low on the horizon, its white light pulsing with every heartbeat that throbbed in his chest and head, while he coasted down the steep hill. His stomach rose, as if he was on the descent of a roller coaster. The traffic lights were with him when he sailed through the intersections, leveling out at Singleton. Ahead, he could see the incline of the bridge that would carry him back across the Trinity. Back to the luxury and safety of his West Village high-rise.

"It's three o'clock," an announcer's voice blared from the radio, startling Danny. He ashtrayed the Thai stick and focused on the radio. When he realized the car was veering, he tried to compensate, but too late. The front wheels had already climbed over the curb, and when he looked up he saw two men frozen in the beam of his headlights. They were standing under an oak tree in the little semicircle of a park in front of the Nash Davis Recreation Center. As the Beamer struck them with a dull thud, they became airborne—one somersaulting, the other spinning as if he'd been shot from a cannon. Danny applauded their acrobatics in his mind, watching them land on their heads and crumple clumsily on the ground in his rearview mirror. They reminded him of some circus show he'd seen in Vegas, but these two needed to work on their landing. When he turned the wheel to keep from clipping an approaching oak tree, he remembered. He wasn't in Vegas tonight.

He brought the car to a stop after he'd jolted over another curb at the rear of the driveway that separated the park from the rec center. He sat for a moment in the double circle cast by the sodium-vapor streetlights that flanked the rec center's entrance. The euphoria and oblivion he'd spent the last few hours working up was draining out of him, but the effects of the meth still gave everything an unearthly, electric glow. *Shit*, he thought. He'd just hit someone. Two someones. He straightened out the car, pulled forward in the driveway, and out of the twin spotlights of the streetlamps. He turned off the engine and his headlights. As far as he could tell, he was okay. He got out of the car. Not much damage. A couple of shallow dents, and it seemed that no one had seen the accident. Still, a feeling of paranoia settled on him while he looked around and listened for movement from the dark park. There was an SUV—a black Tahoe—parked on the side street abutting the rec center. One of theirs, he decided, running over to the tree on the edge of the park.

Oh fuck. They were both young. Midtwenties. He could see that one was already dead. The other was clutching his throat, gurgling, blood running from the side of his mouth in measured arterial ebbs and flows. "Don't worry. Fucking don't worry," Danny said. "I've got a cell phone in the car. I'm going to get you some help." He turned back toward the car, but stopped when he saw a briefcase on the ground behind the gurgling man. He picked it up, instinctively. Heavy, he thought, balancing the briefcase on the rear of the car, as he pushed the buttons that released the locks with a metallic clatter. A whistle escaped his lips. Must be thirty grand. Maybe more. He opened the car door and slid the briefcase onto the passenger seat and took his phone off the charger. He didn't call 911 though—not yet. He was still trying to figure it all out. Besides, what if the other guy was dead now too? If they were both dead, there was nothing Danny could do. Why should he fuck up his life, and anyway, what were they doing with a briefcase full of money, hiding in the trees at three in the morning in this shithole of a neighborhood? He walked back to the man by the tree.

"You okay?" Danny asked, trying to sound composed. A weak gurgle was the man's only reply. "Yeah, yeah, don't worry, help's on the way." Danny glanced around and walked over to the dead guy. There. He was clutching a brown paper bag. Danny bent over and tugged on the sack, but it wouldn't budge. He tried again, pulling harder, and when he let go, he fell forward. On top of the dead guy and the bag. He got to his knees and pried the dead man's fingers from the brown paper bag. "Yes," he said, looking at the collection of tiny baggies it contained. He retrieved one, brought it to his mouth, and ripped it open with his teeth. Powder spilled out onto his tongue. He licked it across his gums and waited. Crystal meth. Good quality too. A couple of drug dealers. *That's who I hit—who I killed*, he thought.

He hurried back to the car with his prize, taking another look at the guy choking on his own blood. "You hang in there, buddy," Danny said, striding past. He deposited the brown paper bag in the trunk with the rest of his stash. Then he put the phone back in the car. He made one more trip over to the hemorrhaging man. The blood had slowed to a trickle. Danny sat down. Reaching over, he cradled the man's bloody jaw in one hand and pushed it up until his teeth met. With his other hand, Danny reached over and pinched the man's nostrils shut. They stayed together in the still darkness that way, until he was sure this one was dead too. After he wiped his bloody hands on the grass, Danny stood and turned to walk away. An audible gasp startled him, and he turned to see the man's jaw dropping back open, as the last of the air in his lungs bubbled out through the congealing blood in his mouth.

He was getting panicky now. How long had he been here? He surveyed the area a final time and decided no one had seen a thing. As he opened the car door, he heard the sound of an engine turn over. His eyes shot to the SUV on the side street just in time to see its headlights flash on as it pulled away into the night. Someone had seen. One of the men must have had an accomplice, waiting in the black Tahoe.

Danny's car started right up. He drove down the curve of the driveway and turned out onto Hampton, toward the bridge. There was a car a few blocks ahead of him, and he could see the glow of the headlights of a couple of others behind him, stopped at the light at Singleton. No cops though. That was good. "You still got it, Danny-boy," he said aloud. As the pounding of his heart in his head began to slow, he started to feel a sense of elation. Started to feel like he'd gotten away with murder, as the euphoric effects of the meth and Thai stick washed back over him—coursed back through him.

At the summit of the bridge the radio crackled alive again, and when he looked out at the skyline with the full moon rising above it, he watched the shadowy silhouette of an enormous bird slowly traversing the pulsating orb. He felt a chill, and a new sensation he couldn't shake. That he was being followed. He rolled down the window and threw the last few inches of the Thai stick out into the night.

Danny was a little sore when he woke. He'd spent a rough night dreaming about the accident. Everything was jumbled up. The faces of the dead men, the shadow of the bird on the moon, the SUV. Someone had seen him. A drug dealer. But what was a drug dealer going to do—go to the police and say he saw somebody kill his accomplices? Not likely. *Calm down*, he told himself. He'd let all this shit get mixed up with the nightmare about his mother and La Lechuza. Rationally, he knew no one had followed him. Otherwise, someone would have shown up to claim the money and the dope. He remembered what his father had told him the first time he'd taken Danny to the cemetery to put flowers on the family graves for All Saint's Day.

"Don't worry about the dead. It's only the living that can hurt you, son."

That's right. He got up. Tried to banish the visions of the previous night when they ran through his mind. Think about the money—a shopping spree at NorthPark. He'd get his Rolex out of hock from Kevin. But nothing worked. He kept coming back to the dream. The nightmare where his mother tried to warn him from the other side. Did he really believe in another side? He believed in what he could snort, smoke, and fuck. But that goddamned bird. That wasn't normal. He'd never seen anything like that. And there was the feeling. The feeling he was being watched.

Danny took the money from the briefcase and stashed it around the apartment. Then he dressed and went to the car wash. He was amazed there was so little damage. Hardly any blood. A tidy job, he thought, as he drove home with a newspaper, after eating a late lunch.

He flipped through the newspaper when he got home. Nothing unusual. It felt like a weight had been removed from him, and he thought how foolish it was to be so paranoid. To believe he was being followed. He laid out a few lines of crystal on the mirrored coffee table and snorted them. He grew luminous again. As he relaxed, he heard the neighbor's dog barking. Old Mrs. Somerset had the balcony two floors below. She'd put the dog out there and go away for hours sometimes, and the little fucker, a Yorkie named Mitzi, would bark nonstop. He wished the dog was on the balcony right below his. He'd drop a poisoned pork chop down to that miserable thing so he could have some peace and quiet. He walked over to the heavy industrial black-out drapes he'd had custom made for the sliding glass door and flung them open. He shook his head, blinked his eyes shut and opened them again. It was still there. Perched on the aluminum curve of the balcony railing. An owl, the size of a small woman.

They stared at each other through the glass, Danny and the owl. As if they were in a contest. A pissing match to see which one could stare the longest without blinking. When his eyes got dry, he whipped the blackout panels together, took a deep breath, and pulled them apart again. The owl was gone.

The closest thing he could find on the Internet was a great horned owl. He printed pictures of owls, tacking them to the walls with pushpins—barn owls, snow owls, burrowing owls. There was some confusion as to whether the eagle owl or the great gray owl was the largest species. The maximum attainable sizes mentioned by the various websites were all wrong too. These owls were runts compared to the one he'd seen. But it was the face of the bird on the balcony that was so different. The ones pictured on the Internet lacked humanity. They were just birds. Yes, it was the face. There was something soft and malleable about its beak. And its sagging, feathered breasts. Do birds have breasts? See, these were the questions he wanted answers to, and the fucking Fish and Wildlife Service website was no help with that.

When the ink cartridges in the printer ran dry, he noticed how quiet it was. All he could hear was a faint whistling noise, like a tea kettle in a distant closet. Two notes. Two syllables. *Dan-ny.* He could hear it distinctly now. He walked to the drapes and eased them apart. It was back. But something was different. The bird wasn't staring at him. He couldn't see the strange beak or the glaring eyes, but the creature's sagging breasts were front and center. He jumped when the bird shook, fluffing its feathers momentarily, and watched its head swivel around, 180 degrees, to meet his gaze. The bird held Mitzi's limp body in its grotesque maw. A hybrid organ. Part nose—part mouth—part beak. Danny watched it grasp the dog's lifeless body in a scaly claw and tear tufts of hair and a little pink bow from the top of her head, before it ripped her head off and swallowed it whole with a gagging motion. He shut the drapes quietly.

That's how the weekend went. He'd open the drapes and sometimes it was there, and sometimes it wasn't. He crashed hard Saturday night, catching nine hours. Sunday afternoon, he snapped a broomstick over his knee and laid the stick into the interior track of the sliding door after he noticed that the bird was tearing away at the metal stripping of the threshold. Sunday night, he decided it wasn't safe to sleep so he sat up, snorting crystal, watching porn, too tired to masturbate. Monday morning, without showering or shaving, he got dressed in his best Brooks Brothers suit and drove to work. He could feel the owl following him. He heard the whistle of his name even though the car windows were rolled up. He was sure a black Tahoe took the same exit he'd taken off Central Expressway.

At the office, everyone was whispering. Staring. Could they hear the whistle? The secretary stopped him and said the boss wanted to see him.

"Danny, my boy, I'm worried about you. I wondered if you still had it, so to speak. But I see you here today, obviously still sick from whatever was ailing you last week. Well, I appreciate loyalty, but I wouldn't feel right letting you work in your condition. No sir, we take care of our own. Have you seen a doctor yet, son? I mean a specialist."

"Ah, no sir."

"Well, that's just what you're going to do. From the looks of you, I wonder if you didn't pick up some fucking parasite over there in Thailand. Filthy place. Anyway, consider yourself on medical leave until further notice."

On his way out, even the secretary was nice for a change. "Take care of yourself, Danny," she said to him as he passed her desk. He thought she looked like she was on the verge of crying. In the office tower lobby, he caught a glimpse of his reflection in the tinted panes of the revolving door. He hardly recognized himself. His face was hollow with deep circles under his eyes, and his clothes hung on him, like a bum. He drove home at the head of the strange convoy, knowing the owl and the Tahoe were following. In his apartment, he paced back and forth between the pictures of the owls he'd tacked on the walls and the mirrored coffee table where he snorted rails of crystal meth, the clarity he sought always just out of reach.

When he peeked through a slit in the curtains, it was there, just as surely as the black Tahoe was parked below. And now the balcony looked different. Cluttered. The bird had been dragging up bits of debris. Pieces of carpet, a pair of old boots. Some sticks. Danny thought there might even be some bones. He recognized the bowl shape taking form. It was building a nest. Was it going to lay a giant fucking egg? Maybe two? Raise a brood of monsters on his balcony, feeding the chicks on neighborhood pets? He'd had enough. He threw up the lock on the sliding door, but then the owl reacted, throwing out its wings, releasing an agitated screech. Its golden eyes dilated to reveal unwavering inky black pupils. He locked the door.

He thought about the dream, his mother. About Uncle Santiago. About what his aunt Mary had said about getting a curandero to lift the curse. It was worth one last effort. He decided to start his search in the botánicas along Jefferson. He retrieved a thousand dollars from his dresser drawer and headed across the river to Oak Cliff.

He stopped at several large botánicas, but met with no success. The proprietors treated him like he was crazy when he told them his story, or shook their heads in resignation and made the sign of the cross. On a side street, between Jefferson and West Davis, he spotted a sign. *Botánica San Ramón.* As he got out of his car, he saw a curtain move in the old house—someone was watching. A string of bells announced him when he walked into the front room. There was a showcase with decks of tarot cards, plaster gargoyles, and crystals in front of shelves of colored candles and jars of potions and powders. Around the walls candles flickered on makeshift altars, illuminating pictures of saints in hammered tin frames. A short man entered the room.

"May I help you?" the man asked with a raspy voice.

Danny stalled, hoping to break the ice before bringing up the giant owl. "Are you a curandero?" Danny asked, then blurted it out: "What do you know about La Lechuza?"

"Yes, I am a curandero. La Lechuza," the man said, drawing out the words. "That is an old Mexican legend. Best to let those kinds of spirits be."

"Is that what it is? A spirit?"

"Yes, an evil spirit. A kind of witch. Do you know someone who has seen the creature?"

"Yes. Me. I saw it. I mean, I still see it. I need help. It's following me. I want it gone." Danny pulled out a roll of cash. "I can pay. Whatever it costs."

"You've come to the wrong place," the little man said. "My business is gossip and love charms. I'm sorry I can't help." He turned to walk away, but Danny sidestepped and blocked him.

"You said you were a curandero. My aunt Mary said a curandero could lift the curse."

The little man shook his head. "I am a curandero, but I don't deal in the black arts. What you need is a bruja—a witch."

"Okay," Danny said, holding out a fifty-dollar bill. "Tell me where to find this witch.

Danny followed the directions the man had drawn on a scrap of paper. The place was near the zoo. There was a sign with an open hand. *Palm Reading by Madame Zora.* He rang the bell, but no one answered. He knocked. The door must have been ajar because it swung open. He remained at the threshold, looking into the room. It was dark, with green shag carpeting. There were two carved chairs with a low table between them in the corner, like a waiting area. In the middle of the room, two more carved chairs sat facing a round table draped with a lace cloth. He was about to leave when he felt something behind him. He turned, and a middle-aged woman with frizzy gray hair, a pinched face, and eyes the color of straw said, "Do you have an appointment? I was at the side of the house. I didn't hear the bell."

"No, do I need one? The man at Botánica San Ramón said you might be able to help me."

She stepped inside. "Did he? I must remember to thank him. No, you don't need an appointment. Come in." The woman closed the door behind them and instructed him to sit in one of the chairs at the table. She had a low center of gravity and short legs, and Danny thought she waddled more than walked, as she went around the room and moved various objects to the center of the round table—some old books, a deck of cards, a silver bowl. "Wait," she said, opening a door and disappearing through it. She returned holding two eggs.

"I guess I should tell you why I'm here."

"Silence," the woman said, and Danny watched her pale eyes and nimble fingers move over the table, placing the eggs in the silver bowl, and the bowl atop the books. She slid the pack of cards from the table, shuffled them, and held them out toward Danny. "Blow on this," she instructed. He did. She cut the cards and began to turn them over on the tabletop in a cruciform pattern, grunting as she went, her pitch signifying either pleasure or distaste. "Choose an egg from the bowl."

"Don't you want to know why I'm here?" Danny asked, lifting an egg from the bowl.

"Blow on the egg," she commanded. He complied, and she removed the other egg from the bowl and cupped it in her hand. "Now crack it—into the bowl."

He hit the egg on the bowl's rim and pried apart the two halves. Blood poured out into the bowl. "What the hell?"

"Now I will tell you why you are here." She pointed to the card at the center of the cross. "This is you." The card depicted a man hanging upside down. "You have been cursed."

Suspicion welled inside him. "Listen, lady, I've heard about tricks like this. You put the blood in that egg somehow. It wouldn't have mattered which one I picked."

Silently, she handed him the other egg. He cracked it. It was a regular egg. The golden yolk rested on the pool of blood in the bowl. It stared up at him like an eye.

"Help me," he said.

"You have come into possession of a sum of money?" she said, telling more than asking, her slender fingers floating above the cards like a cursor, pointing to one diabolic image and then another. "This money is cursed. You must bring it to me, or bury it yourself in a cemetery, over the grave of a recently deceased loved one. This is the only way to lift the curse."

He was sweating. "Wait. I didn't come here to talk about my money. It's a curse. Sure. But it's got nothing to do with my money. It's a bird. An owl. It's called La Lechuza."

She laughed. "Oh yes. I'm familiar with La Lechuza. But the curse does stem from the money. Think. Did you see La Lechuza before you . . . inherited this money?"

"No," he replied, shuffling the puzzle pieces in his head until they made a picture. He hadn't seen La Lechuza until he'd taken the money. "You say if I bury it the curse will be lifted?"

"Oh yes, guaranteed. But it must be over the grave of a loved one." She covered his hand with hers. "Someone recently deceased. I know this can be difficult. You could bring the money to me. I could take care of it for you."

Danny pulled his hand away. "No. I'll take care of it. Tonight. What do I owe you?"

"You owe me nothing," she said. "But donations are gratefully accepted."

Danny reached into his pocket and pulled out the roll of cash. He peeled off five bills and placed them on the table. "That enough?"

"Perfect," she said, examining the money.

Danny knew he'd been followed from Madame Zora's. He saw the black Tahoe in the traffic, sometimes right behind him, other times a few car lengths back. But it was there, just like the owl, whispering his name. At home, Danny did more crystal and drank the last of his vodka. It looked like money would be tight again. He might even lose the Rolex. Fuck it. He didn't care anymore. If burying the money meant he'd never see La Lechuza again, that would have to be okay. He still had the crystal he'd murdered two men for—no, not murder. Just an accident. He picked up a length of Thai stick from the ashtray and lit it. It was working. He was glowing again. They could have been murderers too, he decided, relaxing into the fog of the smoke and the magic of the meth. Maybe he'd done a public service. That's how he was going to look at it.

The hours passed, as he fortified himself on meth and Thai stick. He was glowing so brightly he imagined he might burst into flames. His senses were heightened to the point that he felt he had become one with both the natural and supernatural worlds. The approach of muffled wing beats and the whistle of his name on the wind told him it was so, and that the time had come. He dressed himself, and at ten thirty he left for the cemetery. He'd rehearsed it over and over in his mind. Drive to the cemetery, hop the fence with the briefcase and the shovel he'd bought on his way home from Oak Cliff. He knew his mother's grave was next to his grandmother's.

He brought the roach from the Thai stick along for the drive to Grove Hill Cemetery. Pleasant Grove—a place where nothing good ever happened, he thought, remembering visits to distant cousins in that part of town. They even called themselves *Grove-*

rats. There was the Tahoe. He spotted it several times in traffic, and he could see the shadow of the owl following along, even though it was dark, as he exited off I-30. He was close now, but for some reason he wasn't frightened anymore. He parked across the street from the cemetery, threw the shovel and briefcase over the fence, and vaulted it like a pro—*You still got it, Danny-boy.* As he walked through the dark maze of trees and tombstones, he could hear the downy beating of wings above his head. Above the trees. The sound was soft, almost powdery. *Dan-ny,* the breeze whispered. Just a little further.

At the grave, he fell to his knees, carrying the briefcase in one hand and the shovel in the other. He held his arms out and released a racking, anguished sob. He knelt that way for several moments, as the tree branches rustled their approval near the grave. When he glanced up, a pair of glowing orbs met his gaze. He stood, placed the briefcase on the mound of the grave, and whispered, "Forgive me." He took the shovel in both hands and pulled it back to strike at the soft earth. Before he could complete the motion, he heard someone quietly call his name. He dropped the shovel and turned. It was Madame Zora. She was pointing a gun. Her silver hair and the gun's silver barrel glinted in the light of the full moon, and he was drawn to their luminosity. It seemed as if the graveyard was flooded with light. He couldn't remember a full moon that had lasted this long, or one that had pulsated more invitingly.

"So this is how it goes," he said. "The money's in the briefcase, but I spent some."

"I know," Madame Zora said, pulling a bill from her pocket, holding it up for him to see.

"But how?" he asked. This was too complicated. He needed some crystal. He needed some clarity.

"What if I told you the money had a mark. A shaved corner. Didn't you notice?"

"So this is all about the money? Just take it, I won't go to the police."

"It was never all about the money," she said. "One of the men you killed worked for me. He was my nephew."

Danny was trying to make sense of the pieces when the moon went behind the clouds. He didn't like the graveyard in the dark. He was grateful for the sparks that shot from the gun when she pulled the trigger. They were like fireworks. He'd always liked fireworks. He fell back onto his mother's grave, next to the briefcase. He felt for the leather of the handle and clutched it. *She'll have to pry it out of my hand. Maybe I can overpower her if she tries,* he thought. As he looked up at the sky, he felt cold, but then something warm and wet began to envelope him, and he settled into its embrace.

The clouds were parting now to reveal the full moon again. It was just what he'd wanted most at this moment. Luminosity. He heard something hard strike the grave. It was the gun. She'd dropped it, but his limbs felt useless. He rolled his eyes to watch her when she knelt beside him. Felt a tickling sensation when she pried the handle of the briefcase from his grip. As their eyes met, he knew that this was the part he'd been waiting for.

The change happened right there in front of him. *So that's how it's done.* It was so much simpler than he'd imagined it would be. La Lechuza flew onto his mother's headstone and stared down at him with molten eyes. "Dan-ny," the owl cried. Then it flew away into the tree line.

Time had become irrelevant, and he wasn't sure how long he'd been lying there on the grave. He'd been admiring the moon though. She'd said it hadn't all been about the money, and he was starting to believe her. He listened closely. Could just make out the downy flutter of wings, beating like a pulse in his brain— powdery soft. He watched as the sky faded, and the giant owl pumped its wings, becoming smaller as it flew higher. The shadow of its silhouette traversed the face of the full moon.

LIKE KISSING YOUR SISTER

BY JAMES HIME

Irving

As they pulled into the parking lot of the tittie bar out by the new Texas Stadium, Captain Jeremiah Spur could no longer refrain from commenting on the weather. "I'd be inclined to say it's rainin' like a cow pissin' on a flat rock," he said as he took a drag on his Camel, "but in my experience cows always piss straight down. This here wind has the weather all sideways."

The uniformed officer who was at the wheel of the patrol car, a man by the name of White, nodded at the Texas Ranger. "Weatherman said we was in for a toad strangler."

"How come they're always correct when they predict it'll turn out miserable? Sure 'nough gonna make for a muddy track over at the Cotton Bowl."

"Who you like in that game?"

Jeremiah took a last drag on his cigarette and snuffed it out in the ashtray. "I'm an Aggies fan. When Texas and OU play, I mostly cheer for injuries. That was a joke. I think the crime scene is around back of the place."

It was still morning. The parking lot outside the joint, the Silver Garter, was empty. Jeremiah knew that it was a front for the Dallas Mafia, which was run by Joe Campagnolo out of the Egyptian Lounge over on Mockingbird.

Jeremiah had spent the last year and a half trying to take down the Campagnolo gang, but he didn't have much to show for it so far.

Maybe this morning would represent a turning point. But he was loath to get his hopes up.

They pulled around back and were greeted by crime scene tape, a van from the ME's office, a few police cruisers, and a couple of civilian rides. The tape cordoned off an area around a cream-colored 1984 Oldsmobile 88.

"Nice car," said the driver as he pulled to a stop. "I hadn't seen the new model yet."

"I doubt the man has had it long enough to make the first payment. Guess we better get on with it."

As he stepped out into the monsoon, Jeremiah pulled his slicker to and fastened it. His Stetson all but got away from him in the wind and he had to clutch it to his head. He had covered it in a plastic shell, the better to keep it from being ruined by the rain.

He was not by nature a man much given to vanity, but he set considerable store by his hat.

Jeremiah ducked under the crime scene tape. He made his way around the front of the car to the driver's side, Officer White at his heels. The big Ranger peered in the vehicle at the body lying slumped over the steering wheel. Blood and brain matter smeared the windshield glass from the inside. He eyed it for a few minutes and then straightened up.

"Could have been the work of Joe's boys. Shot at close range behind the right ear. That's about their style. You say he managed this place?" His chin jerked toward the strip joint.

"That's right."

Jeremiah grunted. "Wouldn't have thought they'd left the body here, though. Dumping a vic in an East Texas pasture for some farmer to find—that's more Joe's speed. Who found it?"

"Guy named Paul O'Brien. He works the bar here. Stumbled on it when he came in to open up this morning."

"Where's he at now?"

"Inside."

Jeremiah told White to stay where he was, and he made for the door.

Strip joints tend to be windowless affairs and the Silver Garter was no exception. Most of the illumination came from beer signs hanging behind the bar, and that's where he found O'Brien, sipping coffee.

Jeremiah pulled off his slicker as he crossed the room, and shook the water onto the floor. The barman watched his progress and kept sipping. Jeremiah planted one hip on a stool and set his slicker down on the bar. Pulling an ashtray within easy reach, he helped himself to a book of matches with the joint's name embossed on it in raised gold letters. He lit a cigarette and shook the match out and dropped it in the ashtray. The matchbook he pocketed.

He sat smoking and studying the bartender. The man was young, in his early thirties, with longish black hair, a mustache, pronounced sideburns. He apparently had not let the passage into history of the 1970s influence his grooming style.

"I hear you found the body. What was his name?"

"Larry Karcher."

"Known him long?"

"About a year. That's when I hired on."

"Got any clue who might have wanted to see him dead?"

The man sipped his coffee. "I'm not sure it's such a good idea for me to speculate about that."

"On account of how come?"

"On account of, I might end up like Larry."

Jeremiah pushed his Stetson back on his head and scratched at a spot in his hairline. "But that would only happen if I was to betray your confidence. I been in law enforcement many a year, and that is one thing I ain't never done."

O'Brien dropped his hands into his lap and hung his head for a few moments. When he looked up, he said, "You ever heard of a man named Victor Pirano?"

Jeremiah tapped ash and nodded. "Joe Campagnolo brought him in from New York a few years back, after he'd done a stretch in Sing Sing for manslaughter. Rough customer, despite his fondness for dapper attire. Generally keeps the troops on the west side in line."

O'Brien nodded. "He come in here a couple weeks back, to see Larry. The two of them went in Larry's office and closed the door. I was on my way to get a couple bottles of whiskey from the storeroom in back when I heard 'em goin' at one another. The two of them was screamin' and shoutin' to beat the band."

"What about?"

O'Brien shook his head. "I don't know, and Larry never said. What I do know is that after Victor left, I saw Larry, and he was shakin' like a leaf. The man was pure-D scared out of his mind."

"Pirano been around here since that time?"

"Not till last night."

"You saw him last night?"

"Yeah. We were crazy busy, what with all the college boys in town for the game. He may have been in here somewhere. Taking in the show, for all I know. But I didn't see him till late, when I was leaving for the night. Around two in the morning."

"Where was he?"

"Out back, in the employee parking area. Leaning up against Larry's new 88. I don't know if anyone but me saw him, okay, so if you tell him he was spotted back there, he's likely to figure I'm the one who told you. And that would not be good, man."

Beads of sweat had popped out on O'Brien's upper lip. He was a study in paranoia.

Jeremiah gave a short nod. He made no reply. Instead, he consulted his watch.

Coming up on lunchtime.

Would Victor Pirano really make the rookie mistake of letting himself get noticed right where a body would be found some hours later? Jeremiah had his substantial doubts. But he could think of no reason not to go brace the man while he waited for the forensics to come in.

He stood to go. "If you think of anything else . . ." He produced a business card from the breast pocket of his shirt and handed it to the barman.

The guy looked it over, then set it down on the bar before him. "Texas Ranger, huh?"

Jeremiah made no reply. He shrugged on his slicker and headed back outside where he told Officer White to take him back to his office so he could get his own vehicle.

He figured to follow this case the rest of the way himself. Didn't really need a uniform hanging around, watching his every move. After all, Joe Campagnolo's boys were said to be wired in tight with the DPD.

Vic Pirano was known to be a frequent customer at Dunston's steak house over on Harry Hines. Jeremiah found him there, sitting alone in a booth and fingering a martini that was about half gone. Even though it was Saturday, he was attired as if he had an appointment with his banker—blue French-cuff shirt with white collar, gold cuff links and collar pin, gray pin-striped suit, red tie. Hair slicked back, nails manicured.

Jeremiah hung his slicker and Stetson on a hook that protruded from the side of the booth and slid onto the bench opposite the mobster.

"Captain Spur," the man said, in an accent that was pure Brooklyn. "To what do I owe the pleasure?"

Pirano took a sip while Jeremiah fished out his cigarettes and lit one from the book of matches he'd taken at the tittie bar. Then he slid the matchbook across the table to Pirano. "I'm guessin' you know this here establishment."

Pirano glanced at the matchbook but made no effort to pick it up. "Of course. It sells overpriced drinks to men while entertaining them with shows featuring scantily clad females. I find it surprising, and oddly reassuring, that a morally upright man such as yourself would patronize the place."

"I was over there this morning, all right. But not for the drinks, nor the girls. Last night somebody shot the manager, name of Karcher. The DPD found his body at the wheel of his 88. Do you happen to know anything about that?"

A waiter arrived at tableside with an enormous Caesar salad in hand. He served Pirano and offered him a couple twists of a pepper mill, then retreated. Pirano tucked his napkin in his shirt collar and took a fork to the salad. Jeremiah smoked and watched.

Pirano sat back and chewed and peered around the mostly empty restaurant. He brought a corner of the napkin up to his lips and swallowed.

"Knowing what I do about you and your methods, I am going to surmise that your question is based on more than mere guesswork."

"I have a witness who claims you were recently on the premises over yonder, engaged in a heated quarrel with the vic."

"Ah. That." Pirano drank his martini dry, then caught the eye of the waiter. He made a circular motion over the glass with his finger. The waiter nodded and walked off. "I was asked by the owners of the Silver Garter to have a word with Mr. Karcher about his management practices as relates to the dancing staff. Mr. Karcher had taken upon himself certain liberties where they were concerned. Liberties that were proving to be bad for business."

"You're sayin' he couldn't keep his hands off the exotic dancers?"

"His hands were not the problem. The problem was his dick.

He knocked two of them up in just the last year. This sort of thing has adverse implications for profit margins. It reduces the talent pool. Causes morale problems. The second girl, Rosemary Evans, went so far as to complain to Mr. C. Confronted him personally, at the Egyptian. Said Karcher had promised to marry her, then reneged. Just like a dumb-ass tittie dancer to buy that line. Anyway, the man needed to be spoken to."

"At least until a more permanent solution could be found, huh?"

Pirano made a tut-tutting noise. "Come now, Captain Spur. You speak of my principals as though they have no head for business. Impregnating a couple of strippers is not enough to get you dead if you are an otherwise productive and valuable employee. Sure, you get a strong lecture. Maybe your annual bonus takes a haircut to reflect the fact that you already took your bonus out in pussy. But your job you keep. Not to mention your life."

"You're lying."

"No. I don't believe I am."

"Where were you around two in the morning?"

"This morning? I was over at the Egyptian Lounge, playing a friendly game of Texas Hold'em with Mr. C and some of the boys."

"They'd back you up on this?"

"Hell yes. I make it a policy to stay off the streets on the Friday night of Texas-OU weekend. Too many drunk frat boys driving around town looking to get themselves killed in a car wreck. You cops ought to do something about that, you know. Put a few of those kids in jail. Serve as an example to the rest of 'em."

Jeremiah was sorely tempted to tell Pirano that he had been spotted at the Silver Garter late last night, but that would do violence to his pledge to protect O'Brien. Nor was he sure what good it would do him. He would need more evidence than that to bring down the likes of Pirano.

"Karcher have any family?"

"Not to my knowledge. He was a loner. Spent all his time at the club. Very dedicated to his job. A model employee, leaving aside his raging horniness."

The waiter arrived to remove the salad plate and replace it with a fresh martini and a steak big enough to feed an entire third-grade class.

Jeremiah said, "I'll leave you to your lunch. But you ain't heard the last of this." He got to his feet and took his slicker down off the hook. He shrugged it on as he watched Pirano. The man had tucked into his steak. He sat chewing, a look of dreamy contentment on his face.

He appeared not to have one care in the world.

There were four Rosemary Evanses in the white pages. The first two he called on were dusters. One worked at a big accounting firm and the other was a nurse. They were both sizable women who were in no way exotic-dancer material, even under the most desperate of circumstances.

The third Rosemary listing was an address at a class-C apartment complex off Greenville Avenue, over on the wrong side of North Central. Jeremiah stepped out of his vehicle and eyed the building from the safety of the sidewalk. It was the kind of place where the cockroaches carried sidearms. The rain had all but stopped. He left his slicker in the car as he proceeded up the sidewalk, pausing to study the tenants' mailboxes by the front door.

Rosemary Evans was listed as the occupant of apartment 14B.

When she answered the door, he knew he had come to the right place. Not only was this Ms. Evans possessed of the kind of frame appropriate to a stripper, but she was dabbing at her eyes with a tissue.

Seemed like word about Larry was making the rounds.

Jeremiah doffed his Stetson out of respect. "Ms. Evans? My

name is Jeremiah Spur. I'm a Texas Ranger and I'd like to ask you a few questions about an acquaintance of yours, Larry Karcher. I take it you've heard what's happened."

She nodded her head and led him into the little apartment. It was a studio but she had gone to some trouble to fix the place up and it looked clean enough.

They sat in chairs on either side of a little table and she began to bawl. Jeremiah waited for her tears to subside, which, at length, they did.

"It's just so awful," she sniffed as she wiped the tears from her cheeks. "To love someone and then to lose them like—like that."

"You heard, then, how they found him?"

She nodded again and blew her nose. She stared down at her hands for a few moments, then looked up. "I saw him just yesterday. He seemed so happy. So alive. He was so sweet to me. You see, he had changed his mind and, and—"

The crying commenced again. She fairly shook with it.

"You was hopin' he'd marry you."

"He said he would. And then he said he wouldn't. And then just a few days ago he said he'd like to get together, and when we did he said he'd been thinking about it and he'd decided he was in love with me after all and he'd just been afraid of the, you know, commitment. We would have been so happy together. And now—now he's gone. Gone forever."

She shook her head as though unable to bring herself to believe her own words.

"Leaving you alone. And in a family way, from what I understand. Which brings to mind something else I heard. Karcher managed to get another one of his dancers pregnant. Is that true?"

"Yes. That's yet another sad story!" This exclamation provoked further tears. She cried so hard she bent over double. The woman seemed incapable of holding it together.

Jeremiah stood to go. He figured he might as well leave this woman to do her grieving alone. He put his Stetson on his head and squared it there.

"Thanks for the time. Condolences on your loss." When he got to the door, he paused, then turned back toward Rosemary. "Any chance you might know where I could find this other girl that Karcher knocked up?"

She heaved a sigh. "In a graveyard in Paris, Texas, where she came from."

"You sayin' she's dead?"

"Overdosed on sleeping pills after Larry left her for me. It was just awful. Her own brother found her. She'd been dead for three days. Poor man. He took it terribly hard."

"Any idea where I might find the brother?"

"Yes sir. At the Silver Garter. He's a bartender there, named Paul O'Brien."

It took Jeremiah less than an hour to track down Victor Pirano again. He found the man in a booth at the Egyptian Lounge. Jeremiah slid onto the opposite bench and took out his cigarettes.

"Captain Spur," said Pirano. "Twice in one day, and on a Saturday at that. Have you ever given thought to taking a weekend off? Leave the law enforcement to someone else till Monday? Watch a little college football?"

Jeremiah lit his cigarette and looked around the restaurant. "I might do that someday, when all the bad guys is behind bars. Speakin' of which, where's ol' Joe?"

"He said something about going to a fundraiser for the mayor."

Jeremiah took a drag and tapped ash. "He's plugged in way up the chain, ain't he?"

"I'd find something else to do with my time, were I you, Captain Spur. Like I said. College football. Notre Dame plays later today. I can even place a bet for you, if you'd like."

Jeremiah grunted. "Got something I need to tend to first. If I was to tell you I had an eyewitness that puts you out back of the Silver Garter at two o'clock this morning, what would you say?"

"I would say your eyewitness is a lying cocksucker and a four-flushing son of a bitch."

"You Yankees got a way with words, I'll grant you that. Can you prove you weren't there?"

Pirano held up a hand and motioned for a waiter to join them. "Maurice," he said to the man when he arrived at table-side, "where was I at two o'clock this morning?"

The waiter shrugged. "Out back, playin' poker with Mr. C and a few of the other boys."

Pirano looked at Jeremiah. "You want the names of the others, so you can ask them?"

"I don't believe that will be necessary."

"Thank you, Maurice."

"Any time, Mr. P."

When the waiter was out of earshot, Pirano said, "A man with your superlative deductive skills will no doubt by now have figured out that someone is trying to set me up to take the fall for the recent capping of Mr. Larry Karcher. As you can imagine, I would very much like to know who that is."

Jeremiah stubbed out his cigarette and leaned forward with his elbows on the table. "I'll tell you, but I need you to promise to do something for me first."

By the time Jeremiah got back to the strip bar by the stadium, it was beginning to fill up with college boys dressed in burnt orange and crimson and cream. They all looked waterlogged and whiskey-logged. The game had ended in a draw, 15–15, thanks to a last-second Longhorn field goal.

A tie, the retired Texas football coach Darrell Royal had fa-mously said, is like kissing your sister.

A man kissing his sister—maybe not all that exciting, but certainly not illegal. In some places, it even seemed like it was encouraged.

Arkansas came to mind.

But a man killing another, as revenge for his sister?

That wasn't okay anywhere Jeremiah could think of.

Paul O'Brien was standing at the bar in back and he watched as Jeremiah weaved his way through the place. There were women all around the big Ranger with their private parts on display. Jeremiah paid them no mind. His sweetheart was and always would be his wife Martha, who was back home at his ranch in Washington County.

When he got to the bar, he nodded at O'Brien, who watched him warily.

"You got a phone I could use?" Jeremiah said.

O'Brien reached under the bar and produced a telephone. He set it down on the bar before Jeremiah, who had lit up a cigarette and was shaking the match out.

"How about a phone book?"

Out came the phone book.

"Do me a favor. Look up the phone number for the Egyptian Lounge."

"Joe Campagnolo's place?"

"Yep."

O'Brien paged through the phone book for a few seconds, then handed it to Jeremiah.

"Now," Jeremiah said, "I'm fixin' to call over there and ask for Victor Pirano. And when he comes on the line? I'm gonna let him know you told me you saw him out back last night."

O'Brien's eyes bugged out. "But, but—you promised you wouldn't do that!"

"I did indeed. But since you was lyin' about what you saw, that fact renders my promise null and void."

Jeremiah reached for the phone, but O'Brien grabbed it away. "I can't let you do that!"

"He's bound to find out sooner or later. Might as well tell the man now."

"But what makes you think I'm lying?"

"Because you're the one that done Larry Karcher. As revenge for how he treated your sister: first knocking her up, then dumping her for another gal. And the fact that she took her own life over it."

As the barman spoke, Jeremiah studied his eyes. He could see the guilt that was lodged there.

It was always the same. Their eyes gave them away every time.

The man threw the phone on the floor and went running down the length of the bar. He vaulted over the top and turned and disappeared through a door leading to the back.

He was no doubt headed for his car, figuring to do a runner.

Jeremiah stayed where he was, smoking his cigarette and not looking at the naked women that were everywhere to be seen.

Pirano and the two boys he had brought with him would want a few minutes alone with O'Brien when he came bursting out the back door of the Silver Garter.

When Jeremiah was done with his cigarette, he stubbed it out in the ashtray.

He headed around the bar to the door that led out back. He figured he'd better get out there before Pirano took it upon himself to finish off O'Brien.

That was a job that rightfully belonged to Old Sparky, down in Huntsville. Not to some greasy Big D mobster.

If he got high and behind it, Jeremiah thought he just might get O'Brien booked for capital murder and still make it back to his hotel room in time to catch the kickoff of the Aggies game on the radio this evening.

He figured he'd earned the night off.
He would go back to law enforcement in the morning.

AN ANGEL FROM HEAVEN

BY FRAN HILLYER

Northpark

This is what it came down to, just Luke and the breaths, starting and stopping, with long, silent spaces between. The end was hovering, circling the bed. He took the old man's hand and said what he always said.

"You can go now. You did the very best you could no matter what. It's all going to be good."

He touched the old man's brow, and the breathing stopped. The low growl of Luke's cell phone broke his concentration. It would be a few minutes before the old dude was technically gone. He looked at the second hand on his watch and tried to put the cell phone out of his mind. Two minutes should do it. He had been wearing the stethoscope all night, and he put the two prongs in his ears and touched the old man's chest with his chest piece. No sound. The face slackened, the mouth fell open.

"You're free now, Old Dude." He walked to the oversized chair he had lived in for the last three days and sat down hard.

Three days' work this time. It could have been done so much quicker, but you had to draw it out a little—not too much—to convince them that it was the real deal. They want it soon but slow, the same way women want sex. He could probably be out of here in a couple of hours if the old dude's family came soon.

He removed his cell phone from his shirt pocket and read the text. *R U coming home 2day?* Geez, she'd been sending texts since five a.m. Didn't she ever give it a rest? Now he had to clean up, take the empty vials and syringes to the dumpster, put the unused medications in his car. One thing he had learned was that with the really old ones, no one is paying much attention. When it comes right down to it, nobody cares what kind of drugs these old bodies have in them. He worked around the bed, picking up used wipes, bagging the trash, wiping down the furniture, which the old man had become a part of now. Not such a bad old dude. He put the bagful of medical waste next to the front door, then went into the bathroom to shave. He used the old man's electric razor because it was a really nice one. He'd been using it on the old man, and he liked it. He guessed they'd miss it if he took it with him.

He wanted to put on one of the old man's monogrammed shirts, but that probably wouldn't be such a good idea either. They were the best quality, and he knew they fit him because he'd tried on the old dude's clothes while he was drugged out. Anyway, what if they did give the shirts to him? He'd still have to pull out all those monograms, and that's a lot of work. He'd made his deal, and it was a good one. Hell, get a few more gigs like this, and he could even get a monogrammed shirt for himself. He rubbed his hand over his newly shaven cheek. Nice shave. He had his own toothbrush in the bathroom. He would never use a dead man's toothbrush. He needed to call Cynthia to tell her this job was over, see if she had anything else lined up.

The room on the nursing floor where Anne's mother lay looked like any hospital room except for the chair-rail molding and the vanilla walls. Sally rose from the mahogany dining chair and offered it to Anne. Most of her mother's valuable things—the paintings she had collected, her books, and the remnant of her antiques—had been moved to a storage locker. Her old TV, which she never watched, and the single mahogany dining chair were the only personal items in the room. Her mother had been stripped of everything she ever cherished.

"Just sit down, Sally," Anne said. Anne chose to sit in the wheelchair because it was next to the bed, and from it she tried to meet her mother's vacant gaze. Her mother's arms sagged between the railings of the hospital bed, scaly and speckled with purple splotches. Everything on her body looked wilted: the pouches under her eyes, the droop of her underlip, even her earlobes, which looked too big for her face.

"Well," the old woman said when she saw her daughter, "what's going on over there?"

Over there might describe the gulf between the two women or Anne's house with its broken dishwasher, but it probably didn't mean either one of those things, one being too abstract and the other grounded in a world where people talk with each other about the everyday progress of their lives.

"Where?"

"You know," she said, and her eyes widened. Even the blue of her eyes had faded. Her body hunched into a question mark. She looked at the window, at the vanilla wall, at the framed photo of David's four-year-old. Outside the window, the branches of a live oak reached sideways and reminded Anne of the trees she used to climb on vacation at the coast.

"If you knew what they do to me here. There's a big fight every day." The old woman turned her pale gaze on Anne, pleading. "You have to get me out of here."

Anne looked at Sally. Sally shrugged. "They change her diaper. They dress her. It's over in three minutes." Anne wished she could get her out of there today, but there was wheelchair accessibility in the house to consider. She wished for an angel to carry her mother away.

"We're working on it, Mother. We're having David's old house fixed up for you." It wasn't so much to make her mother happy because happy was something she wasn't going to get, never even had, despite marrying two handsome, rich men and seeing the entire world except the north and south poles, including Kashmir twice. But at least the house would be part of her estate, and with the right kind of care, it could save them all money in the long run, especially if they could get hospice to take her.

"I think we have someone who wants to buy the Livingstone Road property," Anne said. She didn't know why she was bothering to tell her mother this, but there were days when the woman seemed to know things. She knew her daughter. She knew everyone in the family, even when she got their names wrong. Sometime last week Michael had become Matthew, but he was reliably Matthew now. One of these days, she might just check in and demand to have a full accounting of everything: tenants, bonds, her four checking accounts, and what the accountant said to do about taxes.

"We really need to take this offer, Mother. We won't get another one like this."

"Famous last words," her mother chuckled. She lifted her arm and drew her hand to her mouth, picked something invisible from the sheet, and once more lifted her hand to her mouth.

"I mean it, Mother." It occurred to Anne that she could touch the scaled skin on her mother's arm right now, and it could shred like wet newspaper. If the inside of her looked anything like the outside, she couldn't last much longer. "You said that if we got an offer of a million, we needed to take it."

Anne's cell phone growled. The text was from Cynthia. *Bistro N? 11:30?* Anne's concentration was broken, but her mother wouldn't notice. *At the Pinnacle. C U there*, she thumbed.

"Mother, you are going to need to sign these papers so we can sell the Livingstone Road property. We'll bring a notary to your room."

"I don't want to sign anything. Famous last words."

"Yes you do. This is a good thing. It's an opportunity. Remember? You said when we could get a million we should sell? Remember that?"

"No." She heaved her body over to face the wall. "I want to sleep now. Thanks for coming." She closed her eyes to block Anne out. Sally folded her pudgy arms and rolled her eyes. At least Sally understood. Anne needed to leave anyway. Talking to Mother was like talking down a well: hollow, full of echoes, and not going anywhere.

Outside the window, the skinny fingers of the live oak against the pristine August glare made Anne feel trapped. Trapped in a medicated, air-conditioned snow globe without the snow, sealed forever in this last-stop universe. August was the crescendo of summer, like Janis Joplin's famous Texas scream, the white of it soaking through anything it fell on. Just to escape, Anne decided to walk from the Pinnacle to North Park and get some of the unending decay of her mother out of her head.

From the sidewalk outside, the live oak looked less friendly. She walked alone through the heat that lay on her skin like an irradiated sleeve. She was surrounded by people encased in cars. Sealed in every car was a person, rarely more than one person, experiencing exactly the preferred climate, listening to the preferred voices, holding onto the preferred notion of what it meant to be driving into or out of the most splendid mall in Dallas, maybe in the world. Anne looked forward to the sight of normal, shallow people, who drove to the mall and got out of their cars carrying sweaters in the baking heat so that they wouldn't get chilled by the air-conditioning inside.

Beyond the armory of cars reflecting a hundred pings of eye-piercing sun, the chilled haven of tempered sunlight through frosted skylights and the calming sound of inoffensive piano music played by a man in a black suit—the signature of Nordstrom ambience—eased Anne into a land of plenty, where there was no death or sadness, no withering old ladies imprisoned in crepe-paper bodies.

From the escalator, Anne could see Cynthia talking with the hostess. She was wearing white pants and a sleeveless black silk tank. Cynthia—smooth-skinned, bronzer-burnished, honey-lipsticked, with teeth whitened to a perfect ecru—she was Dallas incarnate.

Anne reached to embrace Cynthia in her platform shoes. The music in the bronze-toned bistro was the kind of complicated jazz that Michael liked. A familiar refrain presented itself here and there, and then faded into a jumble of too much.

"Your back feels warm," she said in Anne's ear.

"I walked from the Pinnacle."

"By choice?" She held Anne's hand as the hostess showed them to the booth. Hand-holding was a purely Cynthia pretension, but it won Anne over every time.

The hostess gave them a booth by a tinted window. Outside, the shoppers moved through the thin whiteness like figures in a movie about untroubled prosperity. The leather-bound lunch menu offered a selection of upscale fare. A bison burger cost $12.50. The crab salad was $10.

When the waitress offered drinks, Cynthia said, "Oh, what the fuck. Let's get a bottle of pinot grigio. You walked all the way over here. You need refreshment. How is your mother anyway?"

"The same, I guess. Her doctor says she is shocked by her decline, but then she says she can't give her a diagnosis for hospice and that she could go on like this for a long time."

Cynthia took her cell phone from her purse and frowned, then placed it on the table next to her butter plate.

"Well, I've got some ideas about your situation, but let's have wine first." The waitress offered the wine to Cynthia, who tasted, then twirled the stem of the glass as it filled. She raised it. "Better days."

Anne preferred chardonnay, but Cynthia's choices were usually the ones that trumped. Wine was a good way to put her mother in a sealed envelope for the time being.

The two women had walked the long road from the day they picked up their Theta invitations to the care and stowage of their failing parents, taking their separate paths, avoiding the clashes on the loaded questions, staying neutral and helpful, each silently judging the other's choices, still meeting once a month for lunch after all these years. Anne was godmother to Cynthia's daughter from her second marriage to the anesthesiologist. There was comfort for both women in knowing that someone else shared all the details of the past, knew family, knew all the mundane intricacies of how their lives had moved from there to here.

The waitress approached the table again, flashing her smile, reciting the specials like she was describing a double-feature porn show. "Today's special is salad of baby lettuce with crunchy candied pecans, tossed with seasonal cherries and blanched pears with a balsamic vinaigrette dressing, and for our entrée the roast chicken pomme frites with herb butter."

Anne ordered warm Asian glazed-chicken salad. Cynthia ordered the salmon diablo. The restaurant was filling up with overdressed people, women wearing high heels and men in ties, the business crowd.

"Your father's funeral was beautiful," Anne said. "I haven't told you that."

"Thank you. Daddy wanted it simple. No eulogy." Her staged smile was the same one Anne had seen when she moved through the receiving line three weeks ago. Cynthia sighed, and the smile dissolved. "It's a relief to have him gone. Does that sound bad? He had no quality of life. I'm thankful." Her face suddenly brightened again. "And he died in time to avoid the repeal of the Bush tax cuts."

Did she really just say that? The food arrived, and Cynthia

poured more wine into their glasses, even though Anne's was half-full.

"How is your mother?" Cynthia asked. "You were just with her. You said she was the same. You said the doctors were shocked, but she could last a long time. How much is it going to cost you if she lives past December? Do you know?"

Anne took a bite of her salad. She didn't know what to say. The chicken was arranged in a star shape on top of three kinds of lettuce, pears, and walnuts. It was so lovely it made her want to cry.

"Thirty-five percent, right? As opposed to nothing if she dies before December? Are you telling me you haven't ever considered the estate tax? Never? What's wrong with her accountant?"

The room was getting warmer, the music was getting louder, or maybe it was just the wine. "The only thing she takes any pleasure in is ice cream," Anne said. "Her brain has two channels. One is *I'm going to have a party, and it's going to be all about my family history.* Michael calls it her Deathbed Tableau. Then there's *Get me out of here.* And when she says it, she looks like Linda Blair in *The Exorcist.* She can't walk. She can't hear, and she's losing her mind. Yes. I pray for her to go, and it would be especially convenient if it happened before December." The chicken seemed to swell in her throat.

Cynthia's cell phone moaned, and she looked at its face. "I'm sorry," she said. "I have to take this call." She slid from the booth and strode in her platform heels past the entrance to Bistro N and into the children's shoes department. Anne hated Cynthia's surgical proficiency in finding whatever gangrenous spot her soul housed. Yes, she had thought about the estate tax, and when she was lucid, Mother had thought about it too. She and her accountant had spent years moving assets into limited partnerships to avoid the looming 35 percent. Now Cynthia had made Anne her conspirator.

She pulled her own phone from her purse to make sure Sally hadn't called about Mother. She drained her first glass of wine and poured another. The music was getting louder, probably because of the crowd. It sounded like a duel between the saxophone and the piano. Across the room she thought she saw someone in her book club. For some reason she wanted to hide.

"I'm sorry. That was Luke," said Cynthia as she slipped into the booth. "I have to take his calls. I don't know what we would have done without him. One time one of the caregivers didn't show up, and I called Luke, and he dropped everything and went right over there. He drove Daddy to work out at the Dallas Country Club, he took him out to lunch, he took him to the doctor, he took him to get milkshakes at Highland Park Pharmacy. He never lost his temper, no matter how unreasonable or even abusive Daddy got."

"It's important to have good help," Anne said. "One of the things I didn't know was that I would need a caregiver, even at the Pinnacle. I love Sally. She takes whatever Mother dishes out and just sort of sighs. Mother has fired her three times, and she has come back every time. She's angelic."

"That's what I mean. Luke was an angel from heaven. And it set Charles off into a whole new area of medicine. This business of watching our parents just withering inside and out has given Charles an exciting direction that's a win-win for everybody involved." She was animated, incandescent. She swallowed a large bite of salmon and rolled her eyes. "Some people don't like salmon, but I do. If you eat it three times a week, they say, you'll add five years to your life."

Cynthia grinned at her plate. She was winding up. She looked as eager as a Labrador. "It's good to be married to an anesthesiologist," she chattered. "Charles started working with Luke on Daddy's meds. Charles can write prescriptions for anything. One of the reasons why Luke was perfect was that he has no interest in drugs at all, which is an important factor for us in hiring help because we always have samples around. Charles and Luke just experimented with whatever would keep Daddy contented. It was so much easier than having to persuade some doctor you don't know that he needed Oxy or something like that. We were able to keep Daddy in his house."

"Comfortable," Anne said. She watched as Cynthia poured the last of the wine in her glass.

"Better than comfortable. High all the way to the end. I can honestly say that Daddy had an easy exit. And what's most important *at the right time,* which is something hardly anyone gets. This is the way of the future, and Charles sees it as a whole new market for doctors like him. Of course, when Luke went to work for Charles's cousin, he raised his fee because he'd gotten training from Charles. He still works pretty closely with both Charles and me. He gets a percentage of the estate, but nowhere near what the government would get if the tax cut repeal goes through."

Anne's head was buzzing, either with the jazz or the wine, and she looked around her to see whether the room had contracted. The smell of the salad dressing, the parade of people moving from table to table, the change in the tempo of the music were overpowering, and she breathed deep to calm herself.

"So he's moved on from Charles's cousin?"

"He's with Charles's partner's family now, but he'll be free probably by late September."

The waitress arrived and picked up Anne's empty plate. "Can I get you ladies anything else?" The table between the two women, holding the detritus of their meal, felt as vast as a dance floor to Anne, and she wondered whether she could ever reach across it into the land where the easiest solution to anything was to make it convenient.

"Only the check," Anne replied. "Do you want to just divide it in half?"

"Oh no, I'll pay," Cynthia said. "I treat everybody since Daddy died."

Cynthia amazed Anne, her teeth bleached just enough and not too much, everything about her in harmony with what she wanted to be. She had always managed her whole life that way.

"Let me give you Luke's number." She pulled a card from her purse and wrote on the back with a pink easy-ball pen, then pushed it across the table to Anne as she rose from the booth, straightening her skirt, steadier somehow than she had been at the beginning of the meal. Anne looked at the card with Cynthia's fat pink script on it: an offer of ease and a door into another world. She picked it up and put it in her purse. Picking it up didn't mean she would have to use it.

The two women embraced. "I love you, sweetie," Cynthia whispered into their squeeze. "You're going to be fine."

Luke turned on the sound system to the hip-hop station, a little dance music to work by, and his spirit lifted. He'd made a good job of it. A sandwich would be great right now, and even a beer. There was no need to hurry. The calling list was by the phone, prioritized by Miss Cynthia herself. She was a demon on the phone. She loved this shit. You'd think she got some kind of buzz getting these mummies taken care of. By the time she called everybody, he would be out of the house.

The refrigerator was full, even though nobody ever ate here. There was an entire honey-baked ham in there. He guessed the old dude's family told all their friends that he was on the way out. Great ham, German mustard, thick rye bread, fresh leaf lettuce—a real rich man's sandwich. And a Newcastle ale. He could feel the vibrations of the bass in the floor and in his skin and even his hair, just as he felt the vibration of his phone in his hand. It wasn't Cynthia this time. It was a number he had never seen before. Good old Cynthia. She always managed to line something up.

The old dude's family wouldn't begrudge him the sandwich or even a beer or two. They would be an overflowing fountain of gratitude. They always were.

PART III

MAVERICKS

COINCIDENCES CAN KILL YOU

BY KATHLEEN KENT

Cleburne

The setup was perfect. It should have worked.

Except for the woman. The Good Samaritan with more time than sense on her hands. The kind of woman who would feed a hungry dog on the street while leaning over the homeless guy lying next to it. I've seen it happen. One poor bastard roused himself enough to say, "Hey, lady. What about me?"

Anyway. Just about every officer in our department had been working on this operation for over a year. Five undercovers, positioned around one modest suburban house, hundreds of man hours spent in preparation, a federal wire that had taken months to procure and countless favors called in. Sleepless nights at the office and in the field. Sleepless nights at home, on the couch, because the wife was frosted about the nights spent in the office and in the field.

The house was in a community north of Dallas. McMansions packed tightly together for miles like the Wall of China, only Texas style, with an abundance of American flags and *Vote Republican* signs nestled among the drought-hardy geraniums.

True to our informant, a worn Mercedes pulls up into the driveway, and the driver, an older guy, gets out—he could have been the manager at the local HEB—locks his car door, takes another key out of his pocket, and lets himself into the house.

I'm about to signal over the portable to stand by, when this woman, who's out walking her dog, sprints over to the Mercedes and starts talking to someone, or something, in the car. The driver had opened the windows a crack before locking the car and a furry head pokes its way out of the backseat. It's a small dog. And it's surface-of-the-sun hot outside. The woman, who's picked up her own pocketbook schnauzer, starts pulling on the door handle. She's trying to open the driver's-side door.

She's cooing to the dog inside, talking to him: "Poor baby, poor baby . . ."

Then she marches up to the door and starts ringing the doorbell. I'm not holding my breath at this point. An exhalation of *Fuck, fuck, fucks* are streaming into my radio.

When the owner doesn't answer the door—the guy is probably looking out the window, going *What the fuck?* himself—the woman takes a phone out of her belly bag. And calls the police.

Exactly four minutes later the neighborhood patrolman shows up. Listens to the woman. Goes to the door. Knocks on it. The door opens, there's an argument. And our guy is arrested. On animal cruelty charges and threatening an officer. A guy who was waiting on one of the biggest heroin suppliers in North Texas: a faceless dealer who was going to meet up with our HEB guy and do a Very. Big. Deal. I sat and watched several cars coast slowly by the house as the bust was made. Were they rubbernecking, or was one of the drivers our heroin guy?

The upshot is the HEB guy skips bail, gets on a plane to nowhere, we lose our wire, and over a year's worth of work goes up in flames.

Oh, and did I mention that our guy was a member of the woman's church? She offered to be a character witness for him, feeling badly as she did for calling the cops. A misunderstanding. An unhappy coincidence, as she didn't usually take that route to walk her dog.

In my ten-plus years on the force, I've found that there are three kinds of coincidences that can and probably will befall a case: The happy coincidence. The unhappy coincidence. And the gods-must-be-crazy-bat-shit-weird coincidence. And that kind of coincidence can be very, very dangerous.

Okay. What do a Civil War general, an antique sword, and an AK-47 have in common? Nothing. Unless they all converge during one of my cases.

It was after this case that my fellow officers stopped calling me Brooklyn Betty and began referring to me as Detective Ryczek. I had moved to Dallas from New York with my wife, after spending five years with Brooklyn homicide. My wife was in forensics and happy with her job, but she had grown up in Texas and wanted to be closer to her sick mother. It was not in any sense an easy transition; in some ways the hardest thing was being subjected to my mother-in-law's long-simmering outrage over me, her daughter's lesbian "friend."

The Texas cops were the least of my problems. How do you rattle a female detective who's spent years proving herself to the grandsons of wild-eyed, Fenian, IRA-supporting Irish cops, or with Italian cops whose fathers are "connected"? And they had almost all been connected in some way to organized crime. They all knew someone who knew someone, or had a relative who was in the business.

And how do you antagonize a woman who wears the word *dyke* like a badge of honor? Not to say they didn't try. For a while every proposed undercover scenario, which included me, began with, *Detective Betty's wearing a UPS uniform* . . .

Anyway. I had investigated a lot of strange crimes in New York. A dead naked guy in clown makeup, for one. But usually the trail of clues followed the physics of the known universe, and though all of the pieces may not have fit together right away, they were somehow linked. A small-time heroin user buys from a corner guy, who buys from a neighborhood guy, who buys from a borough boss, etc., etc., on up the chain until you find, if you're lucky, the guys who are unloading it off their boat onto a Brooklyn pier. You don't get to an urban boat dock on a drug bust and find a Civil War general. Unless you're in Texas.

A few years ago, we get a call from the Johnson County sheriff's office, CID unit. An abandoned car—make and model fitting the description of a vehicle belonging to Ignacio Velasquez, a midlevel heroin dealer we had been tracking—had been found outside of Cleburne, about sixty miles southwest of Dallas. Empty, except for what was in the trunk. A local highway patrolman had found the car abandoned on a dirt road, ran a check on the plates, and came up with an outstanding warrant in Dallas. He then popped the trunk and immediately called the sheriff's office. Detective Peavey, their lead criminal investigator, ran a deconfliction report, finding my name. He calls me, tells me what's in the trunk, and asks if I might want to make the trip to Cleburne.

My partner and I drive the sixty miles and meet up with Peavey, who's waiting for us next to the abandoned car: a black Beamer, covered in dust. Forensics is still working the scene; a body bag's on a stretcher. Peavey unzips the bag and inside is an older heavyset man, bound wrists and ankles, shot twice in the head. The corpse has been a corpse for a few hours and Peavey tells us he thinks the guy had been placed in the trunk soon after the shooting.

The corpse is wearing a gray uniform, with shiny brass buttons.

My partner Seth asks, "That a band uniform?"

Seth, an ex–high school football player from Lamesa, tends to frame his thinking according to West Texas practicalities: it's light outside, the sun is up; it's dark outside, the sun has set.

Peavey answers, "No . . . it's a Civil War uniform."

"Civil War," I repeat.

"See those patches and the sash?" he says, pointing to the corpse's shoulders and midsection.

I blink two, maybe three times. "So?"

"A Confederate reenactor," he offers.

"Reenactor," I echo, having no idea what he means.

"It's a group that gets together and stages Civil War battles. Uniforms, armaments, sometimes small cavalry units. Even cannons. They do it a lot around here."

I look at Seth and he shrugs.

"They deal drugs too?" I ask Peavey.

"Not that I know. It's not that kind of group."

I detect a note of defensiveness creeping into the investigator's voice, but I ask, "Then what's he doing in the trunk of Velasquez's car? And where's Velasquez?"

Peavey shakes his head. "I have no idea. But it looks like the asshole ran out of gas. Maybe he took off on foot? Got picked up?" He shrugs. Velasquez is not his problem, yet. But the body is.

He looks around as though to point out the obvious. It's dusk, we're ten miles away from Cleburne, and it's going to be dark soon. One of the local cops who's been murmuring into his car radio comes running with news that the wife of one of the reenactors has called in because she's not heard from her husband in over twenty-four hours.

Peavey informs us that the reenactors do military exercises on several hundred acres of private undeveloped land nearby—used for deer hunting in season—land which is somewhat hilly and densely brushed; boggy after it rains, crisscrossed with small streams. Phone reception is poor.

"They leave their cell phones in their cars and are allowed only one call a day at noon," he tells us. "The parking area is on higher ground where the reception is better. The wife says that some of the other women have called her and they've not heard from their husbands either."

"How many men in the group?" I ask.

The patrolman shrugs. "About fourteen. Give or take."

I point to the corpse. "Was he part of that group?"

He nods. "Probably so."

"Could they be lost?" Seth asks.

Peavey shakes his head. "Not likely. They've all grown up hunting around here."

The ball of light to the west is well below the horizon, flaming a wide band of clouds to a magenta red.

Peavey asks us, "Do you want to trail us to the encampment? See if they know the victim, or Velasquez?"

It's unlikely that Velasquez has headed back again toward the Halloween camp, but it's worth a look-see.

Peavey traces on a map the farm-to-market road that leads to a gate entrance to the deer lease, beyond which, somewhere, is the reenactors' encampment. We drive caravan style: the Cleburne patrol car, Peavey, then us. We're trailing behind for several miles through a curtain of dust kicked up from the dirt road. After fifteen minutes or so, I see through the headlights a high deer fence stretching into the darkness on either side of the road and a tall gate straddling it. The cop stops at the gate, opens it, and signals for Seth to close it after we've passed through.

Now here's where it gets weird.

The road, just beyond the gate, forks and the two cars in front of us veer to the left, in the direction of the base camp. While Seth gets out of the car to wrestle the gate closed, I glance to the right and see in the distance a faint, solitary light bobbing its way toward us. It's not a flashlight beam. It's yellowish and winking, more like a candle flame. Suddenly, it starts swinging crazily as though trying to signal us.

When Seth gets back into the car, I point to the right. "Do you see that?"

Squinting through the windshield, he puts the car into gear, turns to the right, and drives slowly toward whoever is signaling us. He puts on the flashing cherries and within a few minutes a boy, about fourteen, jogs into the headlight beams carrying a lantern and panting like he's been running for miles. And he's dressed like an extra in a Tom Jones movie: high-water pants, linen collarless shirt, and a thumb-buster revolver shoved under a broad leather belt.

When he sees us get out of the car, he drops the lantern in the road, hands on his knees. He points back up the road and gasps (and here I'm quoting exactly), "God Almighty, but they're trying to kill us."

The junior reenactor named Kyle climbs into the car, but not until I make him hand over his pappy's pistol. He calls me "ma'am" and tells us, through choking breaths, that he's with Company E, Fourth Texas Infantry, Hood's Confederate Brigade.

Seth looks at me and mutters, "Seriously?"

We're not on the local Cleburne police radio band so Seth tries calling Peavey on his cell phone. No signal.

I give Kyle some water and he begins to tell us in a rush of words that at eleven o'clock that morning he'd taken a bucket down to a stream to get some water for the camp horses and saw on the far side, at the base of a tree, a bright red duffle bag. He crossed the stream, looked in the bag, and, holy crap, there was a lot of money in there.

"How much?" I ask, beginning to sense that here is the connection between Velasquez and the dead guy in the trunk.

"Looked like thousands."

Kyle took the bag with the cash, forgetting to also take the water bucket, and, being a fourteen-year-old boy, figured finders-keepers. He hid the bag closer to the encampment and returned to his group without the water bucket, and without mentioning the cash. His "sergeant" gave him hell about leaving the bucket behind and went to retrieve it himself. Kyle never saw the sergeant again. Gunshots in the direction of the stream sent the reenactors hurrying to investigate.

"Some Mexicans, five of them, started firing at us from the other side," he says. "We could see a couple of cars parked up on the ridge. One had an automatic rifle, but we returned fire with our muskets."

Muskets, I'm thinking. *They returned assault-weapons fire with Civil War muskets.*

"It's all we had. We couldn't call anyone . . ." He begins to cry. Both his dad and uncle are with the encampment.

I don't want to upset the kid more than he already is, but I have to ask him: "Was your sergeant a heavyset man in a gray uniform? Blue sash around his middle?"

He nods and wipes his sleeve under his nose. "Is he okay?"

Kyle sees the look on my face and covers his eyes with both arms.

I'm wondering right then if, in exquisitely bad timing, the boy's sergeant had stumbled onto the stream at about the time Velasquez was meeting up with his Mexican drug connection. Finding the cash gone, Velasquez & Co. questioned the man until his ignorance quickly ran afoul of their impatience. He was shot and thrown into Velasquez's car. Once the shooting with the reenactors commenced, Velasquez, or someone else, drove the Beamer away from the encampment. The immediate concern at that point was how many Mexican drug dealers were left shooting at a bunch of costumed reenactors.

"We shot one of them," he says. "But two of ours went down at the river trying to make it to the fort . . . I think they may be dead."

"The fort?" Seth asks and looks at me incredulously. He's still trying to reach Peavey on the cell.

"It's what we call it," Kyle says. "It's just an old settlement house and barn we use for defensive maneuvers."

"Go on," I say.

"There were eleven of us barricaded at the house all day." He looks at me, eyes filled with tears, snot running down his nose, and suddenly he appears much younger than fourteen. "The Mexicans kept telling us what they were going to do to us when we ran out of ammunition. Even if they did get their money. When it turned dark, the others told me to go and try and get help. I snuck out, made my way to the road."

If there were five dealers to begin with and one got shot, and one drove the car away, that leaves maybe three armed, pissed-off Mexicans working to get their money back. I peer through the rear window at the road stretching back into the darkness, and wonder when the hell Peavey's going to realize we're not behind him and come investigate.

"At what point did you light the lantern . . . ?" I start to ask Kyle, and right then two things happen at once. I see headlights approaching in the distance behind us; likely it's Peavey coming back to check on us. And the front of our car is sprayed with gunfire, shattering the windshield inward.

I throw myself down over Kyle and hear Seth from the front seat swear and call out: "I'm hit . . ."

So far, it sounds like there may be two shooters with pistols and they're moving clockwise around the car. The front passenger-seat windows shatter and I reach over Kyle, open the door, and shove him out onto the road. Seth has opened his door and he falls out, gun drawn.

"Goddamnit, they shot me!" he yells.

I see that the headlights of Peavey's car behind us have come to a stop, and hear him returning fire. And then the headlights begin to rapidly retreat—"advancing to the rear," as my old captain used to say. Peavey can't see who he's shooting at, and takes the sensible course. I would have done the same thing.

Then the assailants are firing at us again and I feel Kyle's hand tugging mine.

"Come on, come on . . ." he keeps saying. He's pointing to the woods opposite the road.

"Can you move?" I call to Seth, and the three of us crash into the underbrush. It's thick and thorny, and it's dark, but the Mexicans have heard us and they're shooting at us again. They've taken up a defensive position behind our car, and they're relentless. They can't see us in the thicket, but enough sprays of bullets will eventually find a mark.

Kyle is tugging at me again. He says he can find his way back to the barn—set behind the old house where the reenactors are hiding—and we can take cover there. If, that is, the Mexicans haven't also taken up a position there.

We have a choice. We can wait for Peavey's backup, which will take no less than twenty, thirty minutes, or we can advance to the rear. Now I'm wishing I'd let Kyle keep his thumb-buster.

"How far to the barn?" I yank on Kyle's arm and he looks at me, his eyes huge in his head.

He says, "Fifteen minutes, if we run like hell."

Seth nods. He's been struck in the shoulder but he can keep up.

We move deeper into the trees, Kyle's white shirt showing a blur of pale in front of me, and soon we're running a narrow, cleared footpath. It's mid-September, but warm, with a ground-swell of dampness that smells like burnt oatmeal. There's also no breeze and the mosquitoes are swarming. I feel them boring into every bit of exposed flesh and remember Seth saying that Texas mosquitoes could stand flat-footed and fuck a turkey.

We keep moving at a good pace for about ten minutes until Seth's legs give out and he collapses, breathing hard on the ground.

I crouch down, looking back up the path, and in the distance I see a sweep of a flashlight through the trees.

"Shit." I haul Seth onto his feet again. I don't have to tell him that these guys don't give a rat's ass that we're cops.

"We're close," Kyle whispers, and we keep moving.

Another few minutes and we come upon a clearing; the hulk of what must be the barn on a slight rise about thirty yards away. There is no light coming from the barn, no sound. We could stay crouched where we are, but the path leads to us and we're too exposed.

"Well?" I ask Seth.

He takes both my arms and pulls himself up. "We can't stay here."

Crouching, we stagger for the barn across the exposed clearing and hear gunfire coming from behind us, the dull thunk of bullets throwing dirt clods around our feet. I see the barn door but have no idea if it's unlocked, or what's on the inside, and I'm thinking we're better off running for the far side of the building.

Suddenly, from inside the barn, I hear a rifle blast. It's coming from high up, like it's been fired from the roof. We cringe and throw ourselves flat, but from the blackness of the open loft door a man's wavering voice calls out to us, "Run . . . faster . . ."

Then someone in the barn begins firing off a pistol—shots that will prove to come from a LeMat black powder revolver. We scrabble up again, yank at the barn door, and throw ourselves inside. Kyle bolts the doors and we sit, blind and gasping.

For a moment it's total silence. I can't hear our defender up in the loft and so I call out, "Hey . . . hello? Dallas Police!"

"Move toward my voice," the man says. "Toward the ladder. It's safer up here."

We feel our way to the ladder, our eyes adjusting to the dark, and I see a man in a long coat standing in the shadows above me. I tell Kyle to go first, and then crawl up behind Seth, who has to make his way one-armed.

The man helps Kyle up and says, "Hey, boy. Good to see you're still alive." He then hoists Seth off the ladder and reaches down a hand for me. I can see now that he's an older man, in his eighties at least, gaunt and wearing a gray uniform with a lot of medals pinned to his chest. He's also wearing a sword.

Kyle says, "General, these two are the police."

The general gives me the once-over and says, "Uh-hum."

A forceful rattling at the barn door causes the general to draw and fire his pistol through the wood. The explosion is deafening but the rattling stops. I hear the word "putos" screamed in retreat.

The general says, "We're safe here. Unless they decide to burn us out." He tells us that we've entered through the back door of the barn; the front door is situated at the other end, facing the settlement house, which is several hundred feet away.

"You been here all day?" I ask.

The general has taken off his sash and balls it up, pressing it to Seth's bloody shoulder. "Yes. Until now they didn't know I was here. I figured the best offense was a good defense." He hands Seth a canteen. "Good thing they didn't think to check the back door."

"How many reenactors are in the settlement house?"

"Close to a dozen, maybe," he says. "A few are wounded, I think. They've been pinned down all day. Outgunned."

"How many attackers?" Seth asks.

"Three. It was down to one man watching the house with an automatic rifle." He turned an eye to me and sniffed. "Until you led the other two back here again."

"How do you know all this?"

"I'm old, ma'am, I'm not deaf. Those Mexicans have been making enough noise all day to wake the dead."

"Do you know what they're looking for?" I ask.

The general gets up and from under a pile of hay pulls out a red duffle bag. I open it and, holy crap, there must be a hundred thousand in cash, in neat, banded stacks.

"This is all my fault," Kyle whispers.

The general and I agree with him.

"There'll be more police here soon," I say reassuringly. "We just have to sit tight."

A fierce rattling commences at the front door, which is still, fortunately, bolted from the inside.

"We're going to burn you out, putos, if you don't come out now!" A pause and then, "You have one minute!"

I look at Seth and he shakes his head. He's in pain and still bleeding heavily. It's been nearly thirty minutes since we were attacked. Peavey's Cleburne police should be at the encampment soon. The question is, will it be within the one minute we have left before the barbecue?

The general hands Kyle his small sidearm, no doubt another cap-and-ball job, and says, "I'm thinking we have one Mexican at the front, and probably one at the back. I don't think we can make a run for it."

"Fuck it!" the voice outside yells. "We're just going to burn you out!"

The old man puts a hand on Kyle's shoulder. "Well, there's only one thing for it," he says. He walks to the hayloft door at the front of the barn and pitches his LeMat out onto the ground. He yells, "I'm unarmed now!"

"What are you doing?" I hiss.

"Yeah," the voice outside roars, "but you've got cops with you, and they're armed."

"I have what you want!" the general shouts. He turns to me and winks. "Ever heard of Stonewall Jackson?"

"What . . . ?"

"It's September 14 today," the general says gleefully. "Harpers Ferry. Remember?"

I don't remember, and as I'm ordering the general to move away from the open hayloft, he stands up, fully exposed to our attackers outside, one hand resting on a tall, bulky object covered with a canvas cloth. An object I'm assuming is a farm implement. He waves the red duffle bag aloft, pulling out a stack of cash. "You burn us, you burn the money too."

"How 'bout I just shoot you and come up and get the money. Or burn down the house over there, now we know you've got it!"

"Then my officer friends will have to shoot you." There is silence outside the barn and the general continues: "I'll make a deal with you. Give me your word you'll leave and I'll throw down your money."

The old man's got guts, I'll give him that.

"Listen," I whisper fiercely, "you throw that money down and we've lost our bargaining chip."

The general looks at me, the bag hugged to his chest, his face set, and I know I've lost all control or even influence on the outcome.

Crawling closer to the open loft, I dare a quick glance outward and yell down, "Take the deal! Cleburne police are on their way!"

That brings laughter. "Cleburne police. Shut up, bitch! Okay, throw down the money and we'll leave."

Without hesitation, the general heaves the bag with all the cash down into the clearing in front of the barn.

There are a few seconds of quiet and then I yell for the general to get down out of the line of fire because I know they're going to begin shooting at him at any moment. I crawl as quickly as I can away from the open loft, imagining we're going to have to run for it because, sure as shit, the Mexicans are going to flame the barn and try and shoot us as we come out.

The general slips the canvas off the bulky object—like a silken sheet falling off a bed—and it turns out that it's not a farm implement, as I had first thought. It's a cannon. And he's holding in one hand a long string lanyard attached to the barrel. He announces to us that one of the Mexicans is now approaching the duffle bag, gun drawn.

The general unsheathes his sword and declares to the open air, "When it's war, draw the sword and throw away the scabbard!" He bounces on the balls of his feet a few times. "I've always wanted to say that." He then turns to us and adds calmly, "Cover your ears."

He gives the lanyard a good yank and a shattering boom erupts, the explosive recoil sending the cannon careening backward where it plummets over the edge of the loft, crashing into the barn below.

The shooter with the assault rifle starts spraying the loft with bullets, sending wood planks, metal fragments, and strands of hay in all directions around our heads. And then his fire is drawn away from the barn and I realize there are now other shooters in the woods. It's the Cleburne police, and the two remaining Mexican gunmen are shot and killed within a few minutes of engagement. The third man, the gunman who went to retrieve the cash, has to be bagged in pieces. Evidently, a six-pound cannonball will do that.

By the end of the night three of the reenactors who were wounded by the attackers' gunfire had been taken by ambulance to Cleburne. All three recovered. As Kyle had feared, though, two from his group were found dead at the stream. Two other reenactors, both of them overweight smokers, suffered heart attacks during their ordeal, but they survived as well and as far as I know they're still staging Civil War battles outside of Dallas. They have also raised funds through exhibitions and bought themselves a brand-new cannon.

Soon after our Cleburne episode I looked up the battle at Harpers Ferry, West Virginia. It was one of Stonewall Jackson's most brilliant Civil War engagements: a tactical victory which was ensured by cannon hauled over mountains ranges, some of them during the dead of night, so that they could be fired at federal troops from high ground.

I still get Christmas cards every year from the general with quotes from Stonewall. The general's favorite? *My troops may fail to take a position, but are never driven from one.*

And Velasquez? He was not one of the Mexican nationals killed at the encampment. He's still operating in Texas. But then again, so am I.

Seth's shoulder healed quickly, and despite his being such a baby about the pain from the wound, I brought him ice cream every day when I was off duty. In between my baiting him about how tough I think ex–football players are supposed to be, and his baiting me about my ugly shoes, we talked about the Cleburne case and about life being stranger than fiction, filled with cosmic collaborations.

He remembered that someone once said that Thanksgiving dinners take eighteen hours to prepare but are consumed in only twelve minutes. Halftimes at football games are twelve minutes. Coincidence? He thought not.

I didn't have the heart to tell him that he was quoting Erma Bombeck.

By the way, Erma's birthday and mine are on the same day.

Coincidence? I think not.

BIG THINGS HAPPENING HERE

BY DAVID HAYNES

Oak Lawn

The first words she spoke to me were to ask what I had seen. Her voice resonated with a practiced nonchalance, not quite masking an equally practiced aggressive undertone. She spoke like a woman who knew that the hourglass was almost empty and the witch was already at the door—and yet with a solid hint, feigned or otherwise, of warmth and openness. She had greeted us at the door of the rec center and hugged Cooper as if she were a long-lost aunt, the brightness of his eyes shining in contrast to the darkness of hers. Confident that I would verify what she already knew to be true, she reached toward me in that moment and placed her hand gently on my crossed arms. The soft warmth of that hand put the lie to what appeared to be gnarled roughness. Just that easily the words spilled from my mouth.

I told her how Cooper and I had headed out for supper at one of those ubiquitous strips of chain restaurants for which our city is universally famous. Brick cubes tricked out as haciendas, Tuscan villas, Caribbean patios; neon lights and interchangeable fiberglass roofs. We are ambivalent about cuisine, and our plan, as usual, had been the crapshoot of the shortest line. Ahead, midblock on the side street where we parked, the door to a bungalow flew open and three men in dark suits dragged a pair of scraggly young dudes from the house and out toward a white van. Another dark-suited man stepped from the vehicle and covered the captives' heads with what appeared to be pillowcases. They were tossed like last week's laundry into the back of the white van, which lurched from the curb, turned onto the main drag, and headed north toward the freeway.

For the record, we do not reside in a third world backwater, lorded over by corrupt oligarchs and soldiers on the take. This is a major American metropolis in a large Southern-tier state. Freeway flyovers loop our downtown, where glass and steel boxes point toward the sky. It is the nature of this story that I cannot tell you the name of our city, but you would know it by sight and reputation. People have been killed here—famous ones—and the syncopated country/disco rhythms of its theme song may be echoing in your head at this very moment.

The woman—the kind woman with the soft, gnarled, mahogany-colored hands—nodded when I told her what we witnessed on that day. The nod communicated that she knew just what I was talking about: she *understood*. A barely perceptible gesture, that nod, accompanied by a modest swipe of teeth at her full lower lip. It was an expression with which a funeral director might reassure the young widow that he has seen plenty of women with smeared mascara and red-rimmed eyes. Apologies were unnecessary. *You are among friends*, the woman seemed to be saying to me, and for whatever reason I felt like it was true.

It is my nature to be suspicious of moments like this. Sincerity is often ironic, I find, and moments of even marginal mysticism send my eyes rolling and set off in my head the cliché horror-movie soundtrack with the screeching violins. But the world has turned (or so we are told); the old rules have changed, and all bets are off. These are post-ironic times. And so I, with Cooper at my side, accepted her fellowship alongside a cup of watered-down coffee, and followed the warm and sincere and earnest woman to a cluster of open chairs set to one side of an air-conditioned community center in an obscure corner of our fair city. The meeting was about to begin.

What I had not told the woman was that I doubted my own truth; that even still I test the reality of it in my head, continuing to create alternative explanations for the abductions. Coop and I sat on that side street for what felt like twenty minutes, looking at the place where just moments before we had seen two young men snatched from their home. And wouldn't we all like to imagine ourselves doing the right things in this moment—the things that Cooper and I neglected to do: scratching down license plate numbers and details about hair color and clothing. Dialing 911. We replayed it in our heads, again and again: the wresting from the door, the high-pitched squeal from the curb. Eventually I reached for my phone, but Cooper grabbed my hand and pressed it into my lap.

"It's starting," he said to me, and collapsed into a hysterical fit, his open-palmed hand slapping his ghostly shaved head. His torso beat back and forth to a silent rhythm heard only by him. "Oh, man," he said, over and over. The good people of the central city continued with their usual business of deadheading petunias and walking their dogs. A golden retriever sniffed casually at a burgundy-colored stain. Beside me my best friend quivered and rocked and disintegrated and moaned.

I got him home and got him inside, but he could not stop pacing and mumbling to himself. Eventually he collapsed on his bed into some sort of trembling sleep state. I went into the living room and watched the local news on every channel, waiting for a mention of missing persons from somewhere around here—which never came.

Later that night, Coop wandered in and lowered himself stiffly onto the couch. "You're surprised by this?" he asked, but it wasn't really a question. His voice had been enervated with the same deadened but still punctuated edge as late-night callers to AM radio stations. He began chain-smoking, as he would do whenever he got into one of his states. "I keep telling you about shit, but you never believe me."

The blue glow from the television was the only light in the room and I could hear Cooper's raspy draws on the cigarette and the exhalations of smoke. He had always been subject to fits of melancholy and had told me lots of stories over the years—about military-created mosquito-borne viruses that killed only birds and people; about a laboratory not far from where he spent his days processing insurance claims and I taught AP English, where a team of scientists sequestered and trained a group of superintelligent young children. He'd been drawn to such nonsense since our college days. I had been ignoring such bull for the better part of a decade.

"You see for yourself now," he chided, aligning me in that moment with those like himself who have known such things long going. And then he said that he wanted me to come . . . *somewhere* with him, that there were some people I needed to meet. There'd be a woman there, he insisted, who would be someone I should hear.

"She knows things," he assured me. "She knows."

It calmed him that I agreed to tag along, and thus the following evening, there we were: Cooper, me, the woman with the hands. A dozen or so others, as well. A ring of beige metal folding chairs circling us together. Next to me, I felt the calm poise of the woman. Upright she sat, her straight spine standing away from the chair, but in a natural and not uncomfortable way. You wouldn't know that she breathed at all. According to her introduction, she was *not* the leader of this group, but it was obvious that she owned this room and that these were her people.

Before she said another word, I felt the need to speak with her privately. At the first break I implored her to join me for coffee—soon, if she would. She agreed.

The woman (I will not say her name) wore a hand-crocheted vest over a purple turtleneck. Apparently people still crochet. This sort of woman—the kind who hang around the public library, women with recycling bins, these Whole Foods types—my interactions with them had been limited at best. She seemed like the type who would be a quirky friend of my mother's, someone with whom she might get together now and again to do the holiday baking or study Bible verses.

There, that night, in the circle of beige chairs, I felt myself oddly attracted to her, someone not remotely my type. She was older than me (though that has never been a criterion). She was heavy: not fat, but solid, and it looked good on her; still, we must have seemed a Laurel and Hardy match, the two times we would have been observed together in public, me being whichever comedy star was the lanky one.

An older guy, one of those university types, all gray beard and serious-looking spectacles, called us to order and insisted that we knew why we were there. Cooper and the woman moved their heads in grave concurrence. The woman radiated heat, pleasant in that cold community center classroom. I remember leaning into her as the storytelling began.

When it was my turn she caressed my fingers and nodded toward the group. "Tell them," she said, but Cooper interrupted, offering his own version, which was essentially the same as mine, if ever so slightly more turgid and ominous. If any in the group were surprised, you'd not have guessed from their body language; the vague movements of heads and quietly clicked tongues—the low-energy response of people busy accumulating a bit more evidence for a case that to them has long been closed.

"The things people don't know," said another woman, in one of those blue power suits that your lawyer-types wear, ready to take her turn. She stared at her feet the entire time she spoke. She sounded like a parent telling a child that the dog has died.

She said that because of the work she did, "certain information" crossed her desk on a regular basis.

"Large sums of money are moving," she whispered. And then she added, "They think I don't get it. They think that I'm too stupid to understand their codes. They think we're all stupid."

Next to me, the woman with the hands smirked; on the other side, Cooper shivered violently.

The woman suggested a meal instead of coffee, so we went to a vegetarian place she said she liked over in the gayborhood. It's an old bungalow painted in psychedelic graffiti, and all the food is yellow and orange with sprinkles of green. Some guy who acted like the owner nodded at the woman—she was clearly a regular—and showed us to our seats.

"There are good people out here still," she said, almost in a whisper. She told me it was important to remember that. She ordered tea for us, and then soft pureed foods to be picked up with tasteless gray triangles of pita.

She told me this about herself: "My father taught high school biology. In the summer he drove the ice-cream truck and his route sometimes took him deep into the city where we lived. It broke his heart when the children didn't have a quarter for the Dreamsicles and Bomb Pops he sold, and sometimes he would just give them away."

We ate our mildly seasoned foods, spices so delicate as to be imperceptible. We talked about the weather. Later, after dinner, she insisted I drop her at a corner in a part of the city riddled with struggling clubs and galleries and the sorts of goth girls who seemed to only exist within these few blocks. I asked to see her to her door, but she dismissed me with a wave. I watched her walk briskly into an alley between two buildings.

Cooper had begun to keep a bag packed by the front door of the apartment for some reason, and one day I stumbled over it as I entered. I cursed him and his damn suitcase while a stack of spiritless sophomore essays scattered to the floor.

"What the hell's this for?" I asked him.

"It's because you never know anymore. And it's because whenever it comes—whatever it is—I'm going to be ready to go."

I scoffed, as I always would when teasing him, and I assured him that I didn't think anything would be happening on this fine spring afternoon. I suggested we screw the damn papers and whatever the hell was going on with the world and head out for a drink or two.

He made some snide comment about fiddling in Rome. It had a sardonic and ugly tone to it. But even on the last day of the planet, he'll be one you can count on to bend an elbow with you, so he rallied and we walked toward the bars in the trendiest part of town.

"Go to work today?" I asked as we headed past the ranks of new townhomes and boutiques that lined what had once been ghetto streets. I'd been asking this with increasing frequency, and Cooper would always shrug, as he did now. It was a glorious afternoon, and everyone in town had had the same idea, and the streets were full of the young and rich and thin.

We settled into a banquette at an obnoxiously trendy joint that was all velvet and chrome; our regular place—a low-key sports bar—had been shuttered, as had several other places up and down the block. Times were hard in the late '00s: my school had had layoffs too, and more than a few folks had thrown in the towel and just walked away. The rest of us did what we could do, picking up a class during our preps and subbing at after-school activities.

The server dropped off our cocktails and I pressed again at the question of how he'd spent his day.

"What's the point? What's the point of any of it?" he mumbled.

"Oh, I don't know. Keeps us in the hooch, I guess," and I raised my Collins glass in his direction, a half-assed toast. Cooper was always one for self-pity, but he was also an easy mark for the cheering up, and I got something of a smile out of him.

"I got sick days," he rasped, but I couldn't tell if this was an extension of my lame joke or simply an explanation of his idleness as of late.

I fought a strong impulse to mention the fact that our lives, for the most part, continued on their normal trajectory, that we had not been witness to other abductions or subject to mayhem of any kind. Don't get me wrong: this is a big city and any given day finds its share of tragic accidents and random violence with a few odd disappearances thrown in for the good of the order. You develop a thick skin or you leave, and I'd always assumed Cooper had one. But witnessing that . . . abduction had broken him. I fought the impulse to bring it up; any mention of the subject—or of the group meetings or of the suitcase—tended to end poorly.

I asked instead if he wanted to head out to the IMAX after supper, and he said it sounded good to him.

Up at the bar, paying our tab, the TV blared as it always seems to in such places. On the twenty-four-hour news channel, a woman much like the blue-suited woman back at the recreation center interrupted the host's question and looked directly into the camera. "I'm going to say this while I've got the chance. There are things going on . . ." she began, but they cut to a commercial for expensive dog food. I tried to drag him away, but Cooper insisted on seeing the rest of the interview. Back on the screen, a famous football player had taken the lady's seat. Cooper went into the bathroom and vomited into the sink.

I did not return to the "support group," and I told Cooper that I thought it did him no good to hang out with those people. He froze me out after that; the most he offered me was a barely companionable grunt when we passed in the center of the apartment.

I ran into the woman with the gnarled mahogany hands in the produce aisle of a health food store and I found myself happy to see her again. She agreed to let me buy her a smoothie.

We took our drinks to the patio and I chatted with her as if she were an old friend—rather than an odd acquaintance who happened to share the same conspiracy-oriented imagination as my roommate. Still, I felt drawn to talk to her again, and found something soothing about sitting there under the trellises with her.

She asked me about my work and I wondered if she was from here, or, if not, what had brought her to the city.

She'd come in the wake of a corporate giant—"I used to live that life, you know"—where she'd done various kinds of public relations and advertising. She sang a jingle for a consumer staple that she claimed to have a hand in, a song I remembered from early childhood—from the *Transformers* days—and I realized she must be even older than I'd first guessed.

I still found her appealing, in a way somehow not quite sexual. I wanted to be her . . . friend. She made me comfortable in some way.

"These corporations," she said, "they're their own little kingdoms, with their own cultures, their own ethics, their own everything. We had a song we would sing every Friday morning, at ten o'clock sharp. At your desk, at the coffee cart, sitting on the toilet: it didn't matter. The clock struck ten and you stopped what you were doing and sang. It's all about making you feel part of it. One big happy family, and all that garbage. You reach a point and you realize that there is no *there* there. If you're smart, that is. Much like your job, I imagine." With her index finger she tapped at a bead of sweat on her plastic cup as she spoke, releasing a waterfall of condensation to the patio table.

"What are you doing these days?" I asked.

"This."

That was her reply, said as flatly and as matter-of-fact as could be imagined, and while clearly "this" had not meant to indicate idylls on the veranda of a grocery store, there was zero ounce of irony in her voice. I waited for her to say more; but she simply drew on the straw and I watched the tube of peach-colored liquid reach her lips.

"Your turn," she prompted with that same flat tone.

I told her about life in a twenty-first-century high school and how despite all the tests and paperwork and budgetary constraints, the kids were the thing: they were what kept you coming back every day. I told her about a few of my seniors—Tasha, Ramon, Zeke, Kiana—and how hard they were working to get ready for college in the fall. They were great kids, I told her, and I tried to make it clear that my enthusiasm was sincere—which it was.

"They've got great things in store for us, this crew," I told her. "This next generation. They're going to change the world."

I mistook her warm smile as approval of my hard work teaching the city's youth.

Instead she said: "I wasn't sure before, but I'm now pretty sure you are just some kind of a fool."

Around us on the patio shoppers munched on their kale casseroles and organic quesadillas, not noticing, I hoped, the taken-aback look on my face.

What exactly had I done to deserve her reproach? And how the hell was I supposed to respond?

I opened my mouth to speak, but she put up her hand to silence me.

"The complacent burn in the same circle as the complicit," she said. "I've got little time for either."

She glared at something over my shoulder, and before I could tell her what she and her ersatz Dante could do to each other, she rose and pulled me up by the arm and demanded I accompany her to the dry-goods bins.

"Don't turn around," she whispered. "Look like we're together."

In the store she peeled open a plastic bag and began purposefully scraping through a bin of dried cranberries.

I inclined my head toward her ear and implored an explanation.

"You *know*. Don't be stupid." She scooped up oats and hominy and a small cluster of dried apricots. Dutifully she wrote the bin numbers on the strips of paper twist ties and lined them up on the counter. Then she stealthily slipped the last of the ties into my pocket.

"I'll . . . I'm . . . Look, if that gentleman in the madras shirt follows me down the aisle, you know what to do."

She strode quickly toward the meat department, turned the corner, and was gone. That was the last time I saw her.

For a few long minutes I waited there with the food, but I knew she wasn't coming back. The man in the madras shirt bagged up coffee and a selection of dried nuts. He seemed more interested, frankly, in the dried lentils than in me or in whomever I'd been standing with moments earlier. I felt badly about the abandoned dry goods, so I loaded them into my arms and purchased them myself. I don't even like apricots.

I texted some friends to meet me over by the college for pitchers, and we ended up closing the place down for the night.

A few weeks later, cleaning out the change tray, I came across the twist tie, which I'd forgotten she'd slipped me. On the back she'd inscribed nine numbers. One short of a phone number, but I dialed it anyway, trying a few logical digits up front to round it out. "*The number you have dialed . . .*" was the only answer I ever got.

Cooper by this point stayed mostly holed up in his room,

but he would emerge now and then for a glass of water or some crackers. I stopped him that evening, and I realized I'd not seen him at all in many, many days.

"You look terrible, dude. Really terrible."

"Huh?" I'd been perhaps his only human contact for weeks. He seemed to have forgotten how the conversation thing works.

"Say, take a look at this." I handed him the strip.

He looked at it, alarmed.

"I thought you'd be interested. That woman gave it to me. You know, the one from the rec center."

He burbled a bit, like someone with too much liquid in his mouth. "Oh God!" he cried. "God Almighty! Oh my God!" And he collapsed against me.

There was almost nothing to him anymore. Holding him up, I could feel the ribs and elbows piercing through his skin.

The next morning, I acted—did what I ought to have done months earlier. I called his parents, who came that afternoon and fetched him home to the small city in the piney woods where he'd grown up.

For a while there, I would call to check on him. Daily for a while, then days turned into weeks, and so on. The last time I called, it was the "*the number you have reached*" woman again. The Coopers had lived in that town their whole lives. I can't imagine what happened to them.

As for me, I press on with life here in the city—and an odd enough place it is, this *metroplex*. The South, but not really the South; the West, but only sort of. A little bit of everything mixed in, which produces a quirky personality all its own. There are plenty worse places in the world.

Which has not come to an end, at least not yet. There are rooms full of people out there who are expecting it to, soon, at any moment, tomorrow, this afternoon—but the thing is, if you don't know those people you don't ever give it a thought. Which is a good thing, right?

I remain optimistic, then, despite the city's craziness. I teach the kids, who continue to amaze me. I hang out with friends, do the dating thing when the spirit strikes. I am determined to stay in this game, to see it out to the end, whatever and whenever that might be.

There have been no more abductions.

And yet, sometimes I, too, find myself collapsing a bit on the inside, when the noise gets a little too much—when another mother kills her own children, when another bank fails, when another tornado scrapes a town off the prairie—and I find myself, like Cooper, plastered to this couch, exhausted by the thought of it all.

Still, I push through. I like my life here and, as I said, all and all, it isn't so bad when you run the numbers.

So I sit tight. I am resolved, fixed, stolid, and mostly a very satisfied person. Unable to imagine where I might even go that wouldn't be here.

THE STICKUP GIRL

BY HARRY HUNSICKER

South Dallas

I 'm a bandit.

Hands up, sucker, and give me all your money.

A gun and a mask, getaway cars, the whole enchilada.

Call it a family thing, if you want.

My name is Nadine Parker.

I'm twenty-seven years old and the great-great-grandniece of Bonnie Parker. You know, like Bonnie & Clyde?

I used to be a stripper, along with my twin sister Chloe.

Before that I was the night clerk at a twenty-four-hour Stop & Shop on Singleton Boulevard in West Dallas, down the street from the site of Clyde Barrow's family's service station and not too far from where my great-great-aunt grew up.

Now Chloe and I rob places, which, occupational hazards aside, is a lot more fun than dancing. Not always as lucrative but sometimes you gotta make sacrifices for quality of life.

We mostly hit liquors stores, bars, and gas stations, with the occasional fast food joint. I handle the weaponry and the actual stickups; my sister drives.

Speaking of weapons, a gun is a hell of a piece of equipment. Much more than just the bang-bang-you're-dead stuff you see on TV. There's that, of course, but the real juice comes on the other end, the butterflies-in-your stomach feeling of dominance for whoever's grabbing the handle.

That's the part I like, the control that the gun gives me, especially when I'm telling some gold-chain-wearing, convenience-store-working dude to hand over all the cash or I'm gonna pop a cap in his skinny ass.

See, me and Chloe have never had a lot of control in our lives.

First there was Mama with her gambling after Daddy died in the Gulf War in '91. Then there were all those low-life boyfriends of Mama's groping after us as we got older.

All of which was accompanied by a steady downgrade in our living arrangements: the snug two-bedroom cottage with the porch swing replaced by a double-wide near the Goodwill store, followed by a HUD-voucher apartment on Westmoreland, a couple of streets over from the crack houses, the only gringo family for blocks around.

So the guns and the robbing, that gives us a little control.

But not when someone gets shot.

Chloe and I are in our hideout du jour, a motel on Fort Worth Avenue, next to a lube-and-tune shop and a used-tire store.

My sister's lying on top of the covers, and she's in a bad way.

I ease back the bloody bandage from her abdomen. She doesn't open her eyes this time, doesn't grimace in pain. Her breath comes in shallow gasps. Her skin is unhealthy-looking, gray like storm clouds rolling in from Oklahoma.

At least the wound has stopped bleeding.

It's a puckered, ugly little hole a few inches to one side of her navel. The room smells like blood and sweat and human waste.

I mop her forehead with a damp washcloth. Tears well in my eyes.

She's the only family I've got left. Nothing to my name but the three thousand dollars in cash in the closet, the results of our last two months' activities.

I turn the television to the Oprah channel, volume low, and place the remote on the bedside table by a cell phone and a bottle of water.

A feeling of being out of control washes over me, and I realize the danger that comes from this sensation.

I kiss my sister on the forehead—her skin is hot—and walk
to the door. I know where I have to go, and the thought fills me
with dread.

This morning I decided we should rob my second ex-husband,
and that's what started all this.

I actually like Daryl, despite him being an ex and all.

Maybe it's because he actually fessed up about getting chla-
mydia from that waitress at Sizzler, giving me a chance to get on
antibiotics before the STD kicked in full force. Or it could be
because he only slapped me around at the end of our marriage,
and then just a little bit, like his heart wasn't in it.

Or maybe it's because he's not real bright, and I feel sorry
for him.

Hard to say. Emotions are funny things.

Probably the last one. Daryl is—no fooling here—as dumb as
a carton of hair. He believes snow is frozen sand and that fish get
into stock tanks by rain. He thinks Christmas is a celebration of
Santa rising from the dead with his army of zombie elves.

Six months after our split, and Daryl is still assistant manager at Big Odelle's Pawn, Stereo, and Latino Music Store on
Jefferson Boulevard in South Dallas. He still wears short-sleeved
polyester dress shirts, clip-on ties, and a Joe Dirt–style mullet.

At the moment of our glorious reunion, Daryl's polyester-
clad armpits are sweating dark moons as he holds his hands high,
arms shaking, fingers splayed.

There's nobody in the store but the two of us.

I aim the Smith & Wesson 9mm at the name tag clipped to
his breast pocket, my face hidden by a bandanna. Adrenaline
sharpens my senses, makes everything tight and clear.

"P-p-p-please, don't sh-sh-sh-hoot me." Daryl's face turns

pale. His skin color matches the shapeless jumpsuit that hides my figure, a svelte outline he might recognize. To complete the bandit ensemble, I'm also wearing knock-off Wayfarer sunglasses and a frizzy wig, bright red like the color of fresh apples.

"Give me all the money." I alter my voice, throat gravelly.

A glass display case separates us. It's greasy and scratched, contains only three or four car stereos, two fake Rolexes, and a half-dozen radar detectors, most of which are probably stolen.

Daryl gulps, no clue that the robber in front of him used to be his wife. I feel a moment of pity for him. Poor guy's so dumb he doesn't know the difference between his ass and fried chicken.

"And the money in the TV." I point the 9mm at a thirty-year-old set on the back shelf.

Big Odelle, Daryl's boss, runs a betting operation on the side. He keeps the cash from the bookie business in an elderly Magnavox that nobody would ever think of stealing.

Daryl's jaw drops, his hands lower a few inches. Nobody's supposed to know about the money in the TV. The dipwad has obviously forgotten that he told his ex-wife. He shakes his head slowly like that's going to stop me.

The Smith & Wesson is not a Dirty Harry cannon, but it's big enough to make an impression. In the quiet of Big Odelle's shop, it's pretty darned loud when I fire a round. The bullet tears into the wall of CDs on one side of the room.

The power of the weapon, the slap of recoil against my palm, fills my stomach with warmth, makes my thighs tingle.

Clear plastic cases and silvery shards of compact discs scatter everywhere.

Daryl cringes.

Early afternoon on a humid, overcast June day. The light streaming in the front windows makes the linoleum floor look extra dirty. The air smells like dust, gun smoke, and fear-sweat wafting off Daryl's armpits.

He begins to blubber. Tears stream down his cheeks.

This infuriates me. It's not the display of weakness or the terror etched across his face.

It's the visible signs of emotion that make me shiver with anger, remembering the times I wanted to see any expression of feeling from this mullet-haired dimwit, a display of some concept above his hunger or perpetual horniness.

My arms throb with rage.

He senses my fury, rushes to the cash register, scoops up a handful of bills, a hundred bucks or so. From the Magnavox, he removes a thick stack of currency. He shoves everything into the empty McDonald's sack I gave him a few seconds before.

"D-d-don't hurt me. Please." He tosses the sack on the counter. "I got a wife at home."

I grab the sack with my free hand, ponder this new morsel of info.

"What's her name?"

Daryl blinks several times but doesn't say anything.

"Your wife." My words are icy. "What's her name?"

Silence in the store. Chloe is waiting in the side lot in a stolen El Camino. Outside, a car with glass-pack mufflers rumbles by. A heavy bassline from some Mexican rap song rattles the windows.

"I, um, don't know." He licks his lips. The expression on his face is a weasel-caught-in-headlights.

Neither of us speak. The situation is evident: dumb people shouldn't try to lie.

"J-J-Jenny." Daryl wipes his nose with the back of one hand. "That's her name."

Jenny, the waitress from Sizzler.

Anger runs white hot in my veins. I aim the 9mm at his nose. Cock the hammer. The sound of the weapon preparing to fire, metal scraping on metal, is sharp against the hard surfaces of the pawn shop, almost as loud as the shot a few seconds before.

"P-p-please." Daryl cowers. His face is red, cheeks damp from tears. A dark splotch forms on the crotch of his pants.

Then, like a plug's been pulled, the anger inside me drains away, replaced by sadness and disgust and a churning stomach full of should-have-beens, the story of my life.

I lower the gun and leave Big Odelle's.

Jefferson Boulevard used to be the main commercial street of Oak Cliff, a small town just south of downtown Dallas, across the Trinity River. After Oak Cliff got swallowed up by Dallas in the 1950s, Jefferson fell on hard times. Boarded-up storefronts, junkies in the alleys, hookers on the curbs.

Now Jefferson Boulevard looks like Guadalajara during the piñata festival with a little Austin hipster neighborhood thrown in the mix. Lots of signs in Spanish, taco joints. About a zillion Mexican bridal shops and stores specializing in quinceañera dresses.

They're waiting for me when I get to the parking lot. I round the corner of the building, stuffing the wig in my pocket.

By our stolen El Camino stand two gangbangers in white T-shirts and calf-length shorts, La Eme—Mexican Mafia—tats on their faces.

Chloe is against the door. Her hands are up.

Gangbanger One has a knife against to her neck.

"Yo, bitch." Gangbanger Two smiles at me. "What's in the Mickey D's bag?"

I tuck the money under one arm. My right hand stays in my pocket, the 9mm in a tight grip. A robber getting robbed. Didn't I just see this on an episode of *Law & Order?*

Chloe whimpers, eyes wild with terror.

I try to control my fear, the racing heartbeat and ragged breathing.

Here's a couple of facts that are important to know at this

point. Number one: Chloe is not cut out of for a life of crime, hence her role as a driver. Chloe is weak. I'm not saying this as an insult, just as a way things are. When the stepdads were coming into our room late at night, she didn't handle it very well. Moi? I handled that and everything else life threw my way. That's why I'm working the trigger on all our jobs.

Speaking of guns, here's the second important fact: I've never shot anybody. Nearly two dozen armed robberies so far and the most I've ever done is pop a cap into a wall of Mexican conjunto CDs. And that only happened about thirty seconds ago.

"Show me the bag." Gangbanger One presses his knife against Chloe's throat.

I squeeze the Smith & Wesson, start to ease it out of my pocket.

Sweat drips down the small of my back.

The control is slipping away.

I wonder if I can actually pull the trigger on another human being.

The parking lot is small and secluded, empty.

My vision gets blurry and then clear, everything looking like it's been magnified. Sounds are different too. I can hear Chloe's terror as much as see it, the crackle of her lungs, the pinpricks of sweat that erupt noisily on her skin. I grip the gun tighter.

Gangbanger One's feet crunch on the broken asphalt as he moves toward me.

Then, there is nothing.

Blackness.

My limbs are heavy, skin cold.

The palm of my right hand stings as the stench of Aqua Velva fills my nose, the aftershave one of my stepdads used to wear.

Chloe's face is pale.

She's in the passenger seat of the El Camino. I'm driving and I don't remember how that came to be.

I speed down the alley behind Big Odelle's.

At the cross street, I stop and close my eyes for a moment.

In my mind I see the two gangbangers lying on the dirty asphalt, blood pooling underneath their bodies.

My ears ring, and I can now smell burnt gunpowder.

Then I remember the rest of it, the first shot that I fired, the one that missed its intended target.

I look over at Chloe.

She smiles weakly and presses the rag against the wound in her stomach.

I start to cry.

She shushes me, pats my arm with her free hand.

"It's okay, Nadine. Just drive."

We're back at the motel.

The bleeding has stopped. Chloe's face is pale but she appears to be stable.

I offer again for the twentieth time to take her to the hospital. She reminds me again about gunshot wounds and the police and our rather colorful arrest record.

We knew this was a possibility but chose never to dwell on it.

Truth be told, neither of us wants to grow old doing armed robberies. It's not a healthy, long-term plan. Look at what happened to our great-great-aunt.

We do have a goal though—make enough cash, then skip town. Head to Alaska where land is cheap and the men are grateful for female companionship, especially when it's supplied by two blond girls from Texas.

I count the money in the McDonald's bag. One thousand and five dollars.

That's the biggest haul to date, bringing our total nest egg to just over three thousand.

Only one problem. That's not enough cash to finance a getaway to the Great North. We need a whole lot more, ten grand at least. And now we need a doctor who's not too particular about filling out paperwork.

There's only one option and this makes my skin clammy.

My first husband, Quint. A crooked ex-cop I married when I was nineteen.

I shudder just thinking his name. In a town full of hustlers and whackjobs, Quint is in a class by himself. He's evil and twisted, dangerous like a sleeping snake.

"Quint." I whisper the word.

"No." Chloe shakes her head. "You can't do that."

"A hundred thousand. That's how much he carries in the trunk of his car."

Chloe doesn't reply.

A hundred K, give or take, tucked under the spare tire of his Caddy. Then there's the cash in his safe, much more than what he keeps in the car.

"We need to get out of town," I say. "The five-oh is gonna be looking for us hard. And you need a doctor."

Chloe stares at me, a blank look on her face.

"Quint has doctors. People that owe him."

She shakes her head.

"He'll be glad to see me. I'll flash him a little leg, get the name of a doc."

"No, Nadine." She licks her lips. "You can't."

"Then I'll lift his car keys . . . or something." I shrug. "What's the problem?

Chloe knows all too well what the problem is. We're sisters after all, twins. She was there when the marriage ended, helped me put the pieces of my life back together. Helped heal my wounds, both mental and physical.

She shakes her head. "Not Quint."

I stare at the far wall. "We don't really have a choice."

* * *

I'm dirty, coated with dried sweat and Jefferson Boulevard grime.

If I'm gonna charm my way with Quint, I'd better get clean, presentable.

After making sure Chloe is okay for the moment, I go to the bathroom and take a quick shower, scrubbing away the sweat and funk from the robbery of Big Odelle's.

Then I get out, wrap myself in a threadbare towel, and peer at my face in the steamy mirror. After a few moments, I tug at the towel and let it drop to the floor.

The goods are still looking good.

Time goes by.

The steam dissipates and I'm still gazing at my naked self in the mirror, my thoughts empty.

This is not the first time I've done the stare-at-the-mirror routine. Doesn't happen very often or with any warning. It's a sudden thing, like an earthquake no one can sense but me.

I try to figure out what I'm feeling but I can't. Everything's jumbled up inside. I've watched enough *Dr. Phil* to realize I'm searching for an emotion, but I don't know what it is or even how to articulate what it might be.

All I know is there's a coldness inside me that makes no sense.

Another slice of time passes. Snippets of my life drift past on the movie screen in my head.

The stepfather with the bum leg, whose breath stunk of bourbon. That black girl at juvie hall who stole my sneakers.

At the end of the reel, there's a child about ten who's overcome with pain and rage and then more pain. She looks like me but is different somehow.

The AC in the motel room clicks on, a humming noise.

I blink, shiver with cold, wonder what's inside me. A list of possibilities forms in my mind.

Anger at what this body has caused.

Shame at what I've done.

Sadness over what's been done to me.

Some combination of all of the above that no amount of showering will ever wash away.

After a while I break free from the empty place and rummage through a bag of makeup until I find the small bottle of Clinique base tucked in a corner.

The scars are tiny, caused by cigarettes, Winston Lights, if you must know. Over the years, they've almost disappeared. Almost.

I dab a little on the two worst ones, rubbing in a circular motion, hiding the tiny ripples in what is otherwise smooth, flawless flesh.

Then I get dressed and check on Chloe.

She's in a bad way.

A quarter of an hour later the El Camino rattles into the lot in front of a one-story brick building not far from Central Expressway. I park next to a ten-year-old Cadillac, Quint's car.

A few blocks away, there are shiny high-rise offices and nice stores. But here, in the shadowlands of the city, the structures are old and worn. The homes are clapboard, unpainted. The vehicles, battered.

The brick building has blacked-out windows with iron bars, tiny cameras mounted under the eaves. It sits between a Popeye's fried chicken and a place where you can sell your blood for cash.

I get out, pause for a moment so the cameras can get a good look at me. It's not smart to surprise Quint's people.

The front of the building is a legitimate business, a small insurance agency that specializes in monthly auto policies. The front usually has a handful of people working on computers, talking on the phone, selling policies. Sitting to one side of the office workers, on a lumpy leather sofa, will be two heavyset men in tracksuits, armed. They'll be drinking coffee, playing gin, and watching the monitors that show the parking lot.

I should be afraid of walking inside this building, but I'm not. The bullet wound in Chloe's stomach has seen to that. I would, and am about to, do anything to save my sister.

I push open the heavy wooden door. Overhead, a bell clangs.

The front room is empty. The cheap metal desks where the insurance agents sit are vacant.

No one is on the lumpy sofa. A deck of cards lies neatly stacked on the coffee table by two Styrofoam cups.

I step inside, walk past the receptionist desk.

The monitors are mounted on the wall a few feet from the door. They're visible now. They show the main and rear parking lots, empty except for the El Camino and the Caddy by the front door. It's midmorning, a Tuesday. There should be people working, the guards nearby. Maybe the insurance people went to get coffee and Quint is somewhere with his goon squad.

A single door on the back wall leads to the inner sanctum, a large office where Quint runs his operation. The office is wood-paneled with a safe behind the desk and a series of televisions mounted where he can monitor various sporting events.

I stand at the entrance to the office and do the stupidest thing I've ever done. I grab the 9mm from my waistband and push open the door, stepping inside.

The weapon feels comforting in my hand.

A heavy odor of coffee and cigarettes fills the inner sanctum.

Quint is in his late thirties now, a good-looking man, which is how I got into trouble with him in the first place.

He sits with his back to the door in an oversized leather desk chair, watching a soccer game on the television mounted over his safe.

He doesn't move or acknowledge my presence. A power play, typical Quint.

The choice presents itself like a blinding flash of light. I can kill him, shoot the bastard in the back of the head. Revenge is a tasty drug. Every wrong can be righted, every scrap of damage he's inflicted, healed.

But revenge won't get a doctor for Chloe.

For a moment, I don't care. I aim the 9mm at the back of his head, hand trembling.

The son of a bitch doesn't move, supreme in his confidence.

I tighten my finger on the trigger, my breath ragged, chest heaving. The sights line up on the top of his skull, just visible above the back of the chair.

Then I lower the gun.

"Quint." Emotion chokes my voice. "It's me, Nadine." A long pause. "I need your help."

He grunts but doesn't speak, another power play. It's all about control with Quint.

"My sister. She's been hurt, bad. I need a doctor."

He doesn't reply, intent on the TV. One of the soccer teams scores a goal, and the crowd cheers.

"Please, Quint."

He doesn't say anything.

"I-I-I need you." The words come from my mouth haltingly. "I, uh, I miss you."

Sadly, that's the truth. I do miss him. Even during the bad times, and there were plenty, he represented safety. And safety, much like power, is sexy.

I hate myself for admitting this, even in the privacy of my own thoughts.

"What do you want me to say, Quint?" I walk toward him. "That I was wrong for leaving you? That I want you back?"

No reply.

"Well, I was." I reach for his shoulder. "I shouldn't have left."

Quint's wearing a black guayabera shirt, short sleeve, like a waiter at a Mexican restaurant.

I grab his arm and pull. The chair turns but he doesn't, no reaction whatsoever.

The color of the fabric makes it hard to see the blood, but there's no mistaking the bullet hole about six inches directly below his throat.

He's not dead but real near to it. His eyes are open but unseeing, tiny slits. He grunts again. A bubble of blood forms on his lips.

I gasp, jump away, hit a box fan sitting on a side table. Drop the 9mm. The fan falls to the floor. I tremble, knees shaking. I steady myself on the desk.

My hand knocks over an ashtray which lands on top of the 9mm. Ashes and cigarette butts scatter.

Quint gurgles once more. His eyes go empty, and he dies.

I stifle a scream. Stare at the bullet hole.

Every bad decision I've ever made ricochets around in my head, louder and louder and louder. A drum solo of stupidity banging in my brain.

I run, leaving the still-warm corpse of my ex-husband behind.

I'm halfway to the front door when a man I've never seen comes out of the men's room in the insurance office.

He's in his midforties, pudgy, a comb-over so bad it looks like a beaver is dry-humping his scalp.

I stop, stare at him. No one else is in the room.

He's a cop. The cheap, ill-fitting sport coat and Sansabelt pants might as well be a uniform and badge.

"Who are you?" he says.

I don't speak. I realize the 9mm is still on the floor of Quint's room where I'd dropped it.

He stares at me. "You work for Quint?"

I realize what he's asking—am I one of my ex-husband's stable of call girls? I should be angry but I'm not. Too scared.

I shake my head.

His radio squawks. He turns down the volume.

"This is nothing you want to be involved in." He looks around the room. "You understand what I'm saying?"

"Wh-who are you?"

"Just walk away."

I can't help myself. I glance back at Quint's office.

Bad move.

He sucks in a mouthful of air, lips pursed.

Nobody speaks for a few moments.

"You've been in there, haven't you?"

"No." I shake my head.

"You shouldn't a done that." His tone is soft.

"I didn't. I wouldn't—" My breath catches in my throat. "See, I, um, I . . ."

The cop gets the blank look that police have perfected over the centuries.

"Quint." I will myself to be calm. "He's my ex-husband."

The cop arches an eyebrow. He glances at the office and then back at me.

"I hope he suffered." I spit the words out.

His expression changes slightly. A gleam comes into his eyes. "You killed him, didn't you?"

I lick my lips, try to think of a reply.

"Here's the gun you used." He pulls a battered revolver from underneath his sport coat. The weapon is in a plastic evidence bag.

I've been around cops enough, especially the dirty kind, to know what it is: a throw-down piece, untraceable. Serial numbers filed away.

He moves closer so that we're face-to-face.

My stomach churns. I shake my head, stunned, unable to form words.

"The ex-wife." He smiles. "The media will love it."

"No." I shake my head, voice a whisper. "Please. You don't understand. I have to—"

"Shut the hell up." He thumps me on the forehead with his middle finger. "I'm talking."

My skull hurts. I rub the spot where his finger connected.

"My sister, Chloe. She needs a doc—"

He thumps me again, harder. "Shut. Up."

Tears well in my eyes.

"The talk on the street is that Quint keeps a lot of cash lying around." He scans the room. "Show me where."

My failures, the enormity of who and what I am, settle on me like a barbed-wire blanket. The feeling is familiar but painful.

This dirty cop is no different than any other man I've been around. He's rotten to the core like all the rest, the common denominator being me.

"You show me where he keeps the cash," the cop says. "And I'll let you walk."

I nod slowly as a strange thing happens. The ache on my forehead begins to feel warm and worm its way to the pit of my stomach.

I stare at his comb-over and pasty skin. A tingling sensation dances across my thighs.

"In the safe." I nod toward the other office. "There's usually a lot of cash."

"You know the combination?"

I nod again. It's Quint's mother's birthday. Quint wasn't worried that I would rip him off. He knew I understood the consequences of that action.

The cop lifts up my chin so he's looking me in the eye. A sexual energy pulses between us, makes my skin tight.

I'm teary and sad. My lip quivers, not just from emotion. I am also aroused.

Sorrow and sex, they go together in my world.

I lean closer and kiss him.

For an instant, he doesn't respond. Then he kisses back.

We go at it for a few moments. He tastes like spearmint gum and coffee.

I push him toward one of the desks. He sits on the edge, drops the plastic sack with the revolver on the surface by the phone.

"The safe," he says. "The money."

"Later." I drop to my knees.

My thighs tingle as warmth spreads across my body, the two-headed beast tugging at my very core, arousal and control.

I unzip his jeans.

"Damn, you're a nasty ho." His tone is reverential, the words meant as a compliment.

I take them as intended. I like to be nasty; it's where I excel. Nasty is my comfort zone.

He tilts his head back and groans as I engulf his penis in my mouth.

With one hand, I reach for the plastic sack containing the .38.

The cop's groaning morphs into moans of pleasure. His breathing becomes shallow. He grabs the top of my skull with both hands, his head still tilted back.

I jam the muzzle against his testicles.

He looks down. "What the hell?"

I pull the trigger.

Three Weeks Later

The bar sits at the end of Front Street, facing the bitter grayness of the Bering Sea.

Even in summer, with nearly twenty hours of gloomy light each day, the choppy waters at the end of the Seward Peninsula are cold and foreboding, pockmarked with rain more often than not.

The bar's clientele form the bottom of the social strata. Wet-brained white trash, meth-addled Aleuts, drunk Inupiat whalers. They are the dregs, no mean feat in a town of last chances and broken dreams, the figurative and literal final stop for an entire continent.

The higher-end joints, places where you won't get stabbed for your government check and even an occasional tourist ventures, are farther down the street, in what passes for the good part of Nome.

The bartender at the place at the end of Front Street is also the owner, a professional vagabond in his early fifties named Mike.

If life's a TV show, Mike's pretty much seen every episode and knows all the characters: the grifters and sociopaths, lovers and fighters, the terminally despondent, anybody who's ever wanted to lose themselves in the booze-mottled anonymity of a saloon.

There's not a sad tale Mike hasn't heard or a con he can't spot simply by the way a guy holds his head and leans across the bar.

Until The Girl from Texas arrives.

That's what they call her, Mike and a small group of regulars.

The Girl from Texas, or, for short, simply The Girl.

She is clearly a cheechako, somebody new to Alaska.

Beyond that, Mike can't figure her out.

She arrived about two weeks ago, parking in front of his place at the end of Front Street in a dirt-covered Cadillac with plates issued out of Texas.

She's been here every night since, sitting at the end of the bar, a bottle of Budweiser and a pack of Winston Lights in front of her. Three, four beers, the same number of cigarettes, and she leaves.

She is devastatingly attractive. The best-looking woman on

the south shore, opine more than a couple of the regulars. Blond and blue-eyed, she's on the good side of thirty, a body and face designed to make men dream of better times and choices that might have been.

But the eyes betray her. They are a stew of emotion, quick and sad and angry at the same time, hinting at a despondency that has no measure.

She always pays in cash, tips more than she should. She rebuffs the advances of those who want to buy her a drink, the clumsy attempts to take her home. After the first few days, the come-ons stop, and she drinks in peace.

The Caddy disappears at the end of the first week, replaced by an almost new Ford four-wheel-drive pickup with oversized snow tires and a heater plug hanging out of the front grill, the vehicle of someone who intends to spend the winter in Alaska.

Word filters back to Mike that she paid cash for the trade difference, crisp hundred-dollar bills. Mike also hears that she rented a place on the other side of town. A year lease, the security deposit and first month's rent also paid in cash.

This perplexes Mike because people with those kinds of resources don't usually frequent his bar.

She doesn't talk, beyond the minimum to place an order. She just drinks and smokes, an hour or so in the evenings, then leaves, wandering out into the sunny night sky.

Until tonight.

Tonight is different. Sunday evening, two weeks and a day since her first appearance. She has a cell with her, resting on the bar. The phone flashes, an incoming call. From his vantage point by the beer taps, Mike can read the screen: *Parklnd Hosp.*

She answers and turns away, a whispered conversation.

Mike's watched enough History Channel to know that Parkland Hospital is the main medical facility in Dallas, the place where President Kennedy died back in '63.

The Girl ends the call, turns back around. Her face is colorless, eyes brimming with tears.

Mike empties an ashtray, says, "Everything okay?"

"Did I want to leave her?" The Girl's voice is a whisper. She's staring at the label on her beer bottle, speaking to no one.

Mike doesn't say anything.

"Did I have a choice?" She wipes her eyes. "I got her to the hospital. Did what I could."

The jukebox clicks on, Lynyrd Skynyrd, "Sweet Home Alabama."

"You want another beer?" Mike points to her empty bottle.

She looks up like she's seeing him for the first time. "How about a shot of Crown and a little privacy, huh?"

Mike shrugs. He doesn't take offense. Booze makes people ornery, a minor occupational hazard if you work in a bar. He pours a glass of whiskey and brings it over.

She downs the shot, motions for another. "And a beer back."

Mike brings her the drinks and then retreats to the middle of the bar. A good drink-slinger can be invisible when necessary.

She stares at her beer and whiskey for a few moments. Wipes tears again. Then she looks up, catches Mike's eye.

"I, uh, I'm sorry." She clears her throat, sniffs. "Didn't mean to snap at you."

Mike saunters back, polishing a beer mug with a towel.

"I . . . got some bad news." She takes a drink of whiskey.

"Sorry to hear."

"Mike? That's your name, right?"

He nods, continues to polish the mug.

"You got any family, Mike?" She drains the shot. Sips on the beer.

He shakes his head.

"Me neither." She brushes a tear from her cheek. "Not anymore."

"You're from Texas, I hear."

No response for a few moments, thoughts clearly rumbling through her mind.

Then she smiles for the first time in the two weeks and one day she's been coming into the bar, and the very air in the dingy tavern changes like a switch has been flipped.

It's not a happy smile but that doesn't matter. The pain in her face disappears, replaced by a raw sexuality that is like a blast of arctic air, invisible but powerful, impossible to ignore.

She shifts her weight on the barstool and her flannel shirt slides open slightly, revealing pale, freckled cleavage. Her eyes brighten. She runs a hand through her hair, causing the shirt to open a little wider.

"I'm from Dallas." The Girl licks her lips. "You ever been to Texas?"

Mike stands straighter, sucks in his stomach without realizing he's doing so. He's seen people like this before, slept with more than a few, damaged souls who wield their sexuality like a velvet-shrouded sword.

Nothing good comes from a woman like this, but for the moment he doesn't care. He has weaknesses like anyone else. The way she looks at him, the smile on her lips, that changes something inside of a man. Makes danger seem safe, the darkness appear sunny.

Mike lists the places in Texas he's been: Houston, Corpus, Port Arthur. The Rio Grande Valley. Austin.

The Girl and Mike smile at each other, a shared connection.

"The woman at the Century 21 office." The Girl points toward town. "She says you're trying to sell this bar."

Mike doesn't reply. He had indeed told Century 21 he was looking to sell. It's time to move on, the wanderlust is setting in. The Girl from Texas has been busy.

"How much do you want?"

Mike rubs his chin. Then he names a price, a number that is on the top end of reasonable, low six figures.

The Girl nods thoughtfully, a lock of hair dangling in front of her eyes. She uncrosses her legs and slides a heel on the top rung of the barstool, props her chin on the raised knee. Her appearance is an intoxicating mix, sultry innocence.

By the way she holds her body, Mike realizes this woman is his for the night if he wants her. He won't even have to ask, just take her home.

"There's no owner-financing either." He repeats the price.

She nods.

He leans on the bar, hands clasped, eye to eye. "You got that much money?"

"My first husband." The Girl runs a finger down his forearm. "He left me a sizable inheritance."

Her touch is cool and electric. The skin on the tip of her finger makes Mike's flesh tingle, stomach get warm.

"Maybe we could go somewhere and discuss this privately," she says.

Mike smiles. He takes most of the cash from the register and asks the soberest of the regulars to watch the place for an hour or so. Then he and The Girl slide out the back, walking the two blocks to Mike's house down the street from the VFW Hall.

In the bedroom, they don't speak at first.

She peels off her clothes, faded jeans and a flannel shirt, down to her bra and panties.

Mike notices the bandages on her forearm and the scars, circular like burns from a cigarette. Some are fresh, some not so much.

"What happened there?" He points to the injuries.

From her shirt pocket, she pulls out a pack of Winston Lights and taps a cigarette free. "Got a match?" She leans back on the bed.

Mike tosses her an old Zippo.

She lights the cigarette, blows a plume of smoke toward the ceiling.

Mike kicks his shoes off, steps out of his clothing.

She takes another couple of puffs and extinguishes the cigarette against the smooth flesh of her arm. A tiny moan escapes her lips as the glowing knob of tobacco mashes against her skin.

A rare case of paternal concern crosses Mike's mind.

"A pretty girl like you." He winces. "What's so bad that you got to do that to yourself?"

She unhooks her bra, tosses it across the room. "Come to bed, Mike."

He hesitates. Then puts a knee on the mattress, marveling at her body. Batshit crazy in the head, but damn, what a looker. He leans toward her. And stops.

"What's your name? I don't even know your name."

She doesn't reply for a moment. In the dim light of the bedroom, it's hard to tell but it looks like her eyes are filled with tears again.

"C-C-Chloe," she says. "My name is Chloe Parker."

"Pleased to meet you, Chloe Parker." Mike eases down beside her. "You sure are a nice-looking—"

"Don't talk, Mike." She presses a finger against his lips and pulls him close.

DOG SITTER

BY CATHERINE CUELLAR

Love Field

As Xóchitl turned her key in the lock, Buster—a fluffy blond Pomeranian in her care—tugged his leash. She elbowed the latch and backed through the heavy arched wooden door of the Tudor-style cottage. A titanium racing bicycle worth more than Xóchitl's car was tilted against the dining room wall. Giving the door a hip bump closed before releasing Buster's leash, she walked past floor-to-ceiling shelves stacked with art books and CDs to the kitchen. Standing over a trash can, she tossed catalogs, coupons, and postcard pictures of registered sex offenders and missing children, while setting aside bills on the island by the phone. As Emma rubbed against her leg and started meowing for food, Xóchitl stopped at a pink envelope hand-addressed to her.

She put the rest of the mail on the kitchen counter next to stacked cans of Fancy Feast and broke the seal, giving the knuckle of her index finger a slight paper cut. She pressed the stinging wound to her lips, sucking a tiny drop of blood, then slid the card out of its envelope. There was a cartoon of a cute puppy on the front with the caption, *I get so excited when I see you,* and inside, *I can't control myself . . .* with the puppy looking embarrassed next to a puddle, signed, *I Can't Wait To Get Together Again, Love, Jeremías.* This was not an American Greetings or Hallmark card; Xóchitl imagined Jeremías picking it out at a 7-Eleven or truck stop. It bugged her that he capitalized every word. But mostly, she was creeped out because he was writing her at work—and she was opening his card less than twenty-four hours after they had kissed goodnight.

Obviously he'd pulled some strings at the post office where he worked to get this card to her the same day he sent it. Jeremías wasn't a carrier—he sorted packages for shipping at the main post office on I-30 where all the mail in town was processed. Every year on April 15, Xóchitl and her oldest friends Tom and Valda bought beer and tailgated in the parking lot until midnight. They laughed as they watched the traffic caused by frantic taxpayers backing up the exit ramp onto the westbound highway. Although mail carriers stood by the turnoff from the access road, many cars headed past—drivers parking and scurrying inside to have their tax returns metered so they could get the postmark to meet the IRS deadline. The former classmates had been tipsy, sitting on the hood of Xóchitl's old Ford Tempo, when Jeremías walked out to his new Honda Accord, parked next to theirs. He struck up a conversation with Xóchitl (and was very cute) so she offered him a beer. Jeremías accepted. They got drunk, then Valda drove Xóchitl's car back to her house-sitting job while Tom followed, giving Valda a lift home. Xóchitl forgot giving Jeremías her number until he rang her the next day.

They met for drinks at the Inwood Lounge and talked awhile. Xóchitl had thought it was hilarious that sometimes when Jeremías was trying to sound smart or exotic or important, he would affect an ever-so-slight British accent, even though he was as Texan as she was. After he drove her back to Hollywood Heights where she was staying, he walked her to the door and followed her inside. They kissed on the couch until Emma's cat hair made him sneeze. Now, he might be her stalker. At least Jeremías didn't know where Xóchitl would be living next. Her only real address was a post office box in the downtown courthouse.

Xóchitl put the card down, peeled open a can of Fancy Feast, and dumped it in Emma's bowl. Buster pranced in, his leash still trailing behind him. She detached it from his collar and hung it on a doorknob. Buster headed into the sunroom toward Emma's litter box, sniffing for a snack.

"Oh no you don't!" she shouted in the voice she used to talk to animals and babies. She grabbed a tiny plastic shovel and started cleaning out the clumps.

It felt fun and glamorous, playing house in rich people's homes. Xóchitl paid no rent or utility bills. She got to listen to different CDs, read new magazines and books, and usually had cable. Once in a while there'd even be a swimming pool, sauna, or jetted tub. The money was good and the digs were fancy. She knew which prescriptions her clients took, what they kept in their pockets, and where they hid their sex toys. She liked sleeping in their big beds when they traveled and compared the number of pillows, softness of linens, and firmness of mattresses. She loved animals, wasn't allergic, and found comfort in their affection.

But no matter how plush her surroundings, she knew her job was scooping poop.

From Memorial Day through Independence Day, Xóchitl stayed in Lakewood with Salma Hindlick and Angelina Jowlie, a pair of Rhodesian ridgebacks. They woke her up for their walk every morning as the sun was rising, followed by their ritual feeding and a game of catch in the yard. She came to recognize the neighborhood power walkers and pet owners she saw at the same time each morning.

On July 4, after their morning routine, she packed up her car, set the alarm, and returned her house key through the mail slot in the front door. As she backed down the driveway in her Ford Tempo, Xóchitl was jolted in her seat by a huge thud. She was afraid one of the girls had dug out from the yard and somehow gotten behind her car, but she hadn't seen anything in her rearview mirror.

Parking with her engine still idling, she hopped out to see what she'd hit. Xóchitl's heart beat faster as she walked toward her rear bumper, then lurched into her throat when she saw a man's bare-chested torso facedown on the sidewalk under her passenger-side rear tire, with his shorts-clad legs, ankle socks, and running shoes sticking out the other side.

"Goddamn," she said.

She jumped back into the driver's seat and pulled forward to get her car off the runner, then killed the engine. Rolling him over, she saw his nose was smashed and his face was bruised and covered with blood. He wasn't breathing and didn't have a pulse. "Mierda," she muttered.

She ran her hands over his dark plastic shorts searching for an ID, phone, or keys, to no avail. Xóchitl felt like throwing up. She tried to remember if, when, and where she had seen him running on other mornings while she was walking the girls. They were so close to the lake, there were dozens if not hundreds of faces to recall, but his cold corpse bore no resemblance to any of those fit athletes.

Running back to the house, she realized that without her key she was now locked out. She opened her car door and pulled a few T-shirts from her bag. Soaking up some of his blood on the sidewalk with one T-shirt and putting another over his face, she scooched him out of the driveway toward the yard.

Sprinting back to her car, she hopped behind the wheel, started the engine, and backed out, double parking on the street as best she could to obstruct the driveway from view. She used another T-shirt over her hands to drag him back to the blood-stained spot in the driveway where she had found him. Xóchitl turned him back over, facedown.

She looked up and down the tree-lined street for signs of

life. A few firecrackers popped in the distance and she smelled charcoal smoke from holiday barbecues. Apparently, everyone on this block had either already left for their lake houses or were sleeping in. The next door neighbors' house had several newspapers piled in the front yard. She collected and carried them to their front door, stealing one so that she could stuff her bloody T-shirts in its plastic bag. Her clients would be returning at some point later that day.

If she died outside, how long would it take, and who would notice? Would the pets in her care run away, or eat her? Might the neighbors notice when her car remained unmoved for days in the driveway? Or would vultures circle, drawn by the smell of her decomposed remains? She was freaking herself out and needed coffee. And—since life was short—donuts. On her way, she stopped by White Rock Lake. She emptied her newspaper bag of bloody T-shirts into the water by the spillway, then let it float off.

That night, the fireworks were cancelled because of rain. Xóchitl hoped it would wash some of the evidence away. She waited for the call from the Lakewood clients. The next day, she started reading the newspapers she collected, searching for reports about the dead runner. Instead, she found many other haunting stories of people killed, bodies found, or lives tragically cut short. Unless it was a high-profile person or someone with a terminal disease, the cause of death was rarely named. She looked at every photo in the obituaries, but none of them resembled the horrible face she remembered from the driveway. She wondered how her own obituary might read, and if Valda would give her eulogy.

The runner became her first waking thought every morning, and the last thing in her mind as she dozed off each night. She thought about confessing. But the more time passed, the more she feared the severity of her punishment.

* * *

Valda called and asked Xóchitl to come directly to her tiny apartment in Kidd Springs. Valda was sniffling, so Xóchitl asked, "Do you need me to bring anything?" She didn't.

When Xóchitl arrived, Valda's eyes were red from crying and her voice shaky. Valda handed Xóchitl a bottle of beer, then sat with her on the couch.

"I went to the doctor today," Valda said.

"Are you pregnant?"

"I have stage-four cervical cancer."

Xóchitl lost her grip on the bottle. It fell to the floor, breaking into shards and splashing beer all over the place.

Valda leapt up. Xóchitl followed her into the kitchen to grab rags, a broom, and a dustpan. They knocked heads as they stooped over to wipe up the mess. Then they started to weep and hug.

"The doctor said I'm an unusual case because most sexually active women get a pap smear every year," Valda explained. "I didn't even know what that was, except expensive. I didn't want anyone to know I was messing with my boyfriends. I just didn't want to get pregnant. I never saw the doctor until my period wouldn't stop. How stupid am I?"

"You're not stupid," Xóchitl said. "You're wonderful. I've done far worse, I swear. I'd trade places with you if I could."

Xóchitl started driving Valda to testing, treatment, and surgeries, staying with her whenever she wasn't booked with clients. At every doctor's appointment Valda's prognosis grew more grim. The tumors metastasized from her lymph nodes and liver, to her lungs, bones, and brain. Her pain grew so severe, doctors prescribed her synthetic heroin. At Thanksgiving, Valda decided to stop treatment, stop staying home, stop waiting to die—and live a little. She set out on a "farewell tour," visiting her favorite people and places. Valda asked Xóchitl and their old friend Tom to help her plan a New Year's Day open house at Tom's place.

A week before Christmas, Xóchitl's mother Ana called saying she was sick, so she needed her daughter's help making tamales. Xóchitl was slammed with clients traveling for the holiday. She offered instead to prepare some side dishes and bring them with her on Christmas Day.

"If you make them in advance they won't be fresh," Ana chided.

"Could we eat Christmas Eve dinner instead of Christmas Day lunch?" she countered.

"We have Christmas Eve Mass. Christmas Day your nieces will have your brothers up early to see what Santa brought them. They'll be too hungry to last for dinner."

"Potluck?"

"Your brothers will be busy with kids and their toys. I already bought all the groceries. It's a sin to waste food."

"What do you want me to say?"

"I guess I'll see if your brothers can help, or Abuela."

"Keep me posted."

Ana never called. Christmas Eve, Xóchitl called Ana, who was directing Xóchitl's abuela, father, brothers, sisters-in-law, and nieces to avoid handling food while ill.

"So, everything's fine without me?"

Xóchitl got Ana's answer on Christmas morning when she entered her mother's kitchen.

"How dare you not help? At your age, I was married with three children. I still cooked Christmas dinner all by myself. Fortunately, your brothers have good wives. They helped me, unlike you. You should be ashamed. Where did you learn such selfishness, puta?"

Steeling herself against Ana's rare use of coarse language, Xóchitl wanted to kill her. Then, horrified at her own thought, Xóchitl tried una broma.

"Feliz Navidad! I can't bear you a grandchild today, but would you like me to steam the tamales?"

Ana raised her voice: "You must be so proud: letting me know months in advance how you always have to work holidays. Caring for pets and plants instead of your parents. Why don't you live with us like I lived with Abuela until I got married?"

At that moment, Xóchitl's brothers and Abuela entered the kitchen. Xóchitl lost it and excused herself to splash her red face with cold water. Abuela followed her, saying Ana was going through "the change." Ana had a full hysterectomy after her children were born, but Abuela's dementia took that memory. Abuela also said Ana didn't speak for la familia. They were glad Xóchitl was with them.

In blessing the Christmas meal, Ana thanked God for each and every family member by name except Xóchitl. Xóchitl wished she were dead. She thought about confessing to killing the runner—right then and there. If Ana *really* understood why Xóchitl was truly unfit to marry or have kids, she might lay off.

After dinner Xóchitl washed Ana's dishes, heartbroken. She left to walk and feed her clients' dogs and plug in their Christmas lights. Then Xóchitl met Tom at the Inwood Lounge that night for drinks. They talked about how sad they were for Valda. As they drank, Xóchitl got the idea to prove her mother right and seek comfort by seducing Tom. She claimed she was a little nervous about driving all the way to the Munger Historic District from the Park Cities after drinks, so she asked Tom to follow her, promising him a choice of extra bedrooms where he could crash.

After she took the dogs to do their business, she washed her hands and brushed her teeth. Xóchitl went to the spare bedroom where Tom was passed out on top of the covers. She spooned in, then kissed him. It took Tom a moment to realize she wasn't going to leave. He eventually kissed back as she pulled at his clothes—but he was too tired and drunk to get it up. They kicked off their shoes, turned down the covers. Xóchitl started rubbing his back . . . too hard, Tom complained. He wanted her to touch his skin lightly. He dozed off again when she was gentle, sleepily saying, "I'm worried about you."

Because she was a murderer? Or because her best friend was going to die, leaving her alone?

"You might fall in love with me."

How could she begin to explain she chose Tom precisely because he was so weird and immature they couldn't possibly last in a relationship—in part because her secret could be known at any moment. She pursued him only because they'd known each other forever. She knew he was as self-absorbed as she was bereft about Valda.

She wanted a fling with him not because she really liked him, but because she was like him.

On New Year's Eve, they bumped into each other at a party by the rooftop pool at the Manor House. Tom was on a first date with a woman who appeared ten years his junior. After introductions, Tom's date excused herself to find the ladies' room.

"I'm sorry," Tom said.

"There's nothing to apologize for," Xóchitl replied.

"I didn't know you would . . . when she asked me . . ."

"No worries."

"She's home from Austin for the holidays. But we're having fun."

"Of course."

"Thanks, kiddo," Tom said, as he winked and patted Xóchitl on her shoulder.

She smiled, wincing.

On New Year's Day, Xóchitl attended Valda's potluck open house at Tom's place. It felt less awkward than she feared. His New Year's Eve date wasn't there. Xóchitl brought a pie from

Norma's on Davis. The guest of honor arrived without a cane or wheelchair, wearing cute jeans and makeup. Valda fixed her own plate without assistance. And though she had little appetite, she ate a slice of the pie from Norma's.

Tired after making the rounds, Valda perched next to Xóchitl in Tom's smallest room. It was a makeshift office off the kitchen that was once a pantry. Visitors streamed in and out steadily. Valda seemed so uncomfortable; she closed her eyes as people spoke to her. Xóchitl knew her friend's spine was about to crack—the pain in her back was literally killing her. Xóchitl lightly brushed her fingers over Valda's sweater and counted her ribs. Valda weighed less than ninety pounds.

"That feels good," Valda said faintly. "You're very gentle."

Driving Valda home, Xóchitl confessed she'd killed the runner. Valda was hallucinating on painkillers. Xóchitl wasn't sure Valda was conscious, much less able to comprehend what she said.

Then Valda whispered, "Shame and secrets will kill you. Just look at me. Don't keep that to yourself." It was the last time they spoke.

Xóchitl wrote Valda's obituary and gave her eulogy at the funeral. At Valda's request, she scattered her ashes at White Rock Lake, not half a mile from where Xóchitl had tossed the evidence after killing the runner. Then she traded in her murder weapon to buy Valda's Toyota Camry.

That spring, Xóchitl went alone to the post office on tax day with four minibottles of pink wine. Tom was long-distance dating the woman in Austin, so he either forgot or lost interest in their tradition. Xóchitl recognized Jeremías's Honda in the lot and parked beside it. She drank to the memory of the unknown runner and spoke aloud—skyward, to herself, but with faith Valda could hear her.

Jeremías walked out briskly after just midnight. His pace slowed once he saw Xóchitl sitting on the hood of the Camry, talking to herself, surrounded by empty travel-sized wine bottles.

"Hey," he said. "Guess what? I'm moving to California."

"Felicidades!" Xóchitl replied. "Good to see you too. Why are you moving?"

"My brother sold his company to Google. He's a dot-com millionaire now."

"No way!"

"Yeah, he bought a house in San Francisco and wants me to come live with him."

"Wow. What'll you do?"

"I've applied for a job at Banana Republic. That's their headquarters."

"Retail?"

"I want to work in their catalog shipping department, kind of like my job now. Or in their warehouse to supply all their stores."

"That makes sense."

Tiring of small talk at the end of a long day, Jeremías stared at her. "Thanks. Know what? I'm great, and you should've given me a chance."

"It's true," Xóchitl said. "I'm sorry." She realized he still cared enough to be ticked that she'd blown him off. She was sparing him from a relationship with a criminal. She looked east toward downtown. The towering lit skyscrapers were beautiful. The sight made her feel insignificant, like the runner whose name she never knew. She searched the sky for the moon, feeling guilty. For a moment she wondered if Jeremías would follow her home again. She missed Valda.

"Anyway, if you ever visit Frisco," Jeremías said, "you have a place to stay now."

She thanked him, but knew she wouldn't—even if he had an

employee discount at Banana Republic and lived with his millionaire brother.

Xóchitl's Lakewood client called her for the first time in almost a year. She was afraid to answer.

"It's Karen Johnson. Could you stay with my Salma and Angie again this June?"

The thought of returning to the scene of the crime filled Xóchitl with dread. Were they setting a trap to ensnare her? Would declining signal her guilt? She accepted, making an evening appointment to return to their house to get a key. Several hours later she parked on the street and searched their driveway in the dusky evening sun. She saw no bloodstain. Had she imagined it?

Mrs. Johnson invited her inside and offered her a glass of water. Xóchitl's heart was pounding. Her palms were so sweaty she feared she might drop the glass like her beer bottle the night she'd heard Valda's cancer diagnosis.

"Is that a new car?" Mrs. Johnson asked.

"New to me. It was my best friend's," Xóchitl said, her voice breaking. "She passed away." Xóchitl thought she was going to burst into tears, but took a deep breath.

"Oh dear," Mrs. Johnson said, handing her a box of Kleenex. "I'm so sorry. That explains why you never called us to get your check last summer after we got back from Santa Fe."

Mierda, Xóchitl thought. A dead giveaway.

"Oh! How could I forget something like that?" she exclaimed, her mouth dry and her foot tapping fast.

"Please. No worries," Mrs. Johnson said, as she took her checkbook out of her purse and started writing. "We were totally distracted ourselves when we got back. My husband ran over our neighbor in the driveway when we got in that night."

"Dios mío!" Xóchitl shouted. "What happened?" She was

horrified to think the runner had been there all day. Had Dr. Johnson gone to prison in her place?

"It was a terrible shock. But we're okay now," Mrs. Johnson said. "We were quite shaken until the coroner confirmed the man had died many hours earlier. Apparently he had a seizure while running."

"A seizure?" Xóchitl's face hurt. She didn't know whether to laugh or cry.

"Yes, it was awful. We whipped right into the driveway as it was getting dark so we didn't see him at all. His body was just lying on the sidewalk, already gone. We called 911 and the ambulance came. He'd already been gone awhile."

"That's awful," said Xóchitl. "Who was he?"

"We didn't know him, but he lived nearby. He had a history of seizures because of a rare health condition. He was unmarried and didn't have any family in town, so it took awhile to figure out who he was and get his affairs settled. He wasn't carrying any ID."

Mrs. Johnson handed Xóchitl her house key and a check for $1,500.

"That should cover last summer and next month. Anyway, the lesson is always carry ID and an emergency contact number, because—well, you never know."

Xóchitl stared at the check in her hand. "*Verdad.* You never know."

MISS DIRECTION
BY J. SUZANNE FRANK
Downtown

The redhead's hands trembled as she pulled up to the "love shack" on the wrong side of the so-called Trinity River. Music filtered through the night from a dozen shantytown honky-tonks, the sound of cussing and laughing as the colored side of town enjoyed their Saturday night, separated by a floodplain that hadn't had a trickle of water in more than six months.

The house, no curtains, glowed with electric light. Wyatt might hide out over here, but he didn't make himself uncomfortable. He walked in front of the screened window, like a bad dream summoned. He peered out and the redhead waved, saucily, she hoped. He wasn't expecting to see anyone other than his mistress, Cayenne DuPre.

Wait. Cayenne always waited, never jumped her cue. It was like she had a dance coach living between her ears. She just knew how to pick the right moment. The redhead slipped out of the car, carrying her train case and stepping carefully in the "glass slippers" still with their Neiman's tag. The filmy stuff her peignoir was made of caught in the light, and her hair, she knew, gleamed in contrast.

Plastering on the smile of a woman confident in her seductiveness, she knocked.

The door flew open. "Ain't you a hot one," he said. "I thought we were having dinner at your house." But his gaze barely brushed hers; he stayed fixated on her barely covered thirty-eight-inch DDs. A key part in her plan. Something she and Cayenne had in common.

Well, something besides Wyatt.

"A woman has a right to change her mind. Invite me in?"

He stood back and she stepped up. Once the door was closed, there was no going back. The door clicked shut and she reminded herself that he'd brought this on himself.

"Why don't you slip onto something more comfortable," he said with a laugh. She glanced back and saw him gesturing to his groin. He might have been born to wealth and breeding, but it certainly hadn't taken. She laughed.

"Did you decide to not cook?" he asked. "I don't know how I feel about a woman not cooking."

This was the part she hadn't planned on, this was what she'd have to fake: Cayenne's repartee. She excelled in it on stage. "I burned it," she said, spinning around, posing like a mistress who was also a dancer. Cayenne also didn't back down, didn't fear confrontation. "What's the point of your bein' rich and powerful if I have to cook?"

"We're about to be richer, baby. My ex-wife is signing away her alimony."

She had to shake those words off, the slightest moue would betray her. Instead, she laughed. "That woman, giving up money?"

"She won't let me see my son," he said. "So why should I pay?"

"I thought it was the law."

"It's Dallas, baby. Who do you think makes the laws? Me and my buddies. That's what school's for, but you wouldn't know that, would you? Go on—if you didn't cook for me, give me a private show."

"The windows are wide open!"

"You dance for a hundred men a night! What do you care?"

"I perform for money. Not for free."

"C'mon, baby." He got up, placing his hands on her, breathing scotch all over her. "Do it for me."

She forced herself to sink into his grasp, to taunt and flirt. "Well all right," she said, knowing that every move was going to help in the end. Unpleasant but necessary. This was all part of the plan.

Dance. Lights out, then shouts and gunfire. Cayenne arrested at her apartment. No one would know about the signatures. Or her son's shame.

She sashayed and dipped, smiled over her shoulder as she shimmied out of the robe. He was crass and crude, though she knew it was the true man, revealed.

She finished her dance with a high kick, turning off the lights as she brought her foot down. The shack was plunged into darkness, only moonlight and the sole streetlamp lending illumination. She pulled out her gun and cocked the hammer.

"What the hell, Cayenne?"

Then he was on her, brute strength she'd forgotten, mean and vicious, and then . . . realization struck, recognition, and he laughed as he took the gun away, pressed her against the kitchenette's counter, cursing her, fumbling with his pants.

Not again. Not again! She fought and squirmed and found the handle of a cast-iron skillet on the stove. She heard the rip of her peignoir and brought the skillet down, hard on the arms holding her. He swore and leaned forward to attack.

She brought the skillet above her head, and the miles swum at the country club, the tennis matches and equestrienne skills, and underpinning it all, the little girl who'd served family and strangers breakfast since she was eight, and crashed it down on his skull.

Again.

Again.

Again.

And again.

The skillet broke into pieces, Wyatt slumped, and Katherine Wainscott lay there in a stolen wig, shaking.

* * *

The ceiling looked polka-dotted in black and white with the light coming through the window. The room smelled like childbirth, the only other time she recalled the smell of blood. She'd lost so much, soaking through sheets and bed, all to bring her son into the world.

Such suffering couldn't go for naught. *This wasn't part of the plan.* In the stillness she heard a soft whisper, but not conversation. Not . . . On hands and knees she crawled to the window. Droplets of water caught in the screen. Rain.

Dallas had been in drought for months. Her spring flowers hadn't had a chance. *Rain.* She spun around and leaned against the wall. Wyatt lay in a puddle of blood. The skillet . . .

Rain! The convertible! Makeup!

Galvanized, her hands fumbled as she opened the train case, pulling out the papers.

"I won't sign!"

"You have two choices. You want me to go away? You sign. But if you keep my money, I keep seeing my son. Any way I want."

"You, you touched him!"

"And who's gonna believe you? When I met you you were twirlin' your tassels for dinner! I'm fourth-generation! I'm SMU—"

And if she said anything, accused him of the horrible crime, what would she do to her son's life? The boy whose daddy molested him? And what of their second son? Conceived the night she'd begged for a divorce, he already had enough against him.

So she'd signed. No money. No house. But also, no Wyatt. And then the plan she'd made, the one she'd run dress rehearsal on five times in two years, now had a curtain time.

She hadn't planned on the skillet or the rain.

Just a gun. A decoy. An alibi.

Brain suddenly buzzing again, she wrapped Wyatt's bloody fingers around the gun. The stink of blood became normal; the texture of his dying skin and temperature of his body were details she couldn't absorb.

The face in the train case mirror made her flinch as she scooped out cold cream to get as much blood off as possible. It was in her hair, all over her peignoir, hands, and nails. She cleaned what she could to not be repulsive, because Cayenne never was.

Car doors. A knock. "Cayenne?" She froze, then realized it was working—they'd recognized the car.

Smoothing her hair, she snicked across the floor, the soles of her shoes tacky with blood, and opened the door, throwing herself into the man's arms, pressing her breasts against him. He mustn't look at her closely, he must see and feel just what he expected. One hand held her, the other flicked a lighter.

"Holy hell, woman, what have you done?" The voice, the voice? Who was this? She kept her face buried in his chest, striving for Cayenne's West Texas twang.

"I didn't have a choice! He pulled a gun!"

He walked into the single room, looked at the walls and ceiling. "You shot him?"

It didn't smell like gunfire. The pistol wasn't warm. She covered her face and wept Cayenne's tearless but breast-bouncing way. How many landlords had given in to that? How many husbands?

He stared at the body, though it was too bloody to tell if it had been shot or not. "I can help you, babe," he said. "We can make this go away, just you and me." He flicked the lighter again. His suit was too new, his hair too smooth: a mobster, but which one? She'd never seen him at the club, which meant he probably preferred strippers to the flirtation of burlesque.

Mobsters didn't grant favors. "I can do it," she said, keeping her voice small but brave. "Just keep the police and . . . the fire trucks away?"

He smiled, like he was impressed. "Fire trucks." He laughed. "Fire trucks! You're right. Only thing that can clean this up. And you," he added, glancing at her peignoir. "Though I think we should meet later and discuss this. At your house. The two of us?"

There was only one response. She forced herself to smile. "Of course, sugar. Go on now and I'll see you then."

He left out the back and she heard his car slip away. But when he reached Fort Worth Avenue, he turned toward Dallas. Going to the police?

A fire.

She ripped the documents, setting them alight, tucking them around the body, in the combustible couch and beside the stove. A steak lay on the counter, Piggly Wiggly price tag still on it. That reckless man, spending a dollar fifty on a T-bone!

The skillet! The pieces had scattered, and she gathered them together, using the blood to glue them back like a puzzle, and set it on the stove.

His pants caught and she bit back a laugh—of course they did! She poured his high-dollar scotch on his shirt, the couch, feeding the fire that was creeping across the wooden floors and snaking up the walls.

Outside, the rain was still just a patter.

She set the train case, monogrammed *CdP*, on the counter and watched the papers, with her signature, burn to ash. He was dead. Her signature burned away. Now for the final step.

She threw open the door, glimpsing the whites of the eyes that watched from the shadows. The sky rumbled and she ran out the door, gasping, not having to fake fear or sobs as she climbed into the car and reversed, jammed it into first gear, and fishtailed out of the narrow street toward the viaduct.

Once on the other side of the river, she slowed down, took side streets, and at last pulled into a leafy neighborhood with detached garages and single-family dwellings. She parked the car at an angle, then climbed over the side, slipping into the shadows.

The sixth and final "joyride" some youngsters had taken in Cayenne's car. Like a benediction, or a funeral bell, thunder clanged above and the skies opened. The inside of the blue Pontiac Eight was dashed with water and she peeled off the wet peignoir. Blood washed off her hands, poured out of her hair—the wig!

She took it off and swung it like a dead animal into the car.

She could barely see to get to her stash, her clothes, her borrowed bike. But if she couldn't see, she couldn't be seen. Above, the light in the kitchen of Cayenne DuPre's love nest was still on. She'd gone home early tonight, and she was still awake?

Pulling on dungarees and a shirt in the downpour was nearly impossible.

She felt laughter, fearful hysteria, burbling inside her. It was like her guts were full of helium and might burst out of her mouth. She clamped her hands over her mouth, remembering what Cayenne had told her: breathe the helium back in—it made your breasts higher, and higher breasts meant more money. As the two biggest-breasted girls from nowhere Texas, that always made them laugh. But not a fearful laugh, a knowing one.

She swallowed the helium down, making sure the shirt was buttoned to the top. She tucked her dyed-brown hair into a cap and yanked on loafers, displacing the water that filled them. She leapt on her bike and peddled, swerving, sliding, then picking up speed.

Mud ran in rivers down the alleys, but she was only two blocks from home.

Then she saw the lights, flashing red and blue. The police pulled up beside her.

Dropping her voice, she called out, "Here, boy . . . C'mere, boy!"

"Son!" an officer called from inside the car. "What are you doin' out here?"

They were dry inside the car, assuming she was a boy. The policeman shouted, "Your dog is lost?" They'd stopped, turned the interior light on. The driver's hand was on the gearshift to put it in park.

"My mama's cat!" she cried out.

"Boy, you can't find a cat in the rain! Go on home and—"

The radio crackled and they both stared at the receiver. "Go on home, we got real crime here!"

"Yessir," she said, peddling into the darkness.

The patrol car made a three-point turn and sped away. From the darkness, she waited. Drenched to the bone.

Then, two hours later than planned, she rode her borrowed bike into the narrow alley by her window, where the lattice that had been installed years before, the first step of the plan, waited. She finally pulled herself into her bedroom, glad the open windows had soaked the windowsills. Would account for all the water inside.

Stripping off, she squelched into the bathroom, turned on the light, and stared into the mirror. She saw the spots where his fingers would leave bruises, though as her teeth ground, she reminded herself: *The last time*. He wouldn't hurt anyone else, ever again.

She looked at the clock. Church was in five hours. She had to get the boys to Sunday school. Would the police wait until after services, or get here before? With all that had happened, gone wrong, been unexpected, she should plan on early. Would this be her last night here, her cute little Munger Place bungalow?

Nothing had gone according to plan.

She ran a bath.

There were two ways out of being poor, havin' a daddy who didn't keep his hands to himself, and a mama too worn out to care: one was to go to school and make something of yourself until you met a man and got married; the other was to take what you'd been given, put yourself on a stage, and catch a man.

She and Cayenne had both taken the stage route, though it bothered Katherine more; she longed for respectability. When Wyatt Wainscott III, prestigious businessman out of Dallas, wanted to whisk her away, give her a new start, she said yes. Didn't all husbands hit their wives every so often? Didn't all men cat around?

Everyone paid a price. At least she got to shop at Titche-Goettinger and was welcomed into the Garden Club. But Cayenne shopped there too, and Wyatt paid for her gloves just as sure as he paid for Katherine's.

Honestly, she didn't mind. Until she had the boy, until he was two, until he asked his mama to "play with my weenie, like Daddy does" and Katherine knew, just as sure as the vomit filled her mouth, that Wyatt must be stopped. Completely.

Planning a murder, she reasoned, was like planning a dance. Perfect practice meant perfect performance.

Until the rain.

Katherine sluiced cold water over her face. She had time for a catnap before she'd be expected up. With the ease of practice, she rolled her hair, slipped on her nightgown, and told herself: *An hour.* Then she would don her costume, the camouflage she'd worn at the end of her marriage, the decoy coloring she used in her everyday life. A shapeless dress over stockings and a petticoat and what she and Cayenne used to call "church secretary makeup." A stick of eyeliner, a little bit of rouge mixed with lipstick on her cheekbones, a little pink on her lips, and one coat of mascara. With brown hair and light brows, she was frumpy.

There was safety in frumpy. And frumpy certainly couldn't be mistaken for the flamboyant and famous Cayenne DuPre.

Not anymore.

The beating on the door. Katherine had been waiting for it, trying not to snap at the boys as they bounced around, full of energy, ready to unleash on poor, unsuspecting Miss Roy, their Sunday school teacher. Katherine's hands had steadied as she'd ironed Buddy's second white shirt, the first one splashed with mud when he'd discovered it rained all night.

"Mama, Mama, it's Miz Harper!"

Not the police? How could it not be the police? Every single thing had gone wrong, every detail backfired. She'd been *seen* by the policemen! But Katherine bustled to the door, admitting the older woman—the neighborhood gossip—who came with coffee cake and a double-edged smile.

"Boys, boys, you need to take that in the other room," she said, handing them the cake. "Cut yourselves small pieces—"

"Is this small?" asked her youngest, holding his arms a foot apart.

Buddy demonstrated what small was as they negotiated on the way to the kitchen. Miz Harper took Katherine by the elbow and led her into the sitting room. Katherine, surprised, let herself be led, then watched as Miz Harper poured a glass of whiskey and handed it to her.

"I know it's the Lord's day and I know it's not even ten a.m. I also know the First Baptist Church's parking lot is flooded, so there are no services today." She poured herself a glass and drew Katherine to the small settee. "You know my Rodney is a county sheriff, right?"

She had forgotten. They were going to arrange a citizen's arrest? Let her turn herself in? Katherine nodded. "Is he okay?"

"This is why Gannaway is so right. We need to run that trash out of town!"

Katherine wasn't acting anymore. "What?"

"Last night, my dear, well, there's just no other way to put it: your filthy ex-husband met his Maker and I can't imagine that God would have mercy on his soul, as unchristian as it is for me to wish ill on the dead. He deserves the other place."

Katherine drank her whiskey in one shot. It was true. Wyatt was very dead. She bit back the hysteria again. "H . . . how?"

"Well, it appears he was expectin' dinner company, and you know who I mean." Anyone who'd read the paper in recent months had seen the glamorous couple: Wyatt Wainscott and his lady love, Cayenne DuPre, lunching at Neiman's or sharing a bottle of fake champagne at the Colony Club where she was edging out Candy Barr. "The burlesque—"

"That stripper?"

The distinction was lost on anyone who hadn't attended a show. One was shabby: unclean, hungry girls with wounded eyes trying to make a living because education wasn't a possibility.

The other was beautiful, skillful, fun, and sassy. It was a booming business. Six blocks in downtown Dallas hummed every weekend night. Neon dripped from buildings housing clubs like Palace and Fox, Rialto and Capitol. The street was lined with motorcars, gleaming and new. Women in flowing gowns and men suited from Irby's walked from club to club, laughing, squeezing in to see the newest "girl" while sipping "members only" overpriced drinks.

Each girl had a different hook. Shari Angel, the Heavenly Body; Sabrina Star who could spin tassels so fast the audience saw stars; and Cayenne with her firecracker-shooting, red-sequin bustier. Candy Barr with cowboy boots and cap gun reigned, but for every girl with a reputation and a following, there were a dozen nubile, buxom young women just waiting for their moment to come.

Katherine never had a hook, was never that good. Always jumped the cue, gave up too soon, gave too much. Burlesque was about withholding. She was too scared to try. Cayenne excelled at it.

"Katherine? Are you feeling faint?" Miz Harper poured another tot of whiskey.

Katherine looked at the glass, then at her neighbor whose eyes were shiny with salaciousness. "There's more?"

"She came over and set his house on fire. Of course, dumb woman, it didn't catch with last night's storm, but he was felled . . . I'm sorry, is this hard to hear?"

Katherine shook her head.

"He hit his head. That's how he—"

"Met his Maker," she said, sipping at the whiskey. Warmth flowed through her. He was dead. Dead! And they thought it was a fall—no one had noticed the skillet? The gun in his hand, which made no sense at all now.

"Well, I guess Cayenne just can't keep from wantin' folks to watch her," Miz Harper said with a harrumph. "She raced off in her fancy little motorcar. Then the heavens opened like the Lord Himself was trying to wash away her sins."

Katherine forced herself to keep her gaze focused on Miz Harper. That statement wasn't meant for her. Or so she told herself.

"Well, by the time the police got there, they found her sitting, all dressed up, and dry! In her dining room." Miz Harper dropped her voice. "Her bags were packed, everything she owned tucked in suitcases except what she was wearin'."

"What?"

"Well, the police sat down and talked to her. Everyone knew she'd left before her second show. She claimed her car had been stolen, again, and had to take a cab home. Well, she was making dinner for her honey. She said." Again, Miz Harper harrumphed. "Steak and potatoes, just like they're playin' house. But when the officers started slicin' her icebox pie, she screamed."

Katherine leaned forward.

"She claimed she didn't go to Oak Cliff and kill her fiancé, she had baked a pie."

Katherine was certain the woman was drunk. Nothing made sense. "A pie?"

"Not just any pie. Rat poison pie." She sat back. "She was gonna kill him, make it look like a heart attack, right there in her kitchen."

Katherine's hands turned to ice and the laughter, the impossible hysteria, wouldn't be kept down. *I jumped the cue*, she thought. *Again*.

SWINGERS ANONYMOUS

BY JONATHAN WOODS

M *Streets*

We all went over to Pauline's to admire her breasts. She was the newest member of our swingers group. For her coming-out party she was hosting an afternoon barbecue at her place. A small yellow-brick ranch on a cul-de-sac over off of Primrose.

When I got there, five or six members were wandering aimlessly in the backyard, drinking beer or soda pop direct from the can. I walked up to Pauline and kissed her on the cheek. Her chin-length weedy-brown hair smelled of coconut crème rinse, transporting me momentarily to a tropical shore. As I stepped back, her baby blues flashed wickedly.

"That's a cool T-shirt you're wearing," Pauline said. It was a Smiths T-shirt commemorating one of their albums. I'd bought it at a local indie record store.

"I wish I could say the same about yours," I replied. I couldn't because Pauline was naked as a wombat from the waist up.

We were standing at the brick grill in her backyard. Below her exposed belly button she sported a pair of camouflage spandex microshorts two sizes too small (and camouflaging nada). The erotic ebb and flow of her ankles, the delicate arch of her feet, and her toes tipped with tangerine-painted nails were displayed in orange flip-flops. Her breasts hung full and languid and translucent as a tide-worn shell.

"So, Bill, what do you think?"

"Spectacular," I said.

Apparently satisfied with my response, Pauline turned and began flipping the row of beef patties riddled with hormones sizzling on the grill.

When the burgers were done, we all lined up and helped ourselves to deli potato salad, Heinz Boston baked beans, garlic toast, and an assortment of condiments. After dinner everyone got undressed. Six guys; five women. By then there were too many mosquitoes, so we adjourned to Pauline's living room and had a rousing good time. Pauline did all the guys one way or another.

Afterward people casually climbed back into their underwear, then the rest of their clothes, brushed their hair in the mirror above the sink in the single bathroom, and left with a smile or a frown, depending on their psychological bent. In the end there was just Pauline and me and Drew Baker.

Drew was drunk and high on some pills he'd scored down by the Greyhound bus station. He couldn't find his pants anywhere. Staggering back and forth in a vain search, he stumbled over the end of the sofa and rolled onto the carpet, where he lay laughing his ass off at nothing in particular. Through the picture window behind him the sun's fiery orb exploded in climax upon a cloud-strewn sky.

Pauline sashayed into the dining room, ostensibly to fix herself a highball and maybe put on some clothes. I watched her reflection in the floor-to-ceiling mirror on the opposite wall of the living room. Leaning over the brilliant surface of an old walnut table, a family heirloom, she hoovered up the last two lines of blow.

Moments later, still starkers, she walked back across the hall and stood in the arched entrance to the living room, holding a pair of gray slacks. Looking at her, I started to get stiff again.

Scrunching the pants into a ball, she threw them in my direction. "These must be dickhead's," she said.

Her throw was way off. As the slacks arced toward the floor, I made a wild grab. And came up empty. Except my hand hit something solid in one of the pockets, knocking it loose.

The falling object was a stuffed white business envelope. It landed facedown on the hardwood floor. *Ka-thud.* Fat, dumb, and happy.

Kneecaps popping, I scrunched down on my heels like a dishdasha-clad Ali Baba waiting to be executed at the side of a dusty Mesopotamian byway and flicked open the unsealed flap of the envelope. An etching of Benjamin Franklin looked up at me.

I stared back, my blood quickening. I ruffled through the wad of currency like a blackjack dealer with a new deck of cards. They were all brand-new hundred-dollar bills. I guessed around ten thousand dollars' worth. I looked at Pauline and made a gargoyle face. It was a lot of money, ripe for the taking. Her eyes glinted with greed.

Drew stopped laughing and pushed himself up on his elbows. Suddenly he was completely sober. "Hey! I'll take that." Before I could respond, from out of left field Pauline vaulted across the room and, using the side of her foot just like a Manchester United goalie blasting the ball into midfield, kicked Drew in the head. Drew spoke nary another word. His body slumped sideways, head lolling at an odd angle.

What the fuck? I thought. What I said was: "Where'd you learn to kick like that?"

"My three older brothers all played soccer." She looked down at her toes, at her nakedness, which now seemed totally out of place. "I need to get dressed," she said, "but I need a drink first."

Quickly she walked across the dining room and pushed through the swing door into the kitchen. I stared down at Drew. He looked like a goner. Which was a big fucking problem. My brain, emptied of any thought, drifted like a vulture high above the Serengeti. A scream echoed through my head. Then I realized it wasn't just something my mind had dreamed up. It had come from the kitchen. Followed by a heavy crash, the shattering of glass, a harsh exhalation of breath. Then silence. I tiptoed to the kitchen door and pushed it partway open before it struck something unyielding. The door was open enough for me to crane my head around the edge and peer into the kitchen. Directly below, Pauline lay faceup on the linoleum floor, a sleeping naiad, a stoned-out party girl, a dead duck. The fluorescent lights exaggerated the royal-purple capillaries entwined beneath her snow-white skin like veined marble in a gothic tomb. Her head acted as a blunt doorstop.

Near one twisted foot a melting clump of ice glinted in the overhead lighting. To the right of the body, a shattered glass-windowed display cabinet door hung from one mangled hinge. She must have slipped and fallen backward against the cabinet with her full weight.

A splintered segment of the wooden cabinet frame had pierced Pauline from back to front, its jagged point defiling the symmetry of her bodacious chest. A line of crimson spiked downward from the exit wound like the graph of a tech stock in free fall. Eyes wide open in an endless stare signaled the end of the line for Pauline. A pool of dark blood oozed from beneath her cadaver.

Two dead in less than five minutes. One the result of drug-induced random violence; the other a household accident gone rogue.

My brain whirled.

No one was going to fucking believe this. No one in law enforcement for sure. Not coming from the lips of a convicted felon, even if I'd paid my debt to society. *Well, officer, it's like this. I met this woman at a swingers party. Afterward, for no reason that I know of, she kicked one of the participants in the head and broke his neck. Next moment, before I could do or say anything, she slipped on an ice cube on the kitchen floor, impaled herself on a sharp stick, and died instantly. It's God's truth, officer.*

Playing out this little scenario in my head, I located my boxers and slipped them on, followed by a pair of khakis and my Smiths T-shirt. I hefted Drew's envelope of money, then shoved it into my front pocket. As I did so, I wondered what he'd been doing with so much cash, who it really belonged to.

What I needed to do first was get rid of the bodies.

A half hour later both stiffs, wrapped in blue recycling bags, lay in the trunk of Drew's navy-blue Volvo. I mopped the kitchen floor with Spic 'n Span. Wiped the dining room table clear of any coke residue I wasn't able to inhale.

The dead pair could have been ill-starred lovers from a work by James M. Cain, except they were all too real. So was the sweat that had soaked through my T-shirt. And the fear that burned at the bottom of my stomach like battery acid.

During the entire cleanup job I wore a pair of suede garden gloves I found in Pauline's pantry. I was still wearing them as I drove too slowly down Primrose. The Volvo steered like a fucking Sherman tank.

Get a grip, I thought. *Drive normally. If a cop pulls you over, you'll have a hell of a time explaining the gloves.* On further consideration it occurred to me that the gloves would be the least of my worries in the event of a meeting with a traffic cop.

Once I'd merged onto Mockingbird Lane and blended with the usual early-evening traffic, I dialed Suzie on my cell. She answered on the third ring.

"Hello?"

The sound of her voice made everything relax, as though my psych meds had suddenly kicked in. The red-hot nails driven by anxiety into my shoulders turned to cool wintergreen. *Everything is going to be okay.*

"Hello!" came Suzie's voice again, edged with irritation. "Is somebody there? Who the fuck is this?"

"Suzie. It's Bill."

"Hey, Bill. Swell of you to call. How the fuck have you been?" Before I could come up with a retort, her voice exploded across the ether and into my ear. "WHERE THE HELL ARE YOU?!"

Why is she being so adversarial? We slept together; shared bodily fluids. Ate scrambled eggs and whole wheat toast sitting across from each other in the breakfast nook, while reading sections of the local rag. When had things gone south between us?

"I told you before, sweetheart. I'm showing some out-of-town clients around the better neighborhoods."

"Yeah, right. I know you, Bill. I can smell it through the phone. Pussy juice. You're at the Bang! Bang! Club again. That's exactly what you're up to."

"Suzie, I know it's late. Just bear with me. I'll be home soon." I felt the fat envelope of money pressing against my gonads. "And I've got a surprise."

"What kind of surprise?"

"The kind dreams are made of."

A silence descended as Suzie pondered my plagiarism. She didn't have a clue. "Bullshit," she snapped. "You always talk in riddles. A fucking James Joyce you are." Suzie had taken a couple of lit courses at the local community college. In fact, that's where we'd met. Reading and discussing Joseph Conrad's *Secret Agent.* Suzie preferred Colette.

"Maybe this once I'm not bullshitting you."

But she had lost interest.

"Have a good time at the Bang! Bang! Club, Bill. Be sure to catch a life-threatening social disease. And on your way home pick up some OJ at CVS."

The line went dead.

I tossed my cell phone on the passenger seat and slammed

my hand against the steering wheel. *Ow! No fucking surprise for you, baby*, I thought.

Soon I pulled the Volvo onto the soft shoulder in front of a half-built McMansion I knew of. I'd tried to sell the house a few times. But there were no takers in this market. It was one of a dozen or so derelict construction sites located in an abandoned subdivision east of downtown past Buckner Boulevard. These crumbling, partially built homes prevaricated like street people waiting at a bus stop after the last bus has gone. The power company had turned off the electricity to the streetlights a long, long time ago.

When I stepped out of the car, my shoes scrunched on gravel. The sound of traffic far off. The squawk of a nighthawk overhead. I lit a roach I'd found in the ashtray and inhaled deeply.

A prefab shed surrounded by knee-high weeds sagged in the open field behind the house. Its corrugated roof cast the hard shadow of a Nazi officer's cap. The sky behind was a deep-purple bruise on a black woman's thigh.

The shed had been dragged there from somewhere else, so there was no foundation, just a dirt floor.

When night swallowed the world, I eased the Volvo up a rutted dirt track as close as I could get to the shed. I left the Volvo's lights off. Where a ditch cut the driveway in two, I stopped the car. From there the shed was maybe a dozen feet away.

I carried the bodies one at a time from the car to the shed. A bazillion stars, each colder than the diamond solitaire in a porn star's belly button, provided enough light so I didn't break my neck. Pauline I held in my arms like a bride. Stepping over the threshold, I dumped her nude corpse on top of Drew's.

After depositing the bodies, I bolted the shed door with the padlock I used for my locker at the Y. Tomorrow I would be back with a shovel and a couple bags of lime.

Returning to Pauline's neighborhood, I parked the Volvo be-

hind a vacant office building four blocks from her place. Careful
to take the leather gardening gloves, I left the doors unlocked
and the key in the ignition slot. If I got lucky, someone would
steal it. Take it on a joyride to Waco.

Minutes later I slipped behind the wheel of my Lexus, tucked
the garden gloves under the seat, and drove. I thought about
stopping at the Tip-Top Lounge for a vodka tonic and a cheese-
burger. They served till two a.m. But I knew I had to get home
and settle things.

I pulled into my usual parking space behind the aging apartment building on a side street off lower Greenville Avenue where
Suzie and I lived, and killed the engine. On a cautionary note I
slipped the Smith & Wesson slide-action .45 from the glove box
into the back right-hand pocket of my khakis.

When I walked into the apartment Suzie lay sprawled on the living room couch, her robe askew, nothing under. An MTV reality
show at full blast.

She looked at me like I was a hallucination.

"Did you get the OJ?"

"Let's go to Paris," I said.

Her eyes bored into me, reading the tea leaves of my soul like
a laser on a bar code. Her finger hit the mute button.

"Fuck the frogs. Let's go to New York," she said.

I frowned. "You just want to see Wayne again. Personally, I
hate New York." We'd lived there for a disastrous six months.

"Wayne? Wayne who?"

"Wayne the used car salesman." I paused for emphasis. "Jesus Christ, Suzie. I'm talking about Wayne the happy-hour bar
guy at Frag's. The creep you boffed in the third-floor linen closet
of the Chelsea. When you told me you were visiting your girlfriend Ida, who lived there."

Frag's, on the edge of Soho, mimicked the décor of a Saigon

brothel circa 1972. The waitresses and waiters wore baggy black pj's with nothing underneath. Maybe it really was a brothel.

"I've never been to Frag's," Suzie asserted. She suffered from selective recollection discontinuity disorder.

Before I could raise the argument to the next level, the need to take a wicked whiz gripped me by the nads.

"Gotta go! Gotta go!" I shouted, dashing down the darkened hallway to the left.

Afterward, I looked in the mirror over the sink and saw a steaming pile of dog crap. Sex residue, sweat, and dread wafted from every pore and crevice. In desperate need of a bath, I throttled on the hot water spigot of the ancient claw-foot tub.

Waiting for it to fill, I rolled a jay from the stash in the medicine cabinet. I tossed in a few bath toys, some lemon-scented oil. Steam clouded my glasses and the mirror; lay thick as dew on every surface. Moments later I lolled suspended in amniotic bliss, the jay smoldering between my lips.

There was a knock.

The door opened partway and Suzie peered around the edge. A look of sly cunning played across her face. Lime-green baby doll pajamas rustled lasciviously under her robe as she entered.

You know you're in trouble when, upon your arrival, your girlfriend puts on clothes instead of taking them off.

She pushed the toilet cover over with her foot. Old and heavy, it slammed down. *BAM!*

Echoes ricocheted across the porcelain bowl. The seat's loose brass fittings jingled.

Suzie rested her butt on the throne and stared at my privates. For a second or two I wondered if she had a retractable sashimi knife tucked in the pocket of her robe. Then she scanned upward to my face.

"You look comfortable, Bill." She smiled, fake as false teeth. "So, where's the surprise?"

Squinting through a tendril of blue smoke, I lowered my shoulders into the water and smiled up at her. "Just kidding," I said.

"Don't try to bamboozle me. On the phone you were for real. Your voice sounded different from your usual I'm-lying-through-my-teeth voice."

"My clients today were a complete pain in the ass."

"Don't change the subject." Stoned lightning flickered in each eyeball. "I know what it is. You sold a house."

"No."

"No, of course not. Why would I even think that? You haven't sold a house in a fucking year. I've been subsidizing you for as long as I can remember, dancing in that jerkoff bar."

She looked at my clothes scrunched in a heap on top of my new Diesel sneakers she'd bought me for my birthday. Leaning down, she rummaged through the sweaty pile. Found the envelope. Why hadn't I hidden it somewhere?

Found the Smith & Wesson.

Holy shit!

Awkwardly clutching pistol and envelope in her left hand, she thumbed through the block of cash.

"Wow, Bill. Looks like you hit the jackpot."

I sat up, water dripping.

"Give me that before I kill you," I said.

Her brow darkened. She switched the .45 to her right hand and pointed it at me. "You've got it backward, stud."

At that moment my hand touched one of the toys I'd tossed in the bath. A smiling yellow duck with a blue sailor's cap bobbing on the ebb and flow. Driven by self-preservation and instinct, I scooped up the duck and pitched it sideways at Suzie as hard as I could, at the same instant leaping over the side of the tub.

The toy hit Suzie straight in the eye. The money hand

cupped the injury; the envelope fell to the octagonal-tiled floor. Half blind, ravaged by sudden terror, Suzie lurched backward.

I ripped the toilet-seat cover from its hinges, raised it over my head, and brought it crashing down on her noggin.

"UUUhhh!"

She crumpled to the floor, the .45 spinning across the tiles. For an instant I thought about hitting her again. Finishing her off.

But I wasn't the killer type. Never appealed to me. All I wanted now was out. Out of that crummy apartment. Out of our stale, end-of-the-road existence.

Suzie was still breathing, her chest rising and falling. On my knees, I retrieved the pistol from where it had skidded under the tub, collected the cash, my glasses, the stash of weed, my sweat-sodden clothes, and bolted down the hall and out the door. At the top of the stairs, I stopped long enough to yank on my duds, then hightailed it down three flights, sprinted to my Lexus. The transmission squealed as I drove helter-skelter into the night.

Passing through the empty streets, I began to shake. Fore-boding pounded in my head like a stampede. The packet of money burned in my pocket. The owners would be back for it. Back like a bad dream of raging biker mayhem. And what about Suzie? Would she leave town, go stay with her sister in Memphis? Or, consumed by revenge, hunt me down?

At two in the morning I found myself parked at the curb outside Pauline's place. The emptiness of the house seemed to call to me.

I spent the rest of the night tossing and turning on her sofa, a sheet spread over the scratchy velvet, the .45 close at hand.

Too soon the September sun, spewing through the living room's picture window, slapped me awake. I'd forgotten to pull the drapes shut. Exhausted, I lay there contemplating all the shit hitting the fan, wondering what I was going to do with the rest of my life. Then it occurred to me: *Technically, the sofa isn't Pauline's anymore. None of this is.*

Pauline was out of business.

Standing at the picture window gazing at the front lawn, I noticed a folded copy of the *Dallas Morning News* wrapped in plastic lying on the walk. Panic flared. Rushing outside, I retrieved the newspaper and tore it open. But there were no front-page photos of Drew and Pauline's bodies stretched out on gurneys at the city morgue. I breathed a sigh of relief.

At that very moment, one of Pauline's neighbors appeared out of nowhere. One moment she was in absentia, the next clipping dandelion heads in her front yard. As I stood at the curb flicking through the newsprint pages, she sauntered in my direction. Fifty-ish, forehead a maze of tiny wrinkles, brushed-steel hair tied in a bun. Her soft nose and olive skin looked Spanish. She wore a white tube top and the tightest pair of peach-colored capris I'd ever seen. Her lips held a piquant smile.

"God's given us another beautiful day," she said.

"Praise the Lord," I replied.

"How's Pauline?"

"On a trip," I said. "I'm looking after the house for her."

"Nice deal for you."

What did she mean by that?

"Great meeting you," I said.

"My name's Rose. Come over for a drink some time." She turned away and I watched her peach-shaped buttocks wend their way blithely up the curved walkway, until they disappeared into the chiaroscuro of her front porch.

I wondered how much Rose knew about Pauline's sexual predilections.

Finding a carton of OJ and a bottle of Freixenet in the fridge, I made a pitcher of mimosas. Then lit a jay and smoked it at the kitchen sink, staring into the backyard. What I needed to do was disappear, change my spots, become the invisible man.

An hour later I parked my Lexus next to the toolshed in the deserted subdivision. A shovel and three bags of lime lay in the trunk. Bought at different stores. Paid for in cash.

In the sauna of the toolshed, I worked like seven devils to dig a trench for the bodies. I wore the gardening gloves. Sweat ran in rivulets from my body. The odor of decaying flesh made me gag, taste acid on my tongue.

When I was done, I collapsed in the front seat of my car for a while. I must have fallen asleep. My watch said eleven o'clock when I called the office and resigned over the phone. "Opportunity down in Tampa I can't pass up," I said.

Finally, I drove the Lexus to the customer parking lot of the bank where I'd financed it. I put the keys in a business envelope along with a note saying I was moving to Thailand, wrote my loan officer's name on the outside, and left the envelope with the security guard in the bank's lobby.

I took a bus back to Pauline's.

The second night I slept in Pauline's bed, the Smith & Wesson tucked under the pillow.

A week went by. I grew a beard.

I decided not to use Pauline's car, which was parked in the attached garage. If she was on a trip, she would be using it. A small Latino supermarket was within walking distance. I bought some nondescript clothes at a nearby thrift shop. I avoided Rose at all costs.

After a month, I put a *For Sale* sign in the front yard.

During the period of adjustment to my new identity, I slept no more than two hours a night. A pair of psychos haunted my dreams. One tall and lean and cold as outer space. The other a steroid hybrid of rippling muscles and zombie eyes. They burst through the front door, screaming obscenities, demanding the money, wielding high-tech weaponry, razor-sharp Special Forces knives. I jolted awake, drenched in sweat, and stayed up until dawn.

Other times it was Drew and Pauline chasing me through the empty streets of the abandoned subdivision, fetid flesh dripping from their bones, moans escaping their decaying lips. Hollow eye cavities inhabited by swarms of evil wasps.

And sometimes it was my buck-naked swingers group laughing and pointing as I ran in circles, my hand on my swollen dick, begging for relief to no avail.

Without sleep, I had no appetite. Steak, chicken, any kind of meat or fish made my stomach crawl. I was barely able to swallow a few boiled vegetables. A dry slice of multigrain bread, a bowl of brown rice. Chamomile tea.

A shot of booze left me retching in the sink. A snort of blow sent me raging around the house chased by giant carnivorous insects. Weed brought waves of paranoia. Once my raison d'être, sex now repelled me. The thought of it called up visions of Pauline's voluptuous corpse lying in a shallow grave covered in dirt and lime dust.

To keep busy I started taking yoga classes at a storefront studio next to the Latino grocery. The instructor, an aging blonde with the lithe body of a twenty-year-old, lent me books by the Anglo Zen masters. Charlotte Joko Beck and Alan Watts. Pirsig's *Zen and the Art of Motorcycle Maintenance*. Gary Snyder's poems. On sunny days throughout the winter, I sat in the lotus position on the back deck contemplating my fucking navel.

In March I took down the *For Sale* sign and paid a corrupt acquaintance at the Registry of Deeds three hundred dollars to file a forged warranty deed transferring Pauline's property to my name. The house had belonged to her mother. The mortgage had been paid off long ago.

To celebrate I went for a salad at a nearby health food co-op. As I approached, Suzie burst out of the bar next door. I'd lost close to fifty pounds eating vegetarian fare. My bearded face, framed by shoulder-length hair, had grown thin and ascetic. My thrift shop clothes matched the simplicity of a holy man—or a stumblebum. Suzie walked right past me without a glance and climbed into the passenger side of a slick BMW idling at the curb. The guy behind the wheel sported a John Waters pencil mustache and a dimpled chin. I wished him luck.

By the time spring rolled around, with new green leaves, hopping robins, and cooing doves, my nightmares had mostly stopped. Surely whoever owned the ten grand had taken a write-off. Attributed the loss to force majeure. I never went back to the toolshed. R.I.P. Pauline and Drew.

The only dream that kept coming back was the one where my sex club pals were laughing at my swollen schlong. The women rebuffing my entreaties, refusing to grant me the relief of a quickie or a handjob. I wandered in a surreal nightmare of shunga woodblock porn. I knew if I could rid myself of this last haunting from my past, I would be safe, flying under the radar.

One morning I sat at the picnic table in the backyard sipping a cup of green tea and reading the classified ads in the *Observer,* Dallas' free alternative newspaper. And there it was, the answer to my prayers:

Tired of living on the ragged edge of sex addiction? Give Swingers Anonymous a chance. Meeting every Thursday, 7 p.m. at Zion Hall. All who are afflicted are welcome.

Who can understand the twists of fortune, the dharma that brought me to this point in space and time? But one thing my mother told me: never look a gift horse in the mouth. Everything was going to be fine.

ABOUT THE CONTRIBUTORS

Stacy Bondurant

MATT BONDURANT's newest novel, *The Night Swimmer,* was featured in the *New York Times,* the *Daily Beast,* and other media venues. His second novel, *The Wettest County in the World,* was a *New York Times* Editors' Choice, one of the *San Francisco Chronicle*'s 50 Best Books of the Year, and was adapted into a feature film, *Lawless,* by director John Hillcoat. His first novel, *The Third Translation,* was an international best seller and was translated into fourteen languages worldwide.

Sylvia Elzafon Photography

CATHERINE CUELLAR is a third-generation Dallas native with a degree in creative writing from Rhodes College. She cohosted North Texas' literary author interview series *The Writers' Studio* on public radio and has appeared in Dallas' storytelling series "Oral Fixation: An Obsession with True Life Tales." Currently she serves as executive director of the Dallas Arts District.

Richland College

LAUREN DAVIS is a native New Orleanian and noir aficionado with long-standing family ties to Dallas. She is pursuing an MA in history at the University of Texas at Dallas, where she also studies creative writing. She is the recipient of several TIPA awards, and is currently at work on a novel titled *Crescent City Martyrology.*

Thorne Anderson

BEN FOUNTAIN has lived in Dallas for thirty years. His novel *Billy Lynn's Long Halftime Walk* received the 2012 National Book Critics' Circle Award and the *Los Angeles Times* Book Award for Fiction, and was a finalist for the National Book Award. He has received the PEN/Hemingway Award, the Barnes & Noble Discover Award for Fiction, and a Whiting Writers' Award. His short stories have appeared in *Esquire, Harper's,* and the *Paris Review,* among other places.

Peter Larsen

J. SUZANNE FRANK is the author of many novels; the most recent is *Laws of Migration.* Her passion for history has taken her to Egypt, Greece, Israel, and throughout Europe. An eighth-generation Texan who lives in Dallas, she directs the Writer's Path at SMU.

Sandy Drayton

DANIEL J. HALE is an Agatha Award–winning author, the executive vice president of Mystery Writers of America, and a creative writing instructor with the Writer's Path at Southern Methodist University. His short stories have appeared in several anthologies, including Nelson DeMille's *The Rich and the Dead*. A former resident of France, Hale holds degrees from Cornell University, the Bowen School of Law, and SMU. He lives in Dallas.

Hillsman Jackson

DAVID HAYNES teaches and directs the creative writing program at Southern Methodist University and is also part of the faculty of the MFA Program for Writers at Warren Wilson College. He is the author of six novels for adults and five books for younger readers. His latest novel is *A Star in the Face of the Sky*. For more information, visit faceofthesky.com.

Fran Hillyer

FRAN HILLYER is retired from a twenty-eight-year career teaching English and creative writing. She received the Texas Exes Award for Outstanding High School Teachers and the Inspirit Accolade from the Episcopal School of Dallas. Her published works include the poems "Dreaming the Miraculous Baby" in the *Texas Institute of Letters* collection; "Little Lies" and "Four Years Old with Mother and Eternity" in the *Texas Observer;* and What's the Word?, a vocabulary program for SAT.

Paulette Hime

JAMES HIME's debut novel, *The Night of the Dance*, was an Edgar Award finalist. He is the author of three Jeremiah Spur novels, including *Scared Money* and *Where Armadillos Go to Die*. He is the CFO of the real estate department of the Abu Dhabi Investment Authority, but when he's not on an airplane or in an office tower in the Middle East, his permanent address is in Dallas with his wife Paulette.

Nicholas McWhirter

HARRY HUNSICKER, a fourth-generation native of Dallas, is the former executive vice president of the Mystery Writers of America. His debut novel, *Still River,* was nominated for a Shamus Award, and his short story "Iced" was nominated for a Thriller Award. His story "West of Nowhere" appeared in *The Best American Mystery Stories 2011*, edited by Otto Penzler and Harlan Coben. Hunsicker's fourth novel, *The Contractors,* will be published in 2014.

KATHLEEN KENT is the author of two best-selling novels, *The Heretic's Daughter* and *The Traitor's Wife*. In 2008 she was the recipient of the David J. Langum Sr. Award for American Historical Fiction. Her third novel, *The Outcasts*, set in 1870 Texas, was published in September 2013. She lives in Dallas and is working on her fourth book.

OSCAR C. PEÑA, poet, essayist, and jazz musician, was born and raised in Kingsville, Texas. He has published a chapbook, *Fire of Thorns,* and has been a juried poet at Houston Poetry Fest. His work has been published in the *San Pedro River Review,* Austin International Poetry Festival anthology *Di-vêrse'-city*, Rio Grande Valley International Poetry Festival anthology *Boundless*, and *Texas Poetry Calendar.* He lives in League City, Texas, with his wife.

EMMA RATHBONE is the author of the novel *The Patterns of Paper Monsters,* for which she received a Christopher Isherwood Grant. She was born in Pretoria, South Africa. When she was six, her family moved to the Dallas suburb of Plano, Texas. Her work has been published in the *Virginia Quarterly Review* and *Five Chapters.* She lives in Charlottesville, Virginia.

CLAY REYNOLDS is a professor of arts and humanities and director of the creative writing program at the University of Texas at Dallas. His novels include *The Vigil* and *Franklin's Crossing.* In 2012, he was awarded the WWA Spur Award for Short Fiction for his story "The Deacon's Horse." He is a member of the Authors' Guild, Writers' League of Texas, the Texas Institute of Letters, and Western Writers of America.

DAVID HALE SMITH is a literary agent based in Dallas. Since 1994, he has represented some of the most beloved authors in crime fiction. Along with fourteen Edgar Award nominations, his clients have won Edgar, Anthony, Agatha, Shamus, Barry, Macavity, International Thriller Writers, Eisner, and Bram Stoker awards, along with the *Los Angeles Times* Book Prize.

Merritt Tierce

MERRITT TIERCE is a graduate of the Iowa Writers' Workshop and a recipient of a 2011 Rona Jaffe Foundation Award. In addition to telling stories, she works as the executive director of the Texas Equal Access Fund, an abortion fund that serves the low-income women of North Texas. Tierce lives near Dallas with her husband and children, and her first book—a novel called *Love Me Back*—is forthcoming from Doubleday.

JONATHAN WOODS divides his time between Key West, Florida, and Dallas. His stories have appeared in *Plots with Guns, Thuglit,* and *3:AM Magazine,* and in the anthologies *Speedloader, Crime Factory: The First Shift,* and *Noir at the Bar (Vol. I).* His story collection *Bad Juju & Other Tales of Madness and Mayhem* won a 2011 Spinetingler Award. BookPeople Bookstore in Austin, Texas named Woods's *A Death in Mexico* one of the top five debut crime novels of 2012.